Don't Forget to Dance

to Dance

Sylvia Hall

adlib...   Scholastic Limited

For my mum, who loved to dance.

Thanks to Hannah, Colin and Higham Writers.

Scholastic Children's Books,
Commonwealth House, 1–19 New Oxford Street,
London WC1A 1NU, UK
a division of Scholastic Ltd
London ~ New York ~ Toronto ~ Sydney ~ Auckland

First published in the UK by Scholastic Ltd, 1996

Copyright © Sylvia Hall, 1996

ISBN 0 590 54290 7

Typeset by DP Photosetting, Aylesbury, Bucks
Printed in England by Clays Ltd, St Ives plc

10 9 8 7 6 5 4 3 2 1

1.

The aisle of the bus was jammed with school bags and bodies and as it lurched to a halt, Ravenna was thrown off-balance. She struggled to right herself but a bag dug into her side.

"Ouch! Watch what you're doing," she moaned to a boy who was trying to push past her. As she turned to let him by, his hand slipped under her armpit and groped at her breast. Too late, she saw his horrible leer and realized what he was doing. She reached to grab his collar but he scrambled nimbly over the bags, weaving his way to the exit.

From the bus doorway he turned and grinned. "Got ya!" he shouted, then with a whoop of triumph shot down the steps.

Cheeky bastard. She wanted to put her fist right into his freckled grinning face.

Ravenna hated the school bus. Everybody crammed together like sweaty sardines. She'd only caught it tonight to get home early because she had loads of homework. Now that little toe-rag would be boasting, "I felt Ravenna Collins' tits."

Boiling with anger, she wedged herself into a seat beside two girls. As the bus set off again, she closed her eyes and thought of ten ways in which she could murder the nasty little groper. When she opened them she saw Dustin Harrows looking at her. The smarmy sympathetic smile on his face showed he'd seen what the boy had done. Ravenna turned away embarrassed and looked out of the window.

The bus was driving down a leafy avenue on the northern

edge of the town. Pupils getting off the bus here were the lucky ones. The houses were so spread out that it seemed as if each one had its own private bus-stop. Of course, some kids who lived up here didn't bother with the school bus at all. No crush and push for them. They were driven home by parents. Molly, Ravenna's best friend, was probably home already, whisked away by a large, expensive car, changing out of her school uniform, choosing from a row of designer jeans, relaxing on the sofa with a cup of tea.

And here am I, thought Ravenna, being thrown about and groped like a common slag. She braced herself as the bus veered round the corner and bumped into open countryside. Then it drove down the steep hill to turn into the big council housing estate that had been dumped at the bottom.

Ravenna's spirits always plummeted as the rows of concrete houses came into view. "White City" it had been dubbed when it was first built, but anything white had since mouldered into a dank grey. Above it, the town of Maddock cascaded prettily along a high ridge, spilling a few new bungalows and split level houses over its sides. The hillsides were wooded, streams tippled into the valley bottom and moorland rose above the town. Older buildings were scattered amongst the trees or clustered haphazardly. New houses were built in yellow sandstone and carefully designed to blend into their surroundings. Only the council estate was different; the houses slapped into regimented rows, like a military operation. And if she was in charge, Ravenna thought, she'd blow it up.

The bus finally stopped and emptied itself. Ravenna pulled up her jacket collar as she got off, walking quickly away from the noisy gangs. None of her friends lived on the estate.

As she crossed the road a battered Ford Capri roared around the corner. Ravenna ran for the opposite pavement. It was no good taking chances here – drivers would run you over rather than slow down.

"Hey," she heard a voice behind her and turned. It was Dustin Harrows. He was flushed, breathing heavily; he'd run to catch her up.

"I saw what he did. Little creep. I'll hammer him for you."

His face screwed into a pit-bull snarl as he waved his fist in a belligerent manner. Ravenna was flattered that he wanted to defend her honour – he did look pretty powerful – but she didn't want to feel indebted to any lad on the estate.

She tossed back her hair. "I'll deal with him," she snapped.

"Suit yourself," Dustin muttered. He dropped his fist. It dangled menacingly for a moment then he punched it into his other hand, turned away and hurried back to join his mates.

Ravenna watched him go. A tall, lithe figure, his longish blond hair blowing slightly in the wind. She felt a tingle of pleasure – after all, he was the most fanciable lad in year eleven – even if he was trouble.

Turning away, Ravenna made for home. She passed two mangy-looking dogs, ducked a flying chip paper, kicked a rolling tin can and skirted round ragged hedges and broken fences that only partly hid gardens stacked with rusty bikes, prams and old tyres. It wasn't until she reached the back of the estate that the gardens, in contrast, were bright with daffodils blooming from neat diamonds and rectangles. When she turned into her avenue the houses were freshly painted and the windows hung with neat curtains. It was the best kept road on the estate, no problem families here, and it backed on to open countryside. Ravenna was, at least, thankful for that.

Her mum's shout came from upstairs. "Is that you, Ravenna? Put the kettle on, will you? I'm dyin' for a cuppa. Is our Kirsty all right?"

Kirsty was in her high-chair, bashing a dippy egg with a spoon. The shell was shattered into such tiny smithereens that it was impossible to separate egg from shell.

"I got shoulders," Kirsty proudly announced.

"Soldiers," Ravenna corrected.

"Shoulders," Kirsty beamed, trying to dip a small oblong of bread into the mashed egg.

"Hold on. I'll do it for you in a minute. You've made a right mess of it."

Ravenna dashed to hang up her coat and bag in the hall. When she returned, Kirsty had her mouth full of egg and shell and a dribble of yellow yolk was running down her chin. Ah well, Ravenna thought, perhaps she should let her get on with it; she'd read somewhere that eggshell was good for you.

Her mum, Sheila, came clattering into the room, with Brett's head held, vice-like, in the crook of her elbow.

"Once he gets on that computer you can't talk to him," she said, irritably. "I called him three times for his tea and he takes no notice and now his egg will have gone all hard."

"I'd just got on to level five," Brett protested, trying to shake himself free.

"You spend too much time on that damn thing," Sheila retorted. But over his head she was grinning. Ravenna knew she was proud of Brett being, as Sheila saw it, at the forefront of technology.

Sheila ruffled his hair affectionately. "Sit and eat. If your egg's hard then it's your fault. Have you put the kettle on, Ravenna?"

"I've been seeing to Kirsty. She's eating more shell than egg."

Sheila ambled over to the high-chair. "Oh, what a mess. I was only upstairs a minute." She bent and kissed the top of Kirsty's head. "Never mind, you don't care, do you, my duck? I've got you some rice pudding for afters."

Sheila scooped out a spoonful of yolk and shell, feeding it into Kirsty's open mouth. "How was school today, then?" she asked Ravenna.

The same question she always asked – the thing was she hardly ever listened to the answer.

Ravenna stuck the kettle under the tap and put a tea bag in the teapot. "Fine," she answered automatically. Then, remembering the poster Miss Devlin had put up, "Some Bengali dancers are coming. They're going to perform tomorrow, before we do our plays. They look fantastic, so sort of delicate and elegant and. . ."

Ravenna was seized by enthusiasm as she began to describe them to her mother and experienced the same mystic power she'd felt when gazing at the poster. One of the dancers, dark-skinned and shimmering with gold, was caught in mid-air as if floating; her legs and arms hooked like an exotic bird. Just thinking about them made Ravenna want to dance.

"Oh, get us the biscuits will you, love? There's some chocolate digestives."

Sighing heavily, Ravenna reached in the cupboard for the

biscuit jar. She poured the tea and placed the jar on the table as Sheila lit a cigarette.

"I thought you'd given up?"

"Don't tell Ian, will you?" her mother pleaded. "I'm down to five a day but I can't give up completely, Vernie, I can't."

"I won't tell him. Why should I? He'll know soon enough when you get lung cancer."

Ravenna's annoyance sharpened her tongue. She hated her mother calling her Vernie. It made her sound like some gross TV comedian.

"Yeah, you'll die or you'll have to have your leg cut off. I saw this man on telly who had to have his leg off 'cos he smoked," Brett joined in, breadcrumbs spitting from his mouth as he spoke.

Mum turned on him fiercely. "Don't you tell your dad, neither, or you'll get no Easter eggs," she said, taking a long, hard draw on the cigarette and exhaling smoke, which drifted over the biscuits, a loaf of bread and an open tub of margarine.

"Ruins your complexion too. Your face gets all wrinkled," Ravenna said, righteously ignoring the chocolate biscuits and helping herself to an apple.

"Well, thank you all very much. When I'm a haggard old corpse with one leg, you'll all be bloody gloating."

Kirsty was busy thumping her tray and squealing whilst she swiped eggshell all over the floor.

"Ravenna, give Kirsty some rice pudding, it'll shut her up."

"Mum, I've got loads of homework to do," Ravenna protested, but she knew it was no use.

Mum and Brett would disappear just like they did every night to watch TV. Mum was a serious telly addict, knew every pupil Grange Hill had ever had and if Ravenna didn't see to Kirsty, nobody would.

It was eight o'clock by the time she'd fed, changed and bathed Kirsty, washed up, ironed her school blouse and PE kit for the next day. And she still had homework to do.

Before opening her books she stood brushing her hair in front of the mirror that stood on the white chipboard dressing-table in her room. The dim light made a golden pool around her and she gazed back at her own eyes which were gleaming darkly in the mirror. She remembered the shining eyes of the dancers in the poster and waved her arms in front of her reflection.

Behind her in the cot, Kirsty stirred and blew bubbles in her sleep. Ravenna turned from the mirror and twirled in the pool of light, hair and arms floating and swirling. From somewhere in her memory she called up the intricate rhythms of a sitar, the insistent beat of the tabla and she stretched her long legs, curved her body towards the floor then the ceiling, circled her arms and flexed her fingers. She wished she had room to leap and whirl and let her spirit float free.

But a noise from the cot stopped her in mid-spin. If Kirsty awoke now she wouldn't get her homework done. Noiselessly, Ravenna crossed to the cot. Kirsty was lying on her back, arms flung out, her blonde hair fluffed from her bath and her cheeks pink and flushed. She was fast asleep and looked angelic. Ravenna felt a sweep of love but at the same time resented it. Resented having to share her bedroom with a toddler. She thought of her friends in their homes on top of the hill, alone in their big airy rooms with CD players and telephones and asked herself, not for the first time, why couldn't she have been adopted by one of those families?

Falling back on her bed, Ravenna lay, hands clasped under her head, staring at the ceiling. Why couldn't she be part of a civilized family who read books and had conversations, who lived calmly and comfortably with lots of space around them? Not like here where she had to share a bedroom, the television was always blaring out and everybody lived on top of one another. And the estate was filthy. She hated living there: the litter, the broken-down cars in people's front gardens and the way families let their kids run wild. Old Mrs Johnson, who Sheila visited, hadn't been out of her house for weeks. Gangs of kids congregated on her front wall every night, daring each other to knock on her door or ride their bikes across the front lawn. She was frightened to stay in and even more terrified to go out.

Ravenna sighed, and closed her eyes. She pictured Molly finishing her homework, sitting at her own desk in her own room, undisturbed by anybody else's noise, sipping a cup of coffee supplied by her mum. Sheila didn't seem to recognize the importance of homework. Oh, she always made a lot of fuss about Ravenna being bright and doing well at school, liked to take the credit, but how did she think Ravenna achieved it? By magic? Sometimes, like now, after Ravenna had looked after Kirsty and washed, ironed and cleaned, all she wanted to do was sleep.

Teachers at school were already putting pressure on about doing A-levels and going to university. Her English teacher had even mentioned trying for Oxford. How the hell could she achieve that when most nights she had to babysit?

Anyway, people from this estate didn't get to Oxford and if she did get a place, she wasn't sure she'd have the guts to go. Oh, she knew that from the outside she looked confident. Kids at school thought she was so sure of herself, "Snotty, stuck-up Ravenna Collins". But they didn't really know her. How could you feel confident when you lived in a dump like this, branded as a slummy White City kid, and on top of that, you didn't know who your parents were? All the time she was afraid she'd fail; that somebody some time would find out her exam results were just a fluke.

Ravenna sat up, picked up her geography file and thumbed idly through it. All this bloody work to do and no time to do it in. She'd never be able to stay on at school. GCSEs were proving difficult enough and everybody said A-levels were harder. She might as well accept the fate of the rest of the kids on the estate. She'd do some poxy GNVQ course then marry a moron, have five kids and live next door to her mum.

She sat staring blankly at the wall for a few moments. Deep down she knew she wanted more than that. She didn't know exactly what she wanted but she knew she couldn't stand living on the estate for the rest of her life and she was pretty sure that her real mother, when she'd given her away, wouldn't have wanted that for her either. If only she knew where her real mum was. If only she'd come back and claim her. She was sure anything would be better than this.

2.

Morning began with a loud bang – which wasn't unusual. Ravenna was used to having her senses assaulted before she'd even got out of bed. Kirsty was rattling her cot bars and squealing whilst holding up a sodden nappy reeking of ammonia and next door Brett was using his bed as a trampoline. Ravenna recognized the creak of the bed springs followed by an anguished cry as his head thudded against the wall.

She rolled over and buried her head in the duvet. But it was no use. Kirsty's squeals became more insistent. Then the bedroom door was flung open, smacking back against the wall.

"Am I bleeding?" a shrill and fearful voice asked.

Ravenna turned over and opened a bleary eye. Brett, in his Superman pyjamas, was standing in the doorway, holding his head in his hands.

"Come here and let me look," Ravenna said, pushing herself up on to one elbow. Brett trotted forward and she examined the pink scalp beneath tangled blond curls. She couldn't see any wound.

"Where does it hurt?"

Brett pointed to the tender spot and Ravenna ran her fingers over it and felt a lump.

"Come into the bathroom and I'll put some Vaseline on it. Just let me get Kirsty."

Kirsty was impatiently flinging her wet nappy to the floor

whilst trying to scale the cot bars, her Babygro flapping like a two-pronged tail.

"Up, up," she shouted, her arms reaching for Ravenna.

"Come on, then, stinky poos. Let's go and wash you," Ravenna said, as she bent over and Kirsty clung on to her.

As she walked out of the room she noticed the clock. Damn, it was only six-thirty. She could have had another hour's sleep before getting up for school. Some hope in this house, though. Sheila was the only one who ever managed a lie-in.

After dealing with Brett's head and Kirsty's bottom, Ravenna washed herself and then slipped on her school uniform, whilst mentally ticking off a list of props she needed to take in for her drama lesson. She stuffed a sweater, mirror and make-up into a carrier bag then she scooped up a file, swept Kirsty under her armpit and stumbled downstairs.

In the kitchen, the radio was on, pumping out D J diarrhoea and pop music and Sheila was up, frying eggs and smoking her first cigarette of the day.

"Ian's on earlies. I could hear you seeing to Kirsty, so I thought I'd make you some breakfast. Oh, don't you just love this one?" Sheila asked, flipping eggs on to a plate and singing along. *"Even if we're just dancin' in the dark, dancin' in the dark."*

Her voice was as gritty as the singer's. "I love Bruce Springsteen, don't you?" she asked as she tipped beans out of a pan. "Egg, tomato and beans all right?"

Ravenna nodded. She didn't really fancy a cooked breakfast but it was so rare for Sheila to make the effort, she felt she ought to encourage her. She deposited Kirsty in her high-chair and took the warm plate handed to her. Two eggs with bright yellow yolks, a splash of orange beans and a tomato – and no grease in sight. Wow! Perhaps this was going to be a good day.

Ravenna watched the Bengali dancers transform the dusty school hall of Maddock Comprehensive into something exotic, ethereal – a shimmering dream. Their bodies arched and glided to the beat of the tabla; their hands delicately scooped the air and their hips shuddered like silk.

In the front row of the audience, Ravenna leaned forward entranced, her long black hair framing her shining face, her lips slightly apart, her dark eyes riveted to the dancers.

She watched their feet, caramel soles sweeping in intricate patterns; their robes, glowing gauzes, swirling and billowing; their golden hands, curling and flexing as if talking. She saw the dancers twist with limbs lithe as a panther, rippling then settling still, but with a twitch of the neck and a shiver of the shoulder, the body becoming liquid again.

Ravenna imagined in their graceful movements all the pain and beauty of their homeland. Other pupils shuffled and whispered but Ravenna was transfixed, tapping her feet to the rhythm of the drums and swaying slightly in her seat.

As dance followed dance, Ravenna felt herself a part of the magic. Felt as if she were dancing with them. Her wrists and ankles flashing gold, her dark eyes lined with kohl and her bare midriff curling and stretching.

Only when the beat of the drums faded and the dancers were still, was Ravenna aware of the group of boys Miss Devlin had placed beside her on the front row. They were rustling and fidgeting: poor things, they'd had to sit quietly for nearly an hour and watch something beautiful. It must have been torture.

Ravenna heard Dustin Harrows sigh with relief, then he coughed and whispered loudly, "Bet that one's a goer."

His mates sniggered and Ravenna felt their tension release like a long stream of foul air.

"Nice hands, shame about the tits," Malc Orridge quipped and the lads laughed again.

Ravenna was angry. She hated the way they followed one another, chorusing like bleating sheep. Of course, they couldn't admit the dancers were fascinating, beautiful; that would be too much like having an honest emotion. They'd rather take refuge in obscenity.

The dancers regrouped and the music started up again. A young girl in orange tunic and trousers stepped forward smiling nervously, her eyes sweeping the audience. When her gaze met Ravenna's she relaxed, grinned and held out a delicate hand.

Before she realized what she was doing, Ravenna caught the hand, was on her feet and being swept into the midst of the dancers, music cascading around her like a waterfall.

Someone placed a flimsy wrap around her shoulders, and Ravenna draped the gaudy material over her arms, holding it out like a shining river. She watched carefully for a moment, then began to move her body in time to the rhythm – her neck arched, her body glided. The steps were intricate and unnatural but she began to follow. Gold flashed at the dancers' ankles and wrists and the glare of the lights dazzled her eyes.

She stumbled but recovered quickly and then suddenly she

was dancing. Dancing the exact steps. It was as if someone were holding her hand, guiding her. She saw faces with eyes just like hers, strong faces with high cheek-bones framed by a sweep of blue-black hair. She felt a great sense of release and danced confidently, stepping lightly and elegantly. She heard the discordant notes, felt them ripple through her body. She imagined temples, palm trees and dry dusty earth. She was transported; curling her limbs under a hot sun, splashing in deep green pools, dancing to celebrate a mystic spirit. As she twisted and twirled everything became a blur of images.

When the music died away she gazed at the audience with shining eyes until the blur trembled into focus. She was aware of the dancers surrounding her, their jewelled hands clapping delicately, light as flapping birds' wings. Then a heavy thunderous clap split the air.

"Yo, way, Ravenna. Show 'em. Shake it, baby!"

A cacophony of loud claps and cheers hit Ravenna like a wet glove slapping across her face. She saw Dustin's mouth wide open, shouting and cheering; his mates beside him, hands flapping like seals, mouths barking.

For a moment, Ravenna was in a daze. What had she done? Why had she made such a fool of herself? She'd been mad to get up and dance. Dustin and his mates wouldn't give her any peace now. They were laughing, their faces set in mocking grins, their applause overenthusiastic. For a moment, she wanted the floor to open up and swallow her. Dustin was flinging out his arms, waving his hands, mimicking her movements. Pity he was so good-looking – it was wasted on such an ignorant yob.

Ravenna tossed her head. Sod them, she thought. She'd

enjoyed herself. What did she care? Striding back to her seat she fixed Dustin with an icy stare. If he wanted to make something out of it, then let him.

Dustin stuck a leg out across her chair, but seeing Ravenna was about to aim a kick, he moved it.

"Funny," he sneered. "You looked just like one of 'em."

Before Ravenna could reply, Miss Devlin, the drama teacher, stepped forward.

"I'm sure you'll all want to join me in thanking the dancers. They were wonderful and if we can capture one iota of their grace and rhythm in our dance lessons then I'm sure we'll all improve. Thank you for a wonderful display and ... thank you, Ravenna."

Ravenna blushed and was glad of the loud applause to cover her embarrassment. The dancers bowed then left the floor and the musicians began to pack away their instruments. There were a few minutes to go before the bell and Miss Devlin desperately tried to interest the pupils in the culture and wildlife of Bengal. But to Dustin and his mates the irritable Paki at the local corner shop was more real than endangered tigers. They were ready for off and they smirked and whispered Paki jokes.

Ravenna tolerated them until her temper broke.

"Can't you shut your bloody traps for a minute?" she hissed furiously.

She was sick of them. They called anybody who looked vaguely Asian a "Paki". Ravenna wasn't too sure about the exact geography but she knew that Bengalis and Pakistanis were from different countries.

The break-time bell cut across the teacher's words and,

released, the pupils streamed out, elbowing their way towards canteen, tuck shop or smokers' corner.

Ravenna alone stood still, unwilling to give up the magic that clung to the hall. She was breathing heavily, her senses sharpened, aware of her body, lithe and supple. She wanted to dance again. Wanted to try curving her arms and spiking her fingers in those unnatural but amazingly elegant gestures; to lift her legs and shoulders so delicately that it looked as if her limbs were floating independent of her body.

She stood, poised, on tiptoe as chairs rattled and Dockers, Caterpillars and oversized trainers fled towards freedom.

Molly grasped her arm. "Come on, Raven. It's break."

"Weren't they wonderful?" Ravenna breathed.

Molly gave her a funny look. "I wouldn't go as far as that. I liked the costumes but it went on a bit."

"Yeah, it was OK. But when you've seen one dance, you've seen 'em all," agreed Rachael at her side.

"You were brilliant though, Raven," Molly said. "How did you manage all the steps? It was as if you knew them."

"Yeah, you were a natural," Rachael agreed. "I'm glad they didn't pick me. It would've been chaos. We'd have all ended up in a big heap."

"They chose the right one then, didn't they?" Ravenna said, smiling and flicking back her silky hair. Then she brought her hands forward in a twisting motion, curling and rippling the fingers in front of her friends' faces.

Molly pushed her hands away. "You're nuts, Ravenna," she laughed.

After break, Ravenna, Molly and Rachael filed into the black-walled drama studio. They were working on improvisations and it was the turn of Dustin's group to show their play.

"Wonder what it will be like?" Molly asked.

"Dunno, but I bet there's a fight in it," Ravenna replied.

Laughing, her friends went to secure seats in the front row but Ravenna stood for a moment looking at the poster of the Bengali dancers. Flexing her fingers and toes, she plotted steps to the rippling music that still drummed in her head. It was strange, she thought, how she had seemed to know the dances – her arms and legs had moved instinctively. Was she part Indian? It was an exciting thought but hardly likely. The one fact she knew about her mother was that she was Welsh. That was hardly Eastern, was it? But she'd loved the dancing. She'd felt truly herself, truly free. Perhaps that was the connection – dancing was in her blood.

"Looking at your cousins?"

Dustin had crept up on her. She turned to see him smiling smugly, his eyes gleaming maliciously, his eyebrows arched.

"Don't worry. I'll keep your secret. Only I know your mother was an Indian princess." He bent forward as he spoke and laughed. "You're a great mover, anyway," he said as he walked off.

What was he on about? He thought he was so clever but he made her feel uncomfortable. Too late she thought of a sharp reply – he'd gone. He was standing at the opposite side of the room, calmly watching his group scurry around, anxiously positioning blocks and searching for missing props. In an arc of light, he was silhouetted against the wall, his head thrown back, his hands moving expressively as he gave orders. With a shock, Ravenna realized he reminded her of the Indian dancers – elegant, graceful – though, she smiled, he'd probably kill anyone who said so.

Somebody crossed and spoke to him; she saw him shrug, heard him curse, then he swung into action, his strong muscled arms heaving blocks, positioning them carefully. Ravenna noticed how one blond strand of hair kept falling over his eyes and how the golden hairs on his arms glinted as they caught the light. She could see why some girls were attracted to him. But when he turned round he was chewing, his mouth working loosely, his face wearing its usual sardonic expression. He was watching the other group members suspiciously, ready to leap in at any mistake.

Ravenna gave herself a mental shake. What was she thinking? Dustin Harrows was a dork of the highest order.

She only half concentrated on his group's play. It was predictable stuff. They'd been given the theme of "Outsiders" by Miss Devlin and Dustin played a frail old man who was harassed by a grasping Indian landlord.

"It's true though, isn't it, Miss? They come over here, taking our jobs, living on social security?" Dustin said in the discussion which followed.

Ravenna saw Miss Devlin was annoyed about Dustin using the group project for his propaganda. She spoke sharply to him, her chin jutting forward, her hands tightly clasped and her elbows sticking out. She was all fire and sharp edges whereas she was usually relaxed and easy going.

"I guess in this country we were all outsiders at one time or another. We're an island of foreigners. Look around. Who can you say is truly British? We've got blue-eyed blondes, descendants of Norse and Vikings, small, dark-haired Celts, olive-toned Romans etc., etc."

Ravenna lowered her head, aware of Dustin staring at her. Her dark eyes and hair marked her out, but who could say where she came from? If only Sheila would give her a few more details, it would help. But whenever she asked about her background, Sheila clammed up. Even the choice of her Christian name was shrouded in mystery. Ravenna was sure she'd once been told that her natural mother had named her but recently Sheila vowed she'd picked the name because Philip's grandmother had come from a town called Ravenna in Italy. Which was true?

Sometimes she felt she didn't belong to anywhere or anybody. It was strange not looking like anybody else in her family. When there was just Sheila and Philip, her adopted mum and dad, it had been all right, but then Philip had died and Sheila had remarried. A year later, along came Brett. Sheila was thrilled to have a child of her own at last and his blond curls, round face, wide.blue eyes and high forehead – a carbon copy of his mum – made him even more special. Four years later, Kirsty was born: blonde fuzz and bright blue eyes – a perfect match. Even Ian, Sheila's second husband, had blond wisps around his bald head. A matching blond-haired family and Ravenna in their midst – a dark stranger.

Miss Devlin was still pleading for racial tolerance when the lunch bell ended the discussion but, of course, nothing was resolved. Dustin was still blaming immigrants for the fact that his mother had lost her job.

"Who do you think I look like?" Ravenna asked Rachael and Molly over lunch.

"Cher," Rachael replied.

"That's great, Rach, she's about sixty."

"Well, I don't know, who do you wanna look like?"

"I'm not sure," Ravenna said.

"For Pete's sake, Ravenna, if you look like you, you don't need to look like anybody else. Anybody would give their front teeth to look like you," Molly assured her.

"Yeah, but you look like your mum; Rachael looks like her dad. I don't look like any of my relatives."

"Well, think yourself bloomin' lucky," grinned Rachael.

"If that's all you've got to worry about – you *are* lucky," Molly said grimly.

Ravenna looked at Molly in surprise. She sounded depressed and bitter.

"Moll, what have you got to be miserable about?"

"Oh, nothing. I'm the lucky one, remember? Big house, nice parents, foreign holidays. Don't worry about me – forget it."

But Ravenna saw a look of pure misery on Molly's face as she walked out of the drama studio. Something was wrong and Ravenna had to find out what.

3.

Ravenna and Rachael caught up with Molly as she headed towards the dining-hall.

"Slow down, Moll. The nosh isn't that good. What's the matter?" Ravenna asked, catching hold of Molly's arm.

Molly stopped and was about to speak when Faye Mellins and Dustin stepped in front of her, barring her way.

Faye planted herself firmly, hands in the pockets of her denim jacket, one hip sticking out above her short tight skirt. "Hey, you," she said, flicking back her blonde quiff. "My mum's been put on part-time at your factory." She shot Molly a look that was splintered steel.

Molly shrugged. "I can't do anything about it. I'm sorry," she said quietly.

"Sorry? Sorry doesn't pay the bills, does it?" Faye sneered. "Don't suppose your dad's on short time, is he?"

Dustin stood next to her, looking hard and angry with his jacket collar turned up. "She can't go on her skiing trip now," he joined in, "if her mum's not working much."

Molly was blushing and looking as if she wanted to run away. "It's not my fault," she stammered.

Dustin glared down at her. "Don't suppose your dad'll be taking a cut in wages. Oh no, you've got to keep your big house and fancy cars going, haven't you? Even if the workers are broke."

Molly's head went down as if she'd been hit and Ravenna saw a dark shadow cross her face. She stepped forward and put an arm around Moll's shoulder, looked defiantly at Faye and Dustin, then steered Molly away from them.

"Leave her alone. It's not her fault."

Ravenna guided Molly towards the dining-hall.

"Don't worry about them, they're scum. Stupid idiots – as if it's your fault."

Molly looked shaken and Ravenna piled two lots of food on to one tray and carried it to a far table, pushing Molly in front of her.

When they sat down she tried to joke about it. "Ee lass, trouble at mill, ay? They were fair het up."

But Molly wasn't in the mood. She pulled her mouth into a tight line. "Just leave it, Ravenna. I don't want to talk about it."

Ravenna exchanged looks with Rachael and they carried on eating in silence for a few minutes but Ravenna couldn't bear to see Molly looking so upset.

"What's happening, Moll? What's going on at the factory?" she asked again.

Molly sighed and prodded miserably at a fish finger. "Dad's firm had to put some workers on short time last week. And," she whispered, "if more orders don't come in it could get worse."

"But it's not your fault. Your dad doesn't even own the factory any more, does he?" Ravenna asked.

"No, the firm was taken over but everybody still calls it Morgan's. And guess who they'll blame if there aren't any jobs?"

"But that's stupid. Everybody knows there's a recession."

DON'T FORGET TO DANCE

"Might be stupid but if you've got no money, you've got to blame somebody."

"What's Dustin Harrows got to do with it? His family don't work at Morgan's, do they?"

"That won't make any difference to Dustin. You know how he likes to involve himself in other people's affairs. Dustin, the working-class hero," Rachael scoffed.

"Yeah, and now Dustin's made it his business, they won't let me forget it," Molly whispered.

"He likes stirring it. Take no notice of him, Moll," Rachael said.

"Ignore him," Ravenna said, firmly. "I shall."

As the girls picked up their trays and prepared to leave, someone banged into the back of Ravenna's chair. It was Dustin.

"Surprised you can eat," he said to Molly. "Hope it chokes you," he added, as he moved off with Faye and his mates.

"What's he doing in here? I thought he usually went to the chippie," Ravenna asked.

"He comes in sometimes 'cos he gets free dinners," Rachael said.

"How do you know?"

"Obvious, innit? His dad's in prison, his mum's unemployed. Work it out."

"I didn't know his dad was in prison," Ravenna said.

"Well, you live with your head in the clouds half the time. Everybody else knows, it's common knowledge. I'nt it, Moll?"

Molly nodded her head, looking very pale.

The girls cleared their dishes, then Ravenna left the dining-hall alone. She had tennis practice before afternoon lessons.

As Ravenna made her way down the corridors, the school seemed empty and echoing. Nobody was left in the changing room and Ravenna felt lonely and out of sorts as she changed into her tennis kit.

It had been a long and tiring morning. The glow of the dancers was still with her but Dustin had wiped out a lot of the pleasure. The great yob – why did he have to pick on Molly? It was none of his business.

By the time she reached the court, the tennis team were already into their swing.

"Come on, hurry up, Ravenna," Mrs Taylor chided. "You should have been here ten minutes ago."

Ravenna apologized and ran to join her partner. After the upset of the morning, Ravenna was eager to vent her fury and the first ball that came her way she whacked down her opponent's line with an elegant forehand.

"Hold on! We're only practising, not playing at Wimbledon," her opponent yelled, scuttling into the corner of the court to retrieve the ball.

But Ravenna played like someone possessed. Every time she heard that wonderful zing of the racquet when it hit the ball smack in the middle, she rejoiced.

"You'll be a great asset to the team this year, Ravenna," Mrs Taylor enthused when Ravenna came off court. "As long as you arrive on time. Don't forget practice on Saturday morning."

"No, Mrs Taylor," Ravenna said quietly. She hadn't meant

to draw so much attention to herself and could see resentful eyes. She must be careful, it was dangerous to be too good.

Hurrying to afternoon lessons, Ravenna passed the hall and heard dull thudding sounds coming from inside the building and saw a crowd gathered around the doorway. Curious, she headed in their direction.

"It's the band, they're rehearsing for Friday night," somebody informed her.

Ravenna peered over the heads into the hall.

On stage, a band was playing, filling the space with driving drum and guitar sounds. Ravenna pushed through the crowd and saw, centre-stage, a lanky figure hugging a microphone. He was tall, his hair streaked gold under the strip lighting. It was Dustin. He began to sing, his voice rasping with raw energy. Ravenna watched surprised and fascinated, as he moved around the stage, his tall frame lithe, catlike; his movements subtle and shadowy; his voice charged with anger, spitting out the words of the song. He was brash, threatening, dynamic. Then the rhythm changed to a slow ballad and his voice poured like silk over the echoing expanse of the hall. Ravenna had to admit, he was good.

Afternoon school required concentration. In double chemistry, Ravenna found herself thinking back to the morning. Why had Dustin been so horrible to Molly? The factory was nothing to do with him. Rachael had said his dad was in prison? Well, that figured – like father like son. He was a troublemaker. But then a different picture formed – Dustin taking charge, preparing for his play, the light catching the hairs on his arms, speckling them with gold. She thought of the sensitive way he'd acted the part of the old man and then saw him on stage, snaking his body round the microphone, singing with a voice that rippled her insides.

The effort required to keep her mind on her experiment made Ravenna feel dizzy and she was glad when lessons ended and she was walking to the car park with Molly. No rush and push for the school bus tonight; Molly's mum was picking them up in the Range Rover.

Ravenna loved "Badger's Holt", Molly's house; admired the cool, pastel-shaded rooms, the delicate flower arrangements, the comfortable sofas. The kitchen was as big as all her downstairs rooms put together. In the fridge were cartons of unopened juice; on the worktops, bowls of untouched luscious fruit lay like sculptures; in the downstairs bathroom, thick, pale towels lay neatly folded on shelves. The Morgans never seemed to run out of anything. Ravenna knew Molly had packets of unopened knickers in her drawer and once Ravenna had been there when one of the spotlights dimmed and it had been replaced within minutes. To Ravenna, who lived among constant arguments for the last chocolate biscuit or carton of yoghurt, it all seemed like boundless luxury.

And yet it wasn't a fussy house. It was comfortable and Hilary Morgan, Molly's mum, always made her feel welcome. Ravenna had spent more time at Badger's than at her own home before Kirsty was born and Sheila got into the habit of asking Ravenna to look after her. Of course, that had been when Molly's brother, David, was at home and he'd always been able to talk Sheila into letting Ravenna stay over. David was away at university now and she missed him. They had the same stupid sense of humour, always playing tricks on each other, and the same taste in music. Whenever David discovered a new band he'd ring up Ravenna to come over and listen. They'd spent hours in Molly's room listening to records, then tapes, then CDs, and they'd played tennis endlessly until Ravenna improved so much she could almost beat him.

Since he'd been away, Ravenna hadn't spent so much time at Badger's and Mum had demanded more and more of her time. Tonight it was a treat to lie on Molly's bed relaxing and eating apples and chocolate raisins.

Molly's room was vast and organized. It had built-in everything and most things were concealed. Behind doors and panels there were racks for shoes, books and CDs, shelves for sound equipment and wardrobes holding expensive clothes. Soft lights shone from somewhere in the ceiling and Molly's bed was huge.

The girls lay stretched out, munching. They were supposed to be revising for a chemistry test but everyday life interposed between method and conclusion.

"You know, sometimes I think I should have gone to St Bede's when Mum wanted me to," Molly said to Ravenna.

Ravenna felt guilty. It wasn't easy for somebody with a lifestyle as rich as Molly's to attend Maddock Comp, and she knew she'd been largely responsible for Molly's decision to go there. They'd been friends since primary school. Ravenna also knew that certain pupils at school would make it very uncomfortable for Molly if their parents lost their jobs.

She tried to cheer Molly up. "What, and miss out on such a brilliant education? No Dustin Harrows to hate, no Chagger the Chimp to laugh at? It'd be dead boring. Just rows of clean faces in tidy uniforms poring over Latin."

Molly didn't respond but munched miserably on a mouthful of raisins.

"Where else will people find work if Dad's factory closes? There's nothing else round here."

Ravenna could see Molly's point.

"Look, Moll, it might not happen and if it does it won't be your fault or your dad's. And . . . look at it this way, your firm provided them with jobs for years, didn't it?"

"I suppose so. But in a way that's the worst thing. They'd always thought their jobs and money were secure. And so did Dad. We all did," Molly said, dejectedly.

Ravenna flicked a raisin into the air and expertly caught it in her mouth.

"I'll tell you what," she said. "We need something to cheer us up, right? We'll go to the dance on Friday."

Molly's eyebrows shot up. "The school dance?" she asked, incredulously.

Ravenna nodded.

Molly snorted. "You must be joking. You haven't been to a school dance for more than a year."

"Maybe I am," Ravenna said thoughtfully. She had surprised herself. Where had the idea come from?

"You said school dances stink. Last time you went, you said the boys were all yobs and you'd never go again. Do you remember how that stupid lad from the debating team was slobbering over you all night?" Molly reminded her.

"I know, I know, but that was a year ago. I can handle it now. I get propositioned every time I go to a party," Ravenna said airily.

"Lucky you," Molly retorted. Then, looking at Ravenna quizzically, she asked, "Do you really want to go?"

"Just thought it might cheer us up – a night out. Might be our last chance – we could be leaving soon."

"Thank goodness."

"Oh, it's not that bad. Come on, let's go. It'll be a laugh."

"Yeah, a mega joke. The factory'll probably be closing down by then and they'll all spit at me."

"Oh, Moll. Things aren't that bad, are they?"

"No, not quite, but Dad's worried. He's been drinking a lot lately."

Ravenna frowned in sympathy. "Your dad'll work something out. He's a genius. Come on, show them you don't care a damn what they think. Anyway, I'm going to make sure everybody knows Morgan Glassware is no longer your company."

Molly eyed Ravenna suspiciously.

"There wouldn't be anyone important at this dance, would there? Somebody like that rather cool dude in the sixth form?"

Ravenna laughed and flicked another raisin upwards. "Don't be daft. He's studying for his A-levels. He won't be there. Oh, come on, Moll, you can wear your new boots."

"All right. But don't say I didn't warn you. If Dustin Harrows or somebody starts something, you can deal with it."

"He won't be starting anything. It's his band that's playing."

"Oh, my God, what have I let myself in for?" Molly asked, rolling back on the bed in mock despair.

"Don't worry, I'll look after you," Ravenna assured her.

4.

Ravenna sighed as she pulled the iron over the crumpled skirt. She would have liked a new outfit to wear to the dance but she knew it was no good asking Mum for the money. Anyway, it hardly mattered, there was nobody she wanted to impress. Or was there? Tonight Dustin would be centre stage.

Excitement surged through Ravenna at this thought and her body trembled so that she set the iron down before she burnt herself. What was wrong with her? She should feel worried, not excited.

She smoothed the skirt across the ironing-board, trying to calm herself. The skirt wasn't the latest fashion but the material was classy; she'd always loved the way the colours swirled mistily, the way the material hugged her hips before flaring gently. It was a great skirt to dance in.

She laughed out loud as she thought how she would dance, then she snatched up the skirt and held it in front of her. As it caught the light, flashes of gold in the melting whorls reminded her of something: golden streaks gleaming as a head turned, a dark blond head, and a few shining curls creeping over the collar of a jacket. Dustin. She pictured him the way she'd seen him once, in an unguarded moment, smiling without malice. That was the time she'd first admitted to herself that he was really good-looking. And now she filled in other details: the amber eyes fringed by long, dark lashes, the finely chiselled cheek-bones and squared chin, the even white teeth which dazzled when he smiled. But, as Ravenna pictured him, the smile on his face changed to an evil, leering grin.

The iron spat steam and stuck to the material. Ravenna jerked it away. Serves me right, she thought, letting Dustin Harrows get inside my head and unbalance me. She examined the skirt and saw there was no permanent damage done. The fabric was just slightly wrinkled.

"This stupid iron, it's either so hot it sticks or so cold it's useless," she moaned out loud, as she fiddled with the dial.

"No shout, no shout, Venna," Kirsty commanded from the middle of the room, banging her beaker of juice against the table leg.

"Ravenna's not cross with you – just this stupid iron," Ravenna reassured her.

"Dustin is a moron, Dustin is a moron," Ravenna chanted to herself, vigorously rubbing the now cool iron over the wrinkled fabric. Golden hair, amber eyes indeed! Come to your senses, girl – he's not worthy.

She banged the iron down. "There, that'll have to do."

Holding up the long skirt she examined it for creases. It was passable, she decided, and laid it over a chair, then picked up a wispy see-through shirt she'd borrowed from Molly. Could she iron this? She looked for a label. There wasn't one. To be on the safe side she switched the iron off and as she waited for it to cool, the door opened and Sheila came in with an armful of washing.

"I can't understand how he gets so filthy. I mean, surely he spends some of the day sitting at a table. Unless he's such a bloomin' nuisance the teachers send him out to play all day. Just look at these trousers."

Her plump hand held up a pair of grey trousers spattered with mud.

Ravenna made sympathetic clucking noises which changed to a squeal as she saw Kirsty was dripping juice all over her freshly-ironed skirt.

"Oh no, Kirsty, I'm going out in that!" she shouted, snatching the skirt and pulling it towards her.

Kirsty stood still, eyes wide, her bottom lip a ledge, juice dripping on to the lino.

"No need to frighten her," Sheila rapped, scooping up the now trembling Kirsty.

Ravenna took the skirt to the sink and sponged at the juice, hoping that on the multi-coloured fabric, the stain wouldn't show. Kirsty, from the comfort of her mum's arms, began to wail and Ravenna felt a stab of guilt for having shouted at her. After all, no real damage was done. She put down the skirt and reached out for her sister, but her mother turned away.

"You've upset her enough. You can bath her in a minute if you want to make up."

"But, Mum, you know I'm going out. I won't have time. I haven't finished ironing my blouse yet," Ravenna protested.

"It's not going to take you two hours to get ready, is it?"

"No, but I promised I'd go round to Molly's house first."

"Well, just give her a ring and tell her you'll meet her there. I'm going to the Bingo and Ian won't want to bath her when he's only just got in from work."

Ravenna looked at Sheila's face and knew she was in her no-surrender mood. It would be quicker to bath Kirsty than stand and do battle, but it wasn't fair – Kirsty wasn't even her real sister.

On Ravenna's lap, Kirsty lay still for a moment, gazing up at her sister's hard-set face. The child's eyes held questions and it didn't take her long to work out the reason for Ravenna's hurry.

"No out, no out," she began to wail.

Ravenna gritted her teeth and kept her temper whilst she patted dry the squirming, protesting, dimpled little body. She reached for the talcum powder as the bathroom door swung open. It was Ian in his work clothes.

"What's up?" he asked cheerfully.

"I'm just trying to get her into bed," Ravenna said, her voice hissing with exasperation.

"And you're late for the dance?"

Ravenna nodded.

Ian smiled. "Well, go on then. Go and enjoy yourself. I'll take over now and we shall have a story, my petal," he said, lifting a now beaming Kirsty out of Ravenna's arms.

"Thanks, Ian," she said, throwing him a grateful smile as she left. He could be very understanding at times, she thought, unlike Mum.

But on entering her bedroom she was stricken with guilt for that last thought. Lying on the bed were her skirt and blouse, dry, re-ironed and neatly folded. A conciliatory gesture from Mum, even at the risk of being late for Bingo – Ravenna knew what a sacrifice that was.

Half an hour later, Ravenna had made it to Molly's house and was knocking on Molly's bedroom door. Her friend opened it, wearing just bra and pants.

"Hi. Come and help me choose what to wear. I can't decide."

"I didn't have that trouble," Ravenna said drily, looking down at her old skirt.

"Yeah, but you look great in whatever you wear," Molly replied, throwing back the doors of a wardrobe to reveal hordes of trousers, jeans, leggings, shirts.

"Go on, you pick something for me," she asked, standing aside.

Ravenna strode forward and looked through the racks. This could take all night. Molly was so insecure about her appearance, although Ravenna couldn't understand why. She had shiny blondish hair, always well-cut, a cute pointy nose, superb white teeth and a figure that was round and curvy without being fat. But Molly thought her breasts too big, her legs too short, her nose off-centre.

"The black jeans, white shirt and that waistcoat," Ravenna said decisively. "You look good in those."

"Not that it matters, anyway," Molly said, slipping the shirt over her head. "It's not as if we care about anybody who's going to be there."

"No," Ravenna agreed, reaching for some of Molly's expensive perfume.

The dance was well under way by the time they arrived. Music bounced down the corridors to meet them and groups of smokers and would-be troublemakers were skulking in dark corners. At the entrance, ex-pupils were trying to gate-crash. Ravenna smiled as she recognized two of them: a couple of lads who'd been inseparable at school, always causing trouble together. One was small with red hair, freckles and glasses and Ravenna remembered how she'd once heard him tell the PE teacher that he hated school and when he left, he was never coming back.

His mate was taller, more thuggish, and he began to shout as Ravenna and Molly approached the pay table.

Molly clutched Ravenna's arm, trying to pull her back. "I knew we shouldn't have come," she whispered.

"Here, give me your money. You've led too sheltered a life," Ravenna replied, and with a defiant air she stepped forward.

The technology teacher looked cheesed-off. "We've had enough trouble from you in the past, so no messing about. Any trouble tonight and we call the police," he told the menacing lads.

But the lads weren't listening to him now, they were eyeing Ravenna.

"Hallo, my date's arrived," one of the lads boasted.

"Yeah, we're with her," another joined in.

Ravenna never faltered. She looked straight at the teacher and paid the entrance fee without a sideways glance. The lads did a bit of pushing and elbowing around the table but Ravenna ignored them. With perfect poise she collected her change and Molly, and walked away. Neither of them made any move to follow.

Inside, it was hot, dark and incredibly noisy. Pupils seemed to be in herds, standing bleating at each other or shuffling noiselessly to the music. Stick people dancing in time, synchronizing their limbs to the pulsating music. It was difficult to identify anybody at first, faces were shadowy, bodies shifting and clothes unfamiliar.

"There's Rachael," Ravenna shouted above the noise.

She and Molly pushed their way through and tagged on to Rachael's group of dancers, adding their bodies to the silhouettes shadowing the wall.

Ravenna soon lost herself in the insistent beat, moving her body, hips swaying, arms gliding, hair swinging, brushing her cheeks.

Rachael nudged Molly. "There she goes."

They laughed, but with affection. When Ravenna was dancing nobody mocked. She danced with such conviction, such natural rhythm. It wasn't for show but as if she was born to dance. In a film the floor would have cleared for her – even here in the crowded school hall, she had created some space, dancing, whirling inside her own dream.

When the lights went up Ravenna stood oblivious, eyes shining, lips slightly parted, a tiny string of droplets glistening above her top lip.

"Come on," Molly said, gently shaking her. "Let's go and get a drink."

They pushed their way into the classroom where Miss Devlin was supervising the sale of Coke and crisps. Molly saw somebody she knew near the front of the queue and fought her way through, whilst Ravenna waited beyond the crush.

Everyone around her seemed to be part of a group, laughing and drinking, and Ravenna felt conspicuous standing alone. She was aware of several pairs of eyes upon her. Malc Orridge, a friend of Dustin's, stood with a mate, pretending not to notice her whilst obviously talking about her, so she glared and turned her back to them.

"Some stuck-up girls in here tonight, aren't there?" Malc aimed at her back, in his squeaky voice.

"Yeah, think they're too good for us," his friend obligingly joined in.

"Don't know what they're missing, do they?"

Ravenna heard them and she knew exactly. A few pecks on the check, an invitation to go outside, a tongue down the throat and sticky fingers on her breasts. She could do without it, thanks very much.

She wished Molly would come back with the drinks. She could smell something stronger than Coke being passed around a group near to her and two of the girls were pushing each other and lurching into tables.

Ravenna moved away, trying to find a quieter space, but as she stepped back she was almost knocked flying by a body jolting violently against her. It was Malc Orridge.

"Sorry," he squeaked, a stupid grin gaping through his spotty face.

Ravenna wanted to swear at him but she controlled her temper, drew herself up to her full height – which was above his – and gave him one of her withering looks. Malc's spots merged into a general blush as he spluttered another apology and slunk back to his mate.

For the next few minutes, Ravenna had to listen to Malc and friend's whispered argument about whose idea it was to push who into whom. It was a relief to see Molly returning with the drinks.

"Gosh, it was a real crush. Here," Molly said, handing Ravenna a Coke. "Have you seen. . ."

And she began a long list of names and descriptions to

which Ravenna only half listened whilst she scanned the room with a dreamy expression on her face as if she was searching for someone but not really seeing.

"You're not listening to me, are you?" Molly asked.

Ravenna didn't reply. She heard the long bending notes of a guitar, the clash of drums, and sprang to life.

"Come on," she yelled, grabbing Molly's arm. "They're on."

Ignoring Molly's protests, Ravenna propelled her friend out of the classroom and back into the hall.

"Jeez, Ravenna, what are you doing? You left that room where that dishy sixth-former was eyeing you and you drag me out here to listen to some stupid band warming up?" Molly panted.

"I didn't see any dishy sixth-former. Where was he?" Ravenna asked abstractedly, pushing Molly through the crush of bodies.

"He was standing right behind you, you nerd."

Ravenna laughed. "Oh well, I was trying not to look at anybody."

Molly sighed. Ravenna was now dragging her to the front of the stage as if she was some kind of groupie. The lead singer had begun his first song and was leaping and gyrating about the stage, and Ravenna's eyes were riveted to him.

"Isn't he wild?"

Molly's eyes followed Ravenna's and they widened in recognition.

"Ye gods! It's Dustin Harrows," Molly gasped, her face agog. "Yes, I've always thought of him as something wild . . . like an animal . . . but then that's unfair to animals."

Molly's sarcasm was lost on Ravenna, whose attention was glued to Dustin's every twitch. He was leaning forward now, still for a moment, bending towards the hands reaching for him. Ravenna's hand didn't go up but her face was eager, animated, and Molly watched her with growing annoyance. Bodies began to press in on them as people crowded to the front to be part of the act. It was suffocating but Ravenna didn't care. She saw Dustin crouching, his hand slithering over his taut thigh muscles, watched him unwind like a cobra, his tongue licking his lips, saw him dart across the stage, spitting out a frantic tune.

Rachael was thrown up against her as the crowd surged. "They're good, aren't they? Didn't know Dustin had hidden talents," she shouted as the first song ended.

From the other side of Ravenna came Molly's voice, harsh and bitter.

"He's kept them well hidden, if you ask me. I keep expecting him to break into a goose-step or shout, 'Bash the Pakis.'"

As the band went into the second number, a gaggle of girls with moony eyes were now practically throwing themselves on to the stage, and Dustin, egged on by cheers and squeals of ecstasy, leapt about like someone possessed. He swung the microphone, did a body spin and then took off his shirt, showing a muscular body gleaming with sweat. The girls went wild, clapping and screaming, and Dustin lapped up the applause like a smug cat who was used to getting the cream.

The band charged into the next number without a pause and the crowd went with them, dancing wildly to the frenzied beat.

When the lights were lowered and at last the music paused, Dustin stood motionless in a single pool of light which flooded his hair with gold. He leaned towards the audience and began to rasp out a gentle, tender ballad. Ravenna stopped dancing, swaying only slightly as she listened, her eyes clinging to him, her arms hugging her body. When the sound finally died she stood still amidst enthusiastic clapping, whistling and stamping which greeted the end of the band's performance.

She was still entranced, eyes shining, face aglow, when Molly and Rachael pushed their way through to her.

Ravenna beamed at them. "Wasn't he fantastic?"

"Not bad," Molly replied tersely. "Guitars were a bit out of tune."

"Sod the guitars. I mean Dustin," Ravenna said.

Molly shrugged. "He was hoarse at the end," she said.

Ravenna was annoyed at her criticism. All around her people were still cheering and some younger girls were even asking Dustin for his autograph.

"Moll, he was great," Ravenna said. "I know he's a psycho but on stage, he's magic."

Molly glared at her in disbelief, then said abruptly, "I'm going to get another drink. Are you coming?"

Ravenna glanced towards the stage. "No, I'll stay here. Might see that dishy sixth-former."

"Suit yourself," Molly replied, turning on her heel and hurrying away with her arm through Rachael's.

Ravenna stood for a moment, her body tingling all over, glowing with warmth and bathed in trickling sweat. Dustin was now seated on the front of the stage, his long legs dangling, his hair glowing like a halo. He was bending to talk to a group of year-eight girls who were giggling and looking up at him as if he was hot from *Top of the Pops*. Ravenna smiled. He was being really nice to them, signing the back of a T-shirt and kissing their hands – he wasn't as bad as he made out. He had to keep up the macho front or the other lads would slaughter him.

She moved a step nearer and Dustin looked up at her. He grinned, parted the mob of fans that surrounded him and leapt off the stage.

His face was damp and shiny, beaming with triumph; the open buttons of his shirt revealed a bare chest covered with a sheen of sweat. Ravenna could feel the warmth of him rippling towards her, as if he was still pulsating with the rhythm of the music. She wanted to reach out and stroke the glistening skin of his throat and chest.

His teeth flashed pearly white as he bent his head and spoke to her. "That was something, eh? They really liked us," he said. Then he added with a gentle, coy smile, "Did you?"

Ravenna felt her body go soft and heavy, as though it had separated from her head. She was surprised to be still standing upright. She'd thought part of her was on the floor, but her eyes were still on a level with Dustin's chin.

"Yes," she replied shakily. "You were brilliant."

"Was I?" he asked again, as his hand went up to his forehead to sweep back his hair.

"You know you were," Ravenna said. "Fantastic. Destined for great things."

"Oh yeah, recording contracts, number one hits. And where did your career begin? Maddock Comprehensive."

They both laughed but Dustin stopped suddenly and his face became serious, looking down at Ravenna with gentle, searching eyes. The sudden change caught her unawares, and her heart flapped like a wild thing struggling to control its beat. She shivered as Dustin reached out and ran a finger across her shoulder and down her arm.

She gulped. "How long have you been playing together?" she asked, trying to sound as normal as possible.

"About six months. This is only the second gig we've done. First one was terrible. We were all out of tune, then the mike went. We've been practising since then and we've got a different bass player."

"Well, it's paid off. You were excellent, really dynamic," Ravenna said, trying to sound cool and detached, like a local music critic who had just dropped in.

But Dustin's eyes were dazing her. He had fastened them to her and they were glinting and glowing like two amber headlamps. She was aware of the sudden thump of loud disco music and blue and red searchlights dazzling her eyes but the rest was a blur.

Vaguely she heard a DJ urging people back on to the dance floor; around them bodies gathered, bobbing to the pounding electronic beat. Dustin moved towards her and touched her hair; he stroked the palms of her hands and entwined his fingers with hers. He drew her close so that her front brushed his; then he began to dance, shifting slightly from side to side, sliding and snaking, pulling Ravenna with him.

He was loose-limbed, sleek as a leopard, and Ravenna fitted her movements to his, melting into his shadow. They found their own space and everyone else faded away; their hands and hips occasionally touched, their eyes met and smouldered. Ravenna pulsed her body to the beat of the music and the rhythm grew in her. She closed her eyes and gave herself up to it. She felt the warmth of Dustin's body near hers and thought how good it would be to belong to someone.

She moved closer to Dustin and her hand found his. The music slowed and Dustin moved forwards, putting his arms round Ravenna's waist. He pulled her close until she felt the damp skin of his chest against her cheek and his body solidly pressing hers. They swayed together, riding the rhythm. Dustin's fingers massaged magic into her neck and back and she relaxed against him. The music was wistful, yearning, and Dustin gathered her to him, pressing every bump and hollow on her back, making sweet circular motions at the base of her spine. His breath was warm on her cheek and now his cheek was rubbing against hers. She heard the words of the song, the singer's voice, syrupy sweet. It was the type of sentimental ballad she usually hated, "Everything I do, I do it for you." But she was moved by it. It was the best song she'd heard. She loved this song.

And as it faded, Dustin's nose touched hers, his lips covered hers and Ravenna felt herself stray into a world of bursting stars. Dustin's tongue was in her mouth, her whole body wide open to his invasion. She wanted the kiss to go on for ever.

But light blazed through her eyelids and someone close to her began to laugh loudly. She felt a prickle of doubt. What exactly was she doing? The music had stopped, the lights had gone up and people were watching her.

A teacher's voice rang out. "Leave quietly. Don't forget your belongings. Be careful. . ."

Dustin hadn't released her from his arms, but over his shoulder Ravenna saw a pair of piercing eyes glaring at her.

She pulled away from him. "It's Moll," she whispered. "I'd better go."

"Not doing anything wrong, are we?" Dustin said quietly, as he nuzzled her neck.

Ravenna wasn't sure. Moll's fiercely blazing eyes rang alarm bells in her head. Dustin was still holding her tightly, his square chiselled jaw just above her, his lips moist, his eyes tender. But this was Dustin Harrows, the yob from 11C – the lad she couldn't stand.

"Gotta go," she said, twisting herself sideways and breaking his hold. "I'll see you."

And with that she was gone, dashing over to Moll and leaving Dustin holding empty air.

"Come on, let's go home," she said, ignoring Molly's slicing stare.

"Don't tell me you can drag yourself away," Molly snapped. And for once she left the hall first with Ravenna following.

Outside they waited for Molly's father to pick them up. There was a heavy silence between them as they shivered in the cool night air. A gang of younger pupils ran past them, shouting after some girls further down the road.

Ravenna could hear Molly breathing rapidly and knew she was angry.

"Trust Dad to be late. I hope he hasn't been drinking."

Ravenna didn't reply. She was thinking about Dustin. How

did he learn to kiss like that? Was it just instinctive, like his singing? Sensuous, sensitive, passionate – all these adjectives applied. She remembered his heavy breathing, strong snorting breaths down his nose, his chest rising and falling – he'd wanted her.

She glanced down the road, half expecting him to come after her, but knew he'd be helping to load the van, packing away the band's stuff. She could wait for him, tell Molly she'd make her own way home – they could walk home together and. . .?

Gosh, she was trembling. Moll would be furious if she knew what effect Dustin had had on her. She was even slightly cross herself. If she thought about it rationally, she didn't even like him. It was hard to believe that the person who'd sung on stage tonight and melted her insides was the same Dustin who hated Pakis and slagged off Molly.

She glanced at Molly who was tapping her feet. "Moll, I. . ." she began, but she never managed to finish her sentence because Moll jumped in.

"How could you, Ravenna?" she snapped. "With Dustin Harrows of all people! It'll be all round school on Monday, you know that, don't you? Ravenna Collins and Dustin Harrows. Everybody saw you. I can't believe it. All the names you've called him, all the times you've told me that you couldn't stand him. And you fell for him, just because he was up there on stage and all the girls were fancying him. He was all over you and you let him kiss you!"

"Who cares? It was only a laugh," Ravenna said, trying to sound offhand.

"That's rich, coming from you! You're the one who's

always preaching about caring. Calling him a racist, fascist yob. It wouldn't surprise me if he was a member of the National Front and you were slobbering all over him."

Molly stopped abruptly and turned away. Ravenna was too upset and confused to reply. She didn't understand what she'd been up to either.

Large headlights beamed on them and Molly's father skidded the Mercedes to a halt. When they got in the car smelt of stale beery breath. Ravenna hoped that he was sober enough to drive them home safely.

5.

Sunlight was slanting through a gap in the curtains, settling into a bright oblong on the thick pile carpet. There was something so comfortable and peaceful about Molly's house. It was after eight o'clock and yet nobody was up; there was no sound except Molly's soft breathing and a few birds trilling from the garden.

Ravenna sighed with pleasure, rolled on to her side, pulled the duvet around her and curled up, luxuriating in the peace and comfort. It was rare to have a lie-in. Why was it, then, that this morning when she had an opportunity to sleep late, she couldn't? Her mind was being invaded, pricked by the events of last night like sharp splinters. One image filled her thoughts: Dustin Harrows. And not so much a splinter, more like a ruddy big plank.

Ravenna hugged herself and smiled, remembering the way he'd wrapped his arms around her, his breath hot on her lips. She quivered as she thought of the way he'd kissed her softly and tenderly, holding her as if she were precious, stroking her back. A warm shudder shot through her. But the next moment she was furious with herself. You wally! You're thinking like prose from a slushy romantic novel. "Her breath came in tiny gasps as roughly he pulled her to him, kissing her pouting lips." Purple prose, her English teacher called it.

Deliberately, Ravenna made herself remember the other Dustin Harrows, imagined him as he sneered and shrugged his shoulders, spat on the ground; pictured him swaggering and leering with his mates, cutting a swathe through the canteen or corridor. What the hell had got into her last night?

She tried to think of other things but it was hard to control her mind. She turned over quickly to shake off another image of Dustin that was threatening to replace Dustin the yob. It was Dustin on stage last night, his hips grinding to the rhythm of the music, his hands rippling sensuously, his chest gleaming with sweat. Ravenna kicked her feet in exasperation. How could she have let herself be taken in by somebody just because he looked sexy and sang like he had soul?

She tossed and turned and wasn't comfortable any longer. Molly was right. It would be all round school on Monday. *What do you think? Ravenna Collins and Dustin Harrows. Yes, Ravenna Collins, that stuck-up snob in 11T. Thinks she's somebody but she lives on White City. Malc Orridge says Dustin says he...*

No, it was too horrible to think about any more. What an idiot she'd been. She turned over, lay on her back, tried to blot everything out, then decided she'd just ignore Dustin on Monday and pretend it never happened.

But it wasn't going to be as easy as that. For a start there was Molly to contend with. When Molly woke up, Ravenna could tell she hadn't forgotten last night. She slipped out of bed without a word and disappeared into the bathroom.

When she reappeared she threw Ravenna a dressing-gown and averted her eyes.

"I'll make a cup of tea... Would you like a bath...? You can have some of my bath oil."

Her voice was clipped and businesslike. Ravenna couldn't stand it.

"I'm sorry, Moll, I know you're mad at me," she said softly, propping herself up on her elbow and looking at Molly who was pouring water from the electric kettle into two mugs.

"Mad at you? Why should I be mad at you?" Molly protested, feigning innocence.

"I know you are. You're not being yourself," Ravenna replied.

"You can talk! Were you being yourself last night? I certainly hope not . . . or could it be that you really fancy that moron?"

Ravenna was shaken. Molly was the even-tempered one. Even in class arguing her case against closed minds, she remained calm. It was Ravenna who went off the deep end.

"Look, I'm sorry. I know I behaved like an imbecile but I only gave him a quick peck on the cheek. . . I mean it was hardly a passionate affair."

Molly sat down on the end of the bed and stared at Ravenna, and when she spoke her voice was like ice. "Ravenna, you kissed Dustin Harrows in front of the whole school. Everybody saw you. He was practically swallowing you whole . . . and he'll be boasting about it all over the school on Monday."

Molly's body seemed to clench into one gigantic accusing question mark as she stared at Ravenna, then she got up as quickly as she'd sat down, grabbed a mug of tea and thrust it towards Ravenna.

"You might as well have got down on the floor with him,"

was her parting shot before she slammed back into the bathroom.

Sipping her tea, Ravenna looked disconsolately around the vast bedroom. Molly was so lucky having this elegant fitted room and the luxury of her own bathroom. It was difficult to spend ten minutes in the bathroom at home without somebody hammering on the door.

Suddenly, the bathroom door opened and Molly whisked out in a bathrobe, collected a few items of clothing from drawers and began to dress.

"Look, can't we just forget it ever happened?" Ravenna appealed to Molly's back as she slipped her arms into a shirt. "I won't have anything more to do with him, I won't speak to him. I'll insult him, I'll trip him up. . . I'll put salt in his tea, I'll make an announcement in assembly: 'I have seen the error of my ways and know Dustin Harrows is a total dork.' OK? I know I was utterly stupid, I'll. . ."

Ravenna was surprised to hear a loud snort and then a long string of giggles as Molly turned to face her.

"He looked like a demented baboon prancing around the stage, and if he thinks he can sing. . ."

She perched on the edge of the bed, laughing.

"Oh, he wasn't that bad," Ravenna said, and although she joined in Molly's laughter, she was taken aback by how defensive she felt.

"Anyway, he's a good kisser," she giggled.

"Well, I'm thankful to say I shall never find out."

There was a silence between them but Ravenna saw the shadows slipping away and knew it was all right, that Molly had forgiven her.

"It's all right for you, Moll," she said quietly.

"What do you mean, all right for me?"

"Well, you've got your mum, dad, David. This house, your own room. I come here and it's all so ordered, everything has a place, you have a place. You know who you are. I don't. I don't know where I belong. I don't feel I belong on the estate or to my family. I don't know where I come from or where I'm going."

"But, Ravenna, everybody envies you. You're beautiful, clever, good at sport . . . everything."

"They think I'm stuck-up, more like."

Molly sighed. "Well, I might not be so lucky much longer. If Dad's job goes, we'll have to sell the house."

Ravenna, shocked, felt a sudden stab of guilt. She'd been so preoccupied with herself that she hadn't realized things were so desperate with Molly.

"Oh, Molly, I didn't think things were that bad. I'm sorry. I mean, I thought your dad's job was secure. I never thought you might have to lose Badger's."

"Well, it might not come to that but it's a possibility. There's a shareholders' meeting and anything could happen after that."

Ravenna put her hand on Molly's arm trying to think of something comforting to say. Badger's had been Molly's home since she was born and Ravenna knew how much she loved it.

"I'm sure things will turn out OK, Moll. I mean, at least you all have each other."

Molly sighed and bit her lip. Ravenna wished she could say

something more positive. There was silence for a moment, then the telephone rang.

Molly crossed to answer it. "Your mum, Ravenna. She wants to know what time you'll be back."

Ravenna sighed, climbed out of bed and took the receiver. She knew what Mum wanted – someone to take care of Kirsty whilst she went shopping.

Ravenna was in no rush to get home even if it meant risking Sheila's anger. She was just too comfortable at Molly's. She loved the bathroom; stepping into the white-tiled shower cubicle, closing the shiny perspex door, turning on the shower radio and annointing herself with sharp-scented gel. It was so exhilarating, feeling the hot prickly jets of water stinging her body, turning round and round in the spray. But best of all was the wonderful feeling that she was completely alone, that nobody would bang on the door to be let in. No Brett dying for a poo, no Kirsty wondering where Venna was. It was sheer bliss.

After drying herself with a bath towel as big and thick as a carpet, and dabbing herself with Molly's perfume, Ravenna hurriedly dressed and went down to join Molly in the kitchen.

Juice extractors and blenders were whirring and Molly was pressing buttons, peeling fruit and humming happily.

"I'm making my latest creation. Just wait until you taste it. It's nectar," Molly said, spooning some yoghurt into the top of the blender. "By the way, David's home. He got in late last night. Called home to face the crisis, I suppose."

For a moment Molly's face clouded but Ravenna had never known her be miserable for long when she was in the kitchen.

She buzzed the blender again, then spooned the yellow creamy mixture into two tall glasses and grinned with triumph.

"*Voilà!* Mango and apricot shake. A superb breakfast pick-me-up, soft and fruity with a tang of citrus and a hint of malt."

"Sounds exquisite," Ravenna enthused, reaching for the glass.

"Just the thing to clear the palate when the mouth has been contaminated by smoke, alcohol or any other foul matter," Molly announced, raising her glass.

"Don't, Moll," Ravenna said, catching Molly's meaning.

She stuck a straw into the foamy yellow mixture and sucked. It was delicious; tangy and rich but not sickly.

"Yum. You should market this, Molly. You'd make a fortune. It's delicious. I think I like it better than even PG Tips."

Molly smiled and looked pleased. "Should think so. It's got about two pounds of fruit in it, not to mention yoghurt and cream."

"Moll! It must be really fattening."

"Who cares? I told you it's nectar, the secret elixir of life, discovered by Molly Morgan, who will live to be two hundred and twenty, at least," Molly said as she drank hers down and ended up with a creamy moustache.

Ravenna was laughing at her as the door opened and David, in crumpled shirt, jeans and barefooted, wandered in.

Ravenna felt a surge of affection for him and realized how much she'd missed him since he'd been at university. She pulled out a stool and David slumped down beside her. His blond hair was longer, she noticed, and he hadn't shaved. The designer stubble improved him, made him look a bit reckless.

"Hi, Raven. How's things?"

"Fine," she answered, smiling. "How's Manchester?"

"Not bad, not bad at all," David said.

He smiled enigmatically. Something was up, Ravenna could tell, but she knew he wouldn't give anything away until he was ready. She wished she could stay and talk to him.

"You look as if you've had a rough night," Molly said.

"That's a nice greeting when you haven't seen me for three weeks," David replied, rubbing his eyes.

"You know we love you really," Molly said, putting an arm around his shoulders.

"Thanks. I'd kiss you but I haven't cleaned my teeth."

"David! Don't be so gross," Molly yelled.

"What you need is some of Molly's elixir," Ravenna said. "Can I get him some?" she asked Molly.

She scraped the contents of the blender into another tall glass.

"What is it? I've been had like this before," David said, eyeing it suspiciously.

"Go on, try it, it's wonderful," Ravenna urged.

David drank some and nodded. "It's good ... delicious."

"I made it for Ravenna. She needed it after last night."

Ravenna glared at Molly over David's head. She didn't want Molly to tell him about Dustin.

"What happened last night?" David asked.

"Oh, nothing," Molly said. "We just went to the school dance."

Ravenna felt a sudden urge to leave. For one thing she'd be in deep trouble with Sheila if she stayed any longer and if she stayed, she might be tempted to tell David about Dustin herself.

"I've got to go," Ravenna said, rising from her stool. "Sheila will be waiting to go shopping."

"I'll give you a lift," David offered. "Just give me a few minutes to get ready."

"No, it's OK. There's a bus at ten past. I've put my stuff ready in the hall. It won't take me long at all. No use you rushing too. Enjoy your breakfast. I'll see you soon."

And before they could protest, Ravenna walked out of the room and made a quick exit. It was better this way, she thought, as she pelted down the drive, past David's early twenty-first birthday present from his parents – a brand new black BMW. If he drove that on to the estate, someone would put a brick through the window.

"It's taken you long enough," Sheila shouted, when she heard Ravenna let herself into the kitchen. Rushing from the hall in anorak and high heels, she pushed Ravenna aside to peer out of the kitchen door.

"Has she gone? She could give me a lift into town."

"I didn't come back with Mrs Morgan. I came on the bus," Ravenna snapped.

"Oh, just like them. Couldn't they have brought you back? Too busy out playing golf or spending money, I suppose."

"David offered," Ravenna said, "but I said I'd get the bus."

"Well, you would. Don't want them seeing where you live, I suppose."

"Mum, they know where I live. They've brought me back before."

Sheila pulled a crumpled tissue from her anorak pocket and blew her nose.

"I don't know why you refused a lift from David. He's a nice lad and he's got that brand-new car, hasn't he?"

She gave Ravenna a meaningful look.

Ravenna snorted. "Honestly, Mum. Just because you want the neighbours to see a flash car drawing up. And it's no good going on about me and David – I don't fancy him like that – just because you think he's rich. If I get rich it'll be through my own efforts. I'm not relying on any man."

Sheila shook her head and looked as if she were going to say more but Ravenna was thankful to see her look at her watch.

"I'd better go. If I run, I might just make the quarter to. Brett's gone to get some garden stuff with his dad. They're buying some chips for dinner. I'll be back about four. And don't forget we're going to the car-boot tomorrow."

She grabbed her big plastic shopping bag from the hook. "And remember, Miss High and Mighty, money's not to be sniffed at."

Ravenna went through to the lounge where Kirsty was banging a doll's pram into the sideboard. No wonder the furniture was so battered. But nobody else in the house seemed to care – there were biscuit crumbs all over the settee and she noticed a fresh cigarette burn on one of the armchairs. She thought about getting out the hoover but decided against it and just brushed the crumbs off with her hands, clearing a place to sit down.

Seeing it was Ravenna, Kirsty let go of the pram handle and

toddled over. As she pulled herself up on to Ravenna's knee she left wet marks on her skirt. She was dribbling – must be teething again. Oh, no – more sleepless nights.

"Brett gone, Daddy gone, Mummy gone," Kirsty informed her.

"Yes, I know," Ravenna sighed. "There's just you and me left. Come on, we'll go upstairs and I'll change before you ruin my skirt."

Kirsty ignored Ravenna's sharp tone and gave her a broad beaming smile. "Naughty Kirsty," she muttered and hugged Ravenna tightly round the neck. Her face was all wet but she was so eager and loving that Ravenna felt her bad temper melting away. She's a witch, this child, she thought; always knows when I'm in a bad mood, knows just how to get round me.

"Come on, let's go upstairs then I'll take you out," Ravenna said, standing up and moving Kirsty on to her hip.

"Swings," Kirsty said firmly, "swings."

"OK, we'll see. Give me time to change first."

In the bedroom Kirsty bounced on the bed whilst Ravenna changed into an old sweatshirt and jeans. Outside the sun was still shining and Ravenna picked up a hairbrush and wandered over to the window. As she brushed her hair she pushed the window open wider and leaned out, breathing in the fresh, flower-scented air.

She was glad that her bedroom was at the back of the house. You could be in the heart of the country here and never know that just a street away wrecked cars, prams and weeds made the estate look like an urban wasteland. This side the air was full of birdsong; and the fields, humped and hummocked by the workings of old abandoned lead mines, rippled in the shifting sunlight before dipping down into the valley where the water tumbled and wild flowers grew. She wondered if she could persuade Kirsty to walk down to the brook rather than to the rusty old playground.

She stooped to find her trainers from under the bed, put them on, then straightened and caught Kirsty in mid-bounce.

"Shall we go down to the brook, see if there are any tadpoles there? Look for little fishes?"

"No – swings, swings," Kirsty protested from under Ravenna's armpit.

"Let's go and put your wellies on," Ravenna said, madly trying to think of some other way she could persuade Kirsty to abandon the swings. Inspiration came by way of remembering a fishing net and bucket that lingered in the shed from last year's seaside holiday. Ravenna found them, dusty and cobwebbed amongst half-empty paint tins, tennis racquets and gardening tools. She led Kirsty, who was now dancing and shouting "fishes, fishes", to the bottom of the garden and out into the fields.

Of course, Kirsty insisted on carrying the long-handled fishing net, stumbling alongside Ravenna as it caught in brambles and clumps of grass, plodding determinedly downhill, her knees chubby above her red wellies. She placed her sticky fingers in Ravenna's hand and hummed as she walked.

Ravenna was feeling happier. The sunshine was warm on her hair and she tilted her face to catch the rays, drinking it in, feeling it warm her right through, dissolving her bad temper and worries, as she swung down through the fields, calmer, happier.

Sunlight was stippling the water, glancing on rocks and smooth boulders, settling in rainbows where the water cascaded into a deep pool. Ravenna liked to think of this as her special place. Behind her the estate was lost from view and she could imagine it a million miles away.

Above the calm surface of the pool, pond skaters zipped as fast as jets and gnats bobbed. Ravenna let go of Kirsty's hand and stretched out her arms. It was such a beautiful day and the brook looked so lovely that she wished she could dance. Here in the open fields, a stone's throw away from the estate, from the broken windows and warring families, she wanted to leap and pirouette and celebrate the sun.

But Kirsty was tottering down the bank, heading towards the pool.

"Fish, fishes," she trilled and Ravenna reached her just in time to save her from a soaking. Grabbing her round the waist, Ravenna swung her into the air, whirling her round and round. Kirsty shrieked with delight, her arms waving in the air, until Ravenna collapsed dizzy and breathless on to the warm grass.

She lay for a moment feeling the solid earth beneath her, aware of the sharp humps of stones, raking her fingers through the tickling stalks of rye grass. The words "to touch the earth" resounded in her head, repeating themselves over and over like some litany. She closed her eyes and basked in the sun until a loud splash jolted her out of her dream.

"Kirsty!" she yelled, picturing her head first in the water, red wellies pointing skywards. But it was all right. Kirsty was throwing stones into the water, laughing with delight as the spray splashed around her feet. With a sigh, Ravenna lifted herself off the ground and went to fish for tadpoles.

The wriggling little black specks were deposited in the bucket where they swam energetically, circling round and round.

"Look, Kirsty. They're swimming, swimming . . . along the brook, into the pond, through the river, down to the sea."

Ravenna made Kirsty laugh as she mimicked the tadpoles, her arms making swimming movements, her mouth opening and closing. Kirsty tried to copy her, cheeks puffing out, eyes popping. Ravenna laughed at her but stopped suddenly, checked by a crashing splash in the water near her feet. She looked around but couldn't see anybody or anything responsible for it. She was pretty sure something had been thrown into the pond, however, and somebody must be hiding.

"Watch out! Flying fish."

A shout came from behind some bushes and two tall figures appeared on the opposite bank, jetting stones into the water close to Ravenna and Kirsty.

"Stop it!" Ravenna cried. "You'll hit us."

The menacing figures in dark hooded sweatshirts stopped throwing but started laughing like giant mocking crows.

"Haven't you got anything better to do?" Ravenna yelled. She was angry that her pleasant sunny afternoon had been spoiled and annoyed that she couldn't see who the vandals were because the sun was in her eyes.

"Surprised you haven't. Surprised you aren't with Dustin.

From what we've heard you can't keep away from him. Seeing him tonight, aren't you?"

Ravenna knew who it was now they'd spoken: Malc Orridge and his mate, Dean. They'd never leave her alone now and no doubt Dustin Harrows was feeding them lies. Wait till she saw him! She'd tell him what she thought, but for now she knew it was no use denying anything. Malc and Dean wouldn't listen.

"Come on, Kirsty, let's leave this place – it's been polluted," Ravenna said loudly, hauling the protesting Kirsty on to her shoulders.

"Look at that arse! Wish I was shagging it, don't you?" Malc's voice came loud and clear.

Ravenna felt like throwing something back at them but she hurried away, swinging crazily through the thistles back towards the sanctuary of home. Clouds covered the sun. Her day was spoiled.

6.

"I feel sick."

Ravenna looked across the back seat of the car and saw Brett did indeed have the pale green glow of an alien, or someone about to throw up.

"Stop!" Ravenna screamed over the popping exhaust.

Ian, alerted by past experience, put his foot on the accelerator, veered into the nearest grass verge, threw open the car door and hauled Brett from his seat. Brett promptly vomited into a stainless steel sink which some person had thoughtfully abandoned at the roadside.

Ravenna looked the other way. The sight of someone throwing up always made her want to. From the passenger seat, Sheila made sympathetic noises then passed a Milky bar back to Kirsty.

"Oh, Mum, she'll be the next one and she'll get chocolate all over me," Ravenna protested.

"Never mind," said Mum, passing Kirsty a grubby handkerchief. "She's got it now. It'll keep her quiet."

"I thought we were nearly there," Ravenna said hopefully as Brett was returned to his corner.

"Not far now," Ian replied cheerfully.

"I'm better now," Brett announced, visibly pinkening before their eyes.

"Oh good," Ravenna said shortly.

"Have one of these then, love," Mum said, proffering a packet of Kit-Kats to Brett.

"Mum. . ." Ravenna began in protest but swallowed the rest of her words. What was the use? Brett was already undoing the wrapper.

"Right. Well, after that little gastronomic interlude," Ian quipped as he climbed back into the driver's seat, "we'll get on. It's only another couple of miles."

He switched on the ignition, jolting the car back into an explosion of sound, startling the rooks out of the trees.

The journey proved to be more than a couple of miles. They lost their way, ended up in a farmyard, and Ian lost his cheerfulness as he began to worry that all the bargains at the car-boot sale would be sold. Eventually, however, with directions from two kids on bikes, they saw a sign tacked to a farm gate and Ian turned down the rutted track and bumped over the grass towards the rows of parked cars.

"I'll take Kirsty for a walk," Ravenna announced.

The rest of the family didn't stop to argue but set off eagerly to peruse the stalls and car boots.

Ravenna was glad to be alone; she needed some peace and quiet. With practised hands she set up the buggy and strapped Kirsty into it.

"Come on, Kirsty. We'll go and explore."

"Apple, apple," Kirsty chanted, waving her arms wildly towards the distant stalls.

Ravenna knew that Kirsty was remembering the toffee-apple she'd had at last week's sale.

"All right, we'll go for an apple soon. Let's see if we can find any bluebells first."

"Apple, apple," Kirsty sang as Ravenna pushed her over the bumpy grass and out towards the road.

Dodging incoming cars at the gate, Ravenna headed off down a lane enclosed by high hedges. There was no pavement and when a car came up fast behind, swerving on to the other side of the lane to avoid them, Ravenna wondered if the walk had been a good idea. When she reached a point where the lane widened, she paused to catch her breath and glanced around.

"Look, Kirsty, catkins," Ravenna pointed out, tilting the pushchair so that Kirsty could see the wagging tails above her. Kirsty stretched out her hands and Ravenna reached up and broke off one twig for her to hold. Kirsty waved it triumphantly.

"Cat ... thskins, cat ... thskins... I got cathskins," she trilled, waggling the catkins in front of her face so that she smeared a dab of yellow pollen on her nose.

Ravenna felt a spot of rain but didn't want to go back. It was refreshing to be out in the open, after the bumpy, fume-ridden ride in the car. No wonder Brett had been sick. It was a miracle they all hadn't.

She spotted a gate which had a stile beside it.

"Let's see where this leads. Better than walking in the road."

Through the gate a narrow footpath ran down through woods and fields and Ravenna strode down the path, the pushchair bumping along.

By the time they reached the next stile, a watery sun was shining through the clouds and no more rain had fallen. The footpath now ran through a rough tussocked meadow towards a village. Two ponies, an elegant chestnut and rough-coated grey, were grazing in the next field and as Ravenna pulled the pushchair over to the fence, the ponies lifted their heads and trotted towards them. Kirsty squealed with delight and reached out as they nuzzled their noses through the fence, but as soon as the ponies discovered they had nothing for them they trotted away.

"Gone, gone," Kirsty said sadly, "horsies gone," but she continued to watch, leaning forward to peer through a gap in the fence.

Ravenna looked dejectedly into the field too, thinking of yesterday's scene by the brook when Malc and Dean had mocked her and she asked herself for the fiftieth time why she'd let Dustin kiss her. She should have known he'd boast about it, exaggerate their relationship. And even if he hadn't, if it was just Malc's dirty mind, she knew that she had now given people the ammunition they needed to get at her. How could she have been so stupid? Over the years at Maddock Comp, she'd built a reputation for being stuck-up, never going out with any of the Maddock lads, so that now she was hardly ever asked – and she preferred it that way. But after Friday night her reputation was in shreds. She'd be reclassified as a scrubber. Everybody knew Dustin Harrows went out with girls for one reason only – for what he could get out of them.

Now she'd brought herself down to his level – going out with a lad whose dad was in prison. Well, what could you expect from an adopted kid? They couldn't be trusted, could they? Her mother had probably been a real slag – pregnant when she was fifteen – that said it all. And didn't kids take after their parents? Her mother, a dancer? More like the village bicycle. Had she been in love when she got pregnant or was it just overpowering lust, a quick one-night stand with someone like Dustin?

Miserably, Ravenna watched the horses trotting down to the far end of the field. She'd really let herself down, she reflected, and as for that sixth-former, when he heard about Dustin, he wouldn't come near her. She'd be thought of as Dustin's property. Dustin's woman. And tomorrow she'd have to face Dustin and the whole school. Her stomach churned. She imagined meeting Dustin in the corridor tomorrow morning. Could she pretend nothing had happened? She heard again his whispered words, "You are lovely, Ravenna Collins." He'd said it simply, gently, then he'd smiled and kissed her. She shivered as she remembered. Everybody at the dance had seemed to blur and float away until just she and Dustin were left. His eyes had gleamed tenderly, creasing her heart; his fingers had massaged orgasmic circles on to her back and at that moment, she'd wanted him.

Ravenna banged her hand on the pushchair handle. How could somebody be so sensitive and such a pleb at the same time? Damn him. Why was he so complicated?

Well, she thrust her chin out determinedly and flicked back her hair. Tomorrow she'd just have to ignore him, pretend he didn't exist. She didn't need Dustin Harrows in her life.

"No horses, Venna," Kirsty said, twisting her head to look back and up at Ravenna.

Ravenna looked down and her heart melted at the sight of the sad little face.

"No, my pet," she said. "They know we've got nothing for them. They won't come back." She leaned down and kissed the top of Kirsty's blonde head. "I'm sorry if Venna's been bad-tempered. Come on, let's run and see if we can find some flowers."

Kirsty protested but as soon as they got going the motion of the pushchair rocked her into sleepy silence. Ravenna walked on looking out over the fields and feeling a huge yawning gap of loneliness. She didn't want Dustin Harrows but she needed somebody. She wanted to be loved. Why had her mum given her away? Couldn't the family have looked after a baby? How could you give away your own flesh and blood – never knowing what sort of person the baby would grow into? If they'd kept her then she would have had grandparents and maybe, later on, real brothers and sisters of her own.

Questions kept turning in her mind and the feeling of loneliness grew until the breeze chilled tears on her face. She stopped noticing where she was going until the path opened out between gardens and houses to emerge near a crossroads and a cluster of limestone buildings.

Ravenna fished for a tissue and wiped her eyes. There was some sort of festival going on in the village. All the buildings were strung with flags and bunting and crowds of people were spilling over the car park of the pub opposite. As Ravenna steered Kirsty across the road she heard the bouncing chords of country dance music and saw a flash of white in the pub yard. She didn't need to hear the jangling bells to tell her that morris dancers were performing. Not her favourite form of dance but she thought Kirsty would be amused by them, so she joined the watching crowd.

The dancers were jumping in two neat rows, all male and most looking like they were working off six pints too many.

Beards and bald heads seemed to be the fashion, along with knee britches and black shiny shoes and, of course, bell-strewn garters. Ravenna surveyed the surging dancers, bouncing like overweight penguins, but as the music droned on she studied the patterns their feet made and had to admit that despite their bulk they were light-footed and dexterous. Whatever they lacked in elegance, they made up for in energy, jumping high with arms aloft.

Kirsty, awakened by the bells, was enjoying their performance, singing and clapping, almost in time with the thrashing accordion. She shouted encouragement as the dancers whirled to face each other and furiously clashed swordlike sticks whilst their feet never faltered from their drumming beat. Then their heads ducked, their arms entwined and one of them held aloft a star woven from the sticks.

Ravenna stared, amazed to discover the star holder was her science teacher. No mistaking that beard and nose. Who'd have thought it? Mr Barstow, a closet clog dancer!

He spotted Ravenna and she grinned at him. After that, however, she felt slightly embarrassed at standing watching and decided to head back to the sale. Mum would worry if they were gone too long.

On the way back, Ravenna felt cheered by the dancers and giggled at the picture she held of the gallivanting Mr Barstow, his large frame at home amongst the ruddy-faced revellers. She thought what a laugh it would raise at school if she told how she'd seen him morris dancing, but she wouldn't tell – just have a private chuckle over it with Molly.

Sheila and Ian weren't at the car when Ravenna reached the

sale field and were nowhere in sight. She waited a while but Kirsty was restless, so she set off to look for them, wandering desultorily amongst the bargain hunters.

The stalls were full of the usual out-of-date appliances or tat masquerading as valuable antiques or stuff in spanking new boxes that had fallen off the back of a lorry. There were one or two craft stalls where would-be artists had marked outlandish prices on their creations – a mirror decorated with gold-sprayed shells; a crude painting of bluebells in a wood.

Ravenna found it harder to push the buggy over the muddy field than she had done along the footpath to the village because the field was squelchy and people were meandering in aimless clumps. She tried to veer past a stand of gas-filled Mickey Mouse balloons but as she did so, something delicate and shimmering caught her eye.

She turned towards it and saw a dark-haired woman sitting, painting vivid, intricately patterned T-shirts. The woman seemed unaware of her surroundings, concentrating as if in a studio, her gaze intense, her brush making delicate strokes. Ravenna watched, fascinated, but as the wind stirred, she moved her eyes upwards to what had first attracted her attention. It was a beautiful shawl, draped across twine above the woman's head and billowing gently in the breeze. The deep pink silk rippled, shooting starry threads of gold, and its floating fringes twirled like tinsel. Ravenna looked closer and saw it was embroidered with vivid flowers and birds, and dotted with glinting beads.

Below her, Kirsty was trying to clamber out of her push-chair, battering the footrest with her sturdy lace-ups; above her the shawl seemed to sing in the gathering wind.

DON'T FORGET TO DANCE

"How much is the shawl?" Ravenna queried.

The woman looked up and for a moment Ravenna was dazzled by the most luminous green eyes she had ever seen. The eyes shone like dark emeralds and seemed to widen in recognition. At the same moment the woman gave a short gasp.

Ravenna was entranced. It was as if the woman knew her. But she was sure she'd never seen her before — you'd remember eyes like those. She wanted to see the woman's face again but now her head was bowed and she had resumed her painting.

"Six pounds," the woman said, without looking up.

Ravenna's hopes of owning the shawl collapsed. She had only three pounds in her pocket and even if she did find Sheila or Ian, they'd be bound to ask her why she wanted the shawl. To wear, to keep warm? How could she justify it? She wanted it because it was beautiful.

Ravenna stood silently, thinking, watching the shawl shimmer in the breeze and watching the woman painting.

She was startled when the woman spoke again. "You can have it for four," she said. "It was mine. It is lovely, isn't it, but I don't need it any longer."

"It's beautiful," Ravenna breathed. "Why don't you want it any more?"

The woman laughed. An empty hollow laugh like water gurgling in an underground cave. Her earrings of silvery moons and stars jangled in her long, dark hair. "I've done with it," she said. "And you know business isn't great. It costs too much to produce hand-painted T-shirts, more than people want to pay."

Ravenna noticed a trace of a Welsh accent and a hint of bitterness in the woman's voice. She watched her slender hands as they guided the paintbrush, adding golden flecks to dolphins soaring in a rosy sunset. Then the woman wiped her paintbrush on some rag and looked up again. And Ravenna saw she was beautiful. The wide sea-green eyes were iridescent and almond-shaped. Her skin was tawny, her nose long and straight and her ebony hair framed finely sculpted cheekbones. Ravenna thought she was the most beautiful woman she'd ever seen. She was like a Romany princess or mythical mermaid. But on her otherwise perfect skin, there was one flaw – across her cheek was a deep scar.

What happened? Ravenna wanted to ask, but instead she said, "I like your T-shirts."

The woman's eyebrows arched in response. "Wish someone would buy them," she said ruefully.

Ravenna didn't know what to say. She couldn't offer to buy one. She couldn't even afford the shawl and now Kirsty was clutching at a cloth which covered the woman's table and tugging at it, almost upsetting the pots of paint.

Ravenna managed to prise open Kirsty's hands and extract the cloth before she did any damage. She pulled the pushchair back from the table and apologized to the woman for Kirsty's behaviour.

The dazzling smile the woman gave her in return embarrassed Ravenna and she turned quickly away to steer Kirsty towards the balloon stall.

The balloon cost one pound and now Ravenna had even less hope of buying the shawl. Kirsty was happy, however, waving her arm up and down with the bouncing, smirking balloon attached to it, and Ravenna pushed on, avoiding the toffee-apples and hot dogs and turning into the next aisle. She browsed briefly at some second-hand books then saw Ian wandering towards them, holding a bulky package under his arm, with Sheila and Brett following.

Ravenna waited as Ian approached, then found herself saying eagerly to him, "Hi, I was hoping I'd find you. Can you have Kirsty for a minute and can I borrow two pounds?"

Ian smiled and teased her. "Oh, my word, don't tell me that you've found something worthy of your notice. A gem amongst the junk. This must be a first-class sale."

Ravenna waited anxiously, watching as he fished in his pocket and brought out two pound coins. But before Ravenna could take them Mum interrupted.

"What do you want two pounds for?" she asked.

Ravenna scooped the coins out of Ian's hand, saying as she hurried away, "Oh, just something. I'll pay you back from my babysitting money."

"You will too," Mum said firmly. "And what's it for? You spoil her..."

Her words followed Ravenna as she skipped between the tables to find her way back to the woman with the shawl.

But when she reached the spot, the woman had gone. The T-shirts, the pots of paint, the lovely shawl – everything had disappeared. It was as if somebody had waved a magic wand and magicked them away.

Ravenna glowered at the empty space. She'd been away for only ten minutes and everything had disappeared. She whirled around, scanning the rows of stalls behind her. Perhaps she was in the wrong place, she'd remembered the wrong balloon stall. The bloated grinning faces on the bobbing balloons opposite mocked her. She stared at them in horror then ran blindly, panicking, searching between the stalls, pushing past ambling people, tripping over a frying pan and bumping into tables. All the people, dogs, stalls and wares began to merge into one messy tableau as she ran and still she didn't find the woman with the shawl.

Stopping by the hot dog stall for the second time to catch her breath, Ravenna spotted Sheila laughing with a stall owner, her flushed cheeks glowing above her blue anorak, and Ravenna knew she'd circled the entire market and not found the precious shawl. She turned and walked in the opposite direction. She felt stupid and didn't want to join her family yet. Had she imagined the woman? No, that was even more stupid.

One more time she walked back to the empty site near the balloons. She stared again at the empty space but then lifted her eyes and saw, behind the gap where the stall had stood, an old yellow van with rainbows and dolphins painted on its side. The back doors were open and as Ravenna raced towards it she saw long slender legs and a bottom encased in tight jeans sticking out of the back, and above the bottom was a long cascade of bluey-black hair.

"I wanted the shawl," Ravenna shouted.

The figure in the back of the van spun round. It was the same woman and she was holding something, a sliver of silk – the shawl.

"I thought you'd be back for it," she said. "Sorry. Harry turned up and helped me pack away. It's soul destroying sitting there, not selling anything. We're off to the village. There's a dance festival on. Want to come?"

"No thanks, I can't. I mean I'd like to but I can't. My family will ..." Ravenna stammered.

She was taken aback by such an invitation from a complete stranger but the woman said it so naturally that she didn't feel threatened and there was something about this woman that made Ravenna feel as if she already knew her and wish she could go with her.

"Well, another time maybe," the woman said. Then smiling, she held out the shawl and it slipped gently from its folds with a shimmering sigh.

"Take it. Here, go on. It'll look lovely on you. Wear it."

"Thanks," Ravenna said, offering her coins.

The woman laughed, a surprisingly hearty laugh from such a frail, elegant figure. "No, I don't want that. I'd like to give it to you."

Ravenna stood silent and surprised whilst the woman stepped gracefully down from the van and draped the shawl around Ravenna's shoulders.

"There," she said, looking deep into Ravenna's eyes, "it belongs to you. It looks lovely."

The woman's voice was softer now, tender. "Someone special gave it to me and in turn, I gave it to a very special person. But they don't need it any more. I want you to have it."

The woman smiled and motioned for Ravenna to turn around.

Ravenna lifted her arms under the shawl, held them out and

twirled, so that her hair and the shawl spun and mingled, bluey-black flashed with pink and gold.

When she came to a standstill Ravenna and the woman were laughing, as if they were sharing some wonderful, private joke and they carried on until a voice by their side jolted them.

"She'll never make any money."

Ravenna turned and saw the speaker was a tall man with long brown hair curling over his collar. His voice was deep and musical and although he was trying to look stern, beneath his grimace was a playful smile.

"Been here all morning, paid five pounds rent and she gives away what little profit she makes," he joked.

Ravenna returned his smile and the man held out his hand. "Harry Matthews," he said. "Beth told me about you. Said a beautiful young girl had come for the shawl ... and she'd be back and ... you are and you wear it well."

Ravenna was usually embarrassed whenever anyone complimented her but this man spoke in such an open, honest way that it seemed like a simple statement of fact. She shook his hand, saying, "Thank you. I'll keep it always."

The woman who Ravenna knew now to be Beth spoke again. "Until perhaps you find someone to give it to. But do what you like with it. It's yours now."

"I'll take care of it," Ravenna vowed, holding the shawl tight to her body.

"I'm sure you will," Beth replied.

Then she reached forward and touched a strand of Ravenna's hair. Just a fleeting movement and yet Ravenna felt her warmth, and was lit up inside.

But as Beth drew back her hand, Ravenna saw a shadow

pass over her face and her happiness faded as Beth said quickly, "Well, we'd better be going if we're to make the dance festival. Sure you can't come?"

Ravenna shook her head.

"Well, some other time, I hope," Beth said.

As Ravenna nodded, their eyes met and Ravenna realized with a start something she'd known all along. That there was something familiar about Beth's face. And as she looked at her, Beth's eyes, large and luminous, the colour different but the shape the same distinctive, almond shape as her own, looked back at her.

7.

It began even before Ravenna arrived at school on Monday morning. Wolf whistles at the bus-stop, slurping and sucking noises, explosive kisses. On the bus, it was worse.

"I hear Dustin's getting his leg over."

"Says she's a real handful."

Snigger, snigger.

"Yeah, it's always the quiet ones."

"Thought she was too stuck-up for him."

Giggle, giggle.

"What, Ravenna Collins and Dustin Harrows?" gasped someone, obviously the last to hear the gossip.

Ravenna felt like turning round and yelling at them but she controlled herself. She sat still, bending slightly forward, trying not to listen, but it was impossible. Her head prickled as if the boys' insults were barbs stabbing into her scalp.

The air seemed stifling and she turned her face to the cool of the window, pretending to look out, pretending to ignore the scathing remarks, keeping her chin up and hoping the unshed tears shining in her eyes would not spill over and roll down her cheeks.

Ravenna closed her eyes and blinked. A blurred face shimmered in the tears, then stilled into focus. It was Beth. She was smiling and her bright, frank eyes gazed at Ravenna as they had yesterday, seeing into her soul. Ravenna was instantly comforted. She felt Beth's strength. Beth wouldn't approve of Dustin, wouldn't be seduced by his good looks and brittle charm.

For the rest of the journey, she imagined that Beth was beside her – protecting her, caring for her and telling her to ignore the stupid comments. By the time the bus stopped, she thought she was immune to them but as she was getting off the bus, a quiet comment from Faye Mellins got to her.

"Look what the cat brought in. Slag," Faye sneered as Ravenna passed her.

Faye Mellins, of all people. Faye, who'd gone out with almost every boy in year ten and eleven. Ravenna sniffed back her tears and walked on, head in the air, trying to look non-chalant but with her spirits sagging to her shoes. She couldn't seem to think of Beth now. She hoped she might spot Molly or Rachael and gain some support, but she also desperately hoped she wouldn't see Dustin.

In fact, she saw none of them and entered school alone.

"Don't ask me!" she warned as Molly and Rachael watched her enter and dump her school bag with a resounding thump.

"We weren't going to," Molly replied.

"We've agreed not to mention it," Rachael added.

Their faces were a picture of composed understanding but in her misery Ravenna saw it as smugness.

"Oh, bully for you!" she snapped. "What are you training to be? Counsellors or something?"

"Thanks for the sarcasm. We were trying to be thoughtful," Rachael bit back.

Molly got up off the table she was sitting on and put an arm around Ravenna's shoulders. "Don't worry. Just ignore it and it'll go away. Everybody'll give you a hard time today but tomorrow . . . it'll be old news."

Ravenna shrugged off Molly's arm and smile and slumped down in a chair.

"It was only a kiss for God's sake," she complained sullenly.

"Then you've nothing to worry about, have you?" Rachael said, arching her eyebrows to emphasize the last two words.

Ravenna ignored her, slumped down further, stuck out her legs and folded her arms.

"What shall I do when I see him?" she asked. "I'll hit him, I know I will."

Molly snorted and began to say something but Rachael cut in. "No, you won't, he's not worth it. Not worth anything – far beneath you. Don't even speak to him," she advised.

Ravenna sat up slightly. "It's all right for you. He didn't kiss you," she moaned.

"No, thank God he didn't," Rachael said pointedly.

"Don't worry, Raven, we'll stay with you," Molly promised.

"Thanks," Ravenna muttered and tried to look more cheerful. "I'm sorry I'm so grumpy. It just makes me mad that it's been blown out of all proportion. You should have heard the things they were saying on the bus."

"Well, you're safe in here. Dustin avoids this classroom like the plague. He owes Baker loads of work," Rachael said.

Ravenna relaxed slightly and smiled at Rachael, who jumped off the table and bent down to rummage in her bag. She extracted a magazine and waved it at them. "Come on, let's read our horoscopes. Look for some good news."

None of them had the remotest faith in the predictions of the stars but it was a distraction and they sat together forming a tight little group, isolated from any unwanted remarks by their closeness and conversation.

Ravenna laughed wryly when Rachael read aloud to her, "Capricorns are in for a fraught time. Hold on tightly to what you've got or it will slip away."

"Well, if that means Dustin, he's welcome to slip anywhere he likes," Ravenna said emphatically. "Slip on something and break his leg, hopefully."

"Only a broken leg?" Molly asked in mock surprise.

But Ravenna was thinking now of someone else she didn't want to slip away – Beth. She couldn't understand why but Beth seemed to be haunting her thoughts. Her beautiful face kept coming into her mind, and with a rush of sudden enthusiasm she told Molly and Rachael about the car-boot sale, about meeting Beth and Harry, and how Beth had made a present of the shawl.

"It's the most exquisite thing you ever saw," Ravenna enthused. "I'm sure it's really old and precious. It's silk, real silk, covered with birds and flowers and sparkly beads, and she put it round my shoulders and said she wanted me to have it. And she had the loveliest face, all full of kindness, and she was beautiful, really beautiful. And she said she'll see me again."

As suddenly as she'd begun, Ravenna stopped talking. There was nothing more to say really. She had this feeling about Beth that she couldn't put into words. It was as if she'd been touched by something rare and wonderful yesterday but it was impossible to explain this to Molly and Rachael. They didn't even seem to be listening now. Rachael was looking at her magazine and Molly seemed far away, gazing ahead but not seeing. In fact, Ravenna realized, Molly looked rather pale and sad.

First lesson was English which was taught in the tutor room. Ravenna loved English when they were reading plays but this morning she didn't feel like volunteering, and whilst the group were laughing at Victoria Wood's witty dialogue she found her mind on other things.

Images of the previous day shadowed her eyes: the bright yellow van decorated with dolphins, the shimmering shawl fluttering in the breeze, Mr Barstow enthusiastically jigging up and down, Beth holding out the shawl, her face glowing. It was her eyes that Ravenna remembered most, the unusual colour and shape, like some exotic princess and yet apart from the colour, they were so like her own.

One image she couldn't recall, however, was the scar on Beth's cheek. She remembered how startled she'd been by it, and yet now, try as she might, she couldn't picture it. In her mind Beth's face was beautiful and unblemished, the skin a smooth bronze.

As Ravenna thought of Beth she was suffused with a warm glow as if something of Beth's spirit remained with her. It was the best she'd felt all day. She knew that yesterday she'd been offered a special friendship.

She wondered where Beth lived. Not in Maddock, surely, or she'd have seen her around – you couldn't miss someone like that. But Beth said she'd see her again as if she'd known her. Oh, if only she did! Ravenna fidgeted with her hair whilst she tried to recollect what Beth had said and eventually she remembered: "Another time maybe." That was it. She hoped so. Beth would be great to talk to. She'd listen to her, understand her. She wouldn't turn away when she was trying to tell her about Bengali dancers. She'd share the magic. I bet her house is full of wonderful pictures and things. I bet she's travelled, been to lots of countries – France, Italy, Morocco – unlike Sheila who never wanted to go further than Skegness.

Ravenna wound and unwound her hair around a finger and sighed. Then she remembered Beth's smile and relaxed. Somehow she felt everything would be all right. She'd cope with Dustin and she'd see Beth again. At that moment she became aware of the silence. Nobody in the class was reading; they'd stopped and when she looked up, Mr Stanton was staring at her.

"Ravenna. Is Victoria Wood making any serious points here?"

Ravenna thought quickly. "Oh, yes. Beneath the humour there are important comments on society," she answered.

"And what would those be, Ravenna?"

Ravenna was momentarily stumped. She squirmed under Stanton's critical gaze. She had no idea what the play was about but as she turned over a page she focused on a photograph of two women in a sauna.

"Oh, er ... comments about image, what women put themselves through to look beautiful."

"Thank you, Ravenna. When we do get on to that play, your comments will be most pertinent, I'm sure, but at the moment we're considering a convention for cystitis sufferers. Could you follow, please?"

Ravenna was aware of amused glances and people tittering.

It was a joke at her expense. What fun – Ravenna Collins being told off.

At break Ravenna stayed in the tutor room with Molly nibbling on crispbreads and apples. Molly was in one of her slimming phases that Ravenna knew, from experience, would last until lunchtime. It suited Ravenna though; there was no way she wanted to go near the snack-bar where she might bump into Dustin.

All morning she'd been mentally preparing herself for meeting him. She'd decided on a stony, blank expression, devoid of any memory of intimacy on Friday night, and Molly had promised to stay close and intervene if he tried to move in. Luckily, next lesson was history which Dustin didn't take.

Ravenna was so preoccupied with her thoughts that at the end of the morning she realized she'd forgotten to hand in her science project. She left Molly in the dining-room and rushed to the science lab.

Crossing the yard in front of the science block her heart lurched as she saw some of Dustin's friends, but he wasn't with them, and they were too busy fooling around to notice her. She put her head down and hurried towards the labs.

Pushing through the big swing doors, Ravenna heard the silence of the place and was thankful it seemed empty. Her steps echoed as she walked past the physics lab and on towards the chemistry room. Pausing near a notice-board she bent to pull the folder from her bag and then walked on, without raising her head, checking to make sure her work was inside. For this reason she failed to see a tall figure standing in the doorway of the chemistry room – until she collided with it.

"Ouch!" Ravenna exclaimed as the hard plastic folder

jammed into her thigh then fell from her grasp, its cover scraping across the wooden floor. She watched it slide under a radiator, aware that the person she'd bumped into was watching her.

She bent to retrieve the folder, her hair like a thick curtain about her face. Damn! Her leg hurt. She knew that she hadn't been looking where she was going and in this school walking down corridors was a daily hazard. She was always getting thumped by bags or barged into by running kids, but she hadn't expected to be at risk here. She pulled the folder from under the radiator and examined it for dust.

As she knelt, Ravenna felt a hand touch her head. The person she'd collided with was still barring her path.

And she realized who it was. Even before she looked up, Ravenna knew the face she would see. He hadn't spoken and yet she knew.

"Well, seems like we're destined to fall for each other," Dustin laughed.

Ravenna stared up at him in confusion. She felt at a disadvantage. He had surprised her.

"You all right?" he asked, helping her to her feet.

"Yes. I'm OK," Ravenna replied, her voice unnaturally high.

But she didn't feel OK. She was shaking. Dustin's face was close to hers and she saw his amber eyes, soft and full of concern and fringed with those long, dark lashes. He was smiling gently and instead of the cool brush-off she'd intended to give him, Ravenna found herself drawn towards him.

"I was looking for you at break. Where were you?" he asked, putting his hand on her shoulder then stroking the top

DON'T FORGET TO DANCE

of her arm. "I wanted to see you. You disappeared so fast on Friday."

Ravenna wasn't prepared for the way her body responded when he touched her. It went out of control, her stomach somersaulting, her legs wobbling and her throat wanting to swallow but unable to do so.

In another moment she would have leant against him, but behind her a door slammed and a boy's voice interrupted them.

Ravenna couldn't hear what the boy said but she heard his triumphant hoot of discovery and felt Dustin's hand drop from her arm. As Dustin stepped away from her, she saw his face distort with sudden anger, his mouth twist, his chin sharpen. Ravenna felt the strength of him as he braced himself and threatened the hapless intruder, his voice gruff and violent.

"Get lost, you stupid twat, before I smash your head in!"

Ravenna felt sick. Dustin was the pits. You couldn't trust him – he could turn nasty in a moment. And once again she'd nearly been taken in by him.

The door banged loudly as the boy ran off and Ravenna, startled, strode into the lab, hoping to dump the folder and make a quick getaway. But Dustin was behind her, trying to detain her, his hands grabbing for hers. Ravenna dodged around a table and rushed to the empty teacher's desk, speaking frantically as she moved, hoping her words would keep Dustin at bay.

"Sorry, I'm in a hurry. I just came to hand in some work," she said nervously as she dropped the folder on to the table.

Then she kept talking, trying to make her voice sound normal, as she edged towards the door.

"Have you finished your project? It took me ages. Still, it's done now. I'm glad it's out of the way. Hope Barstow thinks I've done enough."

He was behind her as she reached for the door handle and she was helpless as he gripped her shoulders and turned her around.

"Wha' abou' tonight, then?" he asked, propelling her back into the room.

The words were slightly slurred, provocative. Ravenna shuddered as his arms snaked around her. She tried to wriggle from his grasp but he held her tightly.

"Let me go," she pleaded.

In answer, he laughed, tightened his grip and lifted her from the ground as if she were no heavier than a child.

"You don't really mean it," he laughed. "Come on, remember Friday night. It was great."

He squashed Ravenna against his chest as he held her in an iron grip.

"Put me down! Put me down!" she shouted. She kicked out, hoping she'd catch something vital. But she was no match for his strength and she quickly became breathless, dangling like a puppet from his arms.

Dustin laughed as he felt Ravenna go limp and then he whirled her around, dancing with her, neatly swinging her between the stools and tables as if she weighed nothing. Ravenna heard him singing as the room swirled into a blur of taps and sinks and tabletops. She cried out as her swinging foot struck a stool and knocked it over. But he didn't stop.

He kept on laughing and swinging her around until a voice boomed from the doorway: "I think you'd better put her down, Dustin."

Instantly, Dustin let her drop to the floor and Ravenna landed with a thump.

"What's going on here?" Mr Barstow asked, crossing towards them.

Ravenna picked herself up as Dustin backed away, saying, "Just messing about, sir."

Dustin's voice was surly and Mr Barstow gave him a long look to silence him.

"I don't think Ravenna was appreciating the joke, Dustin. It didn't look like she was laughing. I think you were bothering her."

Ravenna tried to gather some dignity and stand upright without shaking. She was thankful for Barstow's intervention but felt humiliated and all she wanted to do was get out of the room as quickly as possible.

"It's OK, sir. We were just messing around," she muttered, smoothing her hair.

The teacher paused, looking from one to the other before answering, "All right. I'll let it go this time, but remember, Dustin ... I've got your number."

Dustin had already begun to slope out of the room and Ravenna reluctantly followed but Mr Barstow called her back.

"Sit down a minute," he said, pointing to a stool, and when he was certain Dustin was out of earshot, he continued. "Don't put up with anything from him. Don't let him hassle you. You should never have to put up with anybody's attentions you don't want. Too much of that stuff goes on here and it's time it stopped."

"Yes, sir," Ravenna replied meekly. She looked at his broad face full of concern and knew he meant well but even so, she was uncomfortable.

But now it was Mr Barstow's turn to shuffle and look uneasy. He cleared his throat. "Hrm. I don't want you to take this the wrong way but a . . . friend of mine, Selina, has started self-defence classes for girls on a Thursday night. Might be something you'd like to consider."

"Thank you, sir," Ravenna said uncertainly as she rose to go.

"I'd go out that way if I were you," Mr Barstow said, indicating a fire door that led out on to the yard near the dining-hall.

Ravenna thanked him and turned to leave. He was all right for a teacher. She wondered if she should mention seeing him yesterday. Perhaps he would think her rude if she didn't, or would he be embarrassed if she did?

She turned back to face him. "I enjoyed the dancing yesterday, sir," she said.

"Thank you, Ravenna. I enjoy it too."

He said it simply, naturally. Well, of course, why shouldn't he? It wasn't as if morris dancing was anything to be ashamed of. What was the matter with her? She was beginning to think like the rest of the pupils at Maddock, always looking for something to make fun of. John Barstow wasn't strange, he was just different. Like Beth. Beth's clothes, her looks, her warmth, everything set her apart. And Molly too. Molly wasn't like the rest of the girls at Maddock, boy mad, fashion mad. Molly made her own mind up about things. And me, Ravenna thought – that's why people don't like me, because I'm different too. Not just because I'm adopted but because I don't want to be like everybody else.

Slipping across the yard to the dining-hall to join Molly and Rachael at lunch, Ravenna kept a look-out for Dustin. She'd have to be on her guard. Damn Dustin Harrows!

"And where've you been?" Molly asked suspiciously when Ravenna sat down at their dinner table. "Didn't I notice Dustin come in just seconds before you?"

"Yes, you probably did," Ravenna replied coolly. "And the reason I'm not in the dinner queue is that I'm avoiding him. And thank you, Molly, for your support. He dived on me in the science lab whilst you were in here stuffing your face."

"I didn't know he was going to be there, did I? You left me, remember?" Molly protested. Then, her face full of curiosity, she asked, "What happened?"

"He pretended to be all nice, asking me about my project, then before I could escape he put his arms round me and swung me off my feet like I was a doll or something. It was horrible. I felt so helpless, but then Barstow came and interrupted and I felt dead embarrassed," Ravenna said angrily.

Molly and Rachael stopped eating and regarded Ravenna with wide eyes.

"Fancy him trying something in the lab!" Rachael said, all agog. "He didn't kiss you again, did he?"

"No, he didn't get the chance and he's not going to. I hate his guts, the slimy toad. I don't trust him so stick close to me. We've got Drama tomorrow afternoon and knowing him, he just might set something up – so we'll have to be careful."

Ravenna realized she was trembling as she said this and she felt suddenly filled with rage as she remembered how Dustin had lifted her off the ground as if she was nothing. Her voice wavered as she told Molly and Rachael about the self-defence classes.

"I want to be able to defend myself. Next time he or anybody else comes for me, I want to be able to deal with them."

"OK, you've convinced me, I'll join you," Molly said and after a bit of persuading Rachael too agreed to give the classes a try.

Ravenna waited as Molly and Rachael finished their salads. She didn't want to eat. Her mouth was dry and her insides were gurgling and gyrating as if trying to rearrange themselves. She wanted to get out of the dining-room and walk off her nervousness.

The girls left in a threesome. As they passed the table where Dustin was sitting, Ravenna was aware of his golden head and broad shoulders rising above those of his mates. She could feel the boys' stares hot on her back and there was a loud explosion of laughter.

"Don't worry," Molly said as she linked arms with Ravenna outside the dingy canteen. "Wait till we start these classes. You'll be able to fling him to the floor and stamp on him."

Ravenna gave a wry smile, remembering the way he'd lifted her off her feet. "I think we'll need faith as well as training," she sighed.

The girls walked across the large windy expanse of asphalt into the library. Here, under the watchful eye of Mr Stanton, they could browse along bookshelves, or sit in the quiet study area, undisturbed by yobbos. Rachael went to use the careers computer whilst Ravenna and Molly lounged at a table near the radiator.

Ravenna needed to talk. She couldn't get Dustin out of her head.

"I hate him, Molly. I can't think what possessed me," Ravenna moaned. "Why am I so stupid?"

Molly smiled. "You're not stupid, Ravenna. Everybody knows that. You're clever and sensible ... you just occasionally suffer from lapses of judgement."

"You mean Dustin?"

"Exactly ... Dustin."

Ravenna leaned over the table and thumbed some magazines. "I wish I hadn't kissed him, Moll. He's foul. I was helpless when he grabbed me in the lab. I couldn't do anything. And I know it's not finished with. He won't take no for an answer."

"Have you told him you don't want anything to do with him?"

"Yes... Well, no, not exactly, if I'm honest. But surely he could tell I was fighting him off?"

"He probably just thought you were messing about. Lads like Dustin can't believe anyone wouldn't actually fancy them."

"Well, I'll tell him. I'll go and find him now and tell him." Ravenna's voice was strident. Two pupils who were trying to study looked across meaningfully as she pushed back her chair and rose to go.

Molly grabbed her arm and spoke gently as she pulled her back down. "I don't think that's a good idea."

Ravenna pursed her lips and sat still. "No, you're right. I need to think about it." She flicked back her hair and sighed. "I do go a bit weird sometimes, don't I?" she asked Molly.

Molly smiled wickedly and squeezed Ravenna's elbow. "Like the time you danced on the roof of Miss Devlin's car, you mean?"

Ravenna grinned. "It wasn't my fault Miss Devlin showed us *Fame*. Seriously though, Moll, I don't know what gets into me. I wish I'd never gone to that dance last Friday."

Molly fixed Ravenna with her clear blue eyes and spoke firmly. "Forget it, Ravenna. Ignore Dustin and he'll soon find somebody else to upset."

Ravenna looked down at the magazines on the table, studying the cover of *Motor Cyclists Monthly*. "It's OK for you, Molly," she said. "You're so sensible. You never do anything stupid."

"No, well that's probably because I'm so boring."

"No, you're not," Ravenna protested. "You're just sure about what you want. You wouldn't have got into this mess."

Molly was leaning on the table, her chin in her hands. She sighed. "Oh, come on, Ravenna. I do daft things too."

Ravenna leaned forward, her elbows touching Molly's. "No, you don't. Not like me. Not like kissing Dustin Harrows." As she finished speaking, her head sagged and she looked thoroughly miserable. "I've brought myself down to his level and maybe that's where I belong. I don't know who I am, do I? I could have come from anybody. You've got a family – your mum, dad, David. You know where you come from – you belong. I don't belong to anybody."

Molly turned and looked at Ravenna. "You can't always use being adopted as an excuse, you know," she said.

Ravenna snorted. "Do you know what it's like to be given away? To know that your mum didn't want you?"

Around them people began to mutter about the noise and Molly huddled closer to Ravenna as she whispered, "That's probably not the truth and you know it. Your mum was young, maybe younger than we are now. You told me. She could have desperately wanted to keep you but how could she? What would you do with a baby?"

"Well, I wouldn't give it away for a start," Ravenna almost yelled so that more insistent comments were aimed at the pair, and Molly put her finger to her lips then pulled Ravenna to her feet and behind some bookcases.

Behind the barrier Molly's voice was louder. "Oh, so you'd give up new clothes, school, university? Stay in night after night to look after a kid when all your friends were out raving?" she asked Ravenna.

"I'd get a job," Ravenna countered.

Molly shook her head in disbelief. "You're being unrealistic."

"How do you know? You don't know what I'd do. You can only think of how you'd feel and you'll never have to face anything so bloody difficult, will you?" Ravenna retorted.

To Ravenna's astonishment, Molly's face reddened and her eyes filled with tears. "Oh, of course not. Oh, no... Everybody thinks my life is so easy – all you think of is yourself, Ravenna Collins. Me, me, me. My dad might lose his job and soon we might not even have a house to live in."

Ravenna was startled to see Molly so upset. She should

have guessed something was wrong, should have read the signs. "Oh, Molly, I'm sorry. I'm a selfish sod. I've just been thinking about myself all day."

"I know," Molly said bitterly. She was breathing rapidly, trying to calm herself. When she spoke her voice was quiet so that Ravenna had to bend forward to hear her.

"Well, it might not be as hopeless as we thought last week, but Dad's worried. He's really hitting the bottle. That upsets Mum more than the thought that he might lose his job."

Ravenna reached out and put her hand on Molly's arm. "I'm sorry. I won't say any more about Dustin and my poxy little problems."

Molly looked at Ravenna's woeful face and smiled. "Cheer up, we're not beaten yet. Pals for ever," she laughed, giving the secret sign they used to share when they were little.

Ravenna responded with hand on heart and then the girls fell into silence, Molly returning to the study area ostensibly to sort out some maths homework and Ravenna leafing through a book, but each busy with their own thoughts.

Ravenna felt battered, as if she had been put in a tube and rolled over and over. The past few days things had been unsettling. Last week she had been going about her life calmly and confidently, looking forward to completing her GCSEs and possibly going to sixth-form college with Molly. Now their lives seemed to have been tipped upside down. How could she account for her sudden attraction to Dustin when she'd always despised him before, and why was she so obsessed about her adoption and wondering who her real mother was?

She couldn't concentrate on anything because either

Dustin or Beth was in her mind. Her hands went to a sore place where Dustin had squeezed her and then she thought of Beth's hands touching her, gently placing the shawl around her. She saw Beth's face, beautiful and smiling, and she wanted to talk to Molly about Beth. But Molly seemed engrossed in her maths and anyway, Ravenna thought, what else was there to say?

She focused on some phrases in the book in front of her but they didn't make any sense. It was Beth's face she saw again and she remembered Beth's smile, so gentle and tender. Her heart ached for that tenderness.

But now it was Molly's hand on her arm, shaking her, saying something. Molly seemed excited, her words hesitant but urgently spoken.

"Raven, I've been thinking. Why don't you ... I mean, it might make you feel better if you. . ." She paused, swallowed, then continued, her eyes fixed on her friend's. "Raven, what about looking for your real mother?"

It was as if Molly had read Ravenna's mind and voiced her thoughts. Ravenna was already tingling with excitement when she pushed back her hair and, looking at Molly with shining eyes, announced, "My mother was Welsh. Remember that's what Sheila said. A Welsh schoolgirl. And Beth is Welsh. I heard her accent. Molly, I know why she wanted to give me the shawl. I know why I keep thinking about her. I know why she was at the car-boot sale."

Molly looked at Ravenna questioningly.

Ravenna continued, "She was looking for me. Don't you realize? She's found me. She's my mother."

8.

All afternoon Ravenna was ecstatic. In study period, sitting beside Molly, she retold everything she could remember about Beth. This didn't amount to much but Ravenna embroidered the few precious details, weaving myths around Beth and Harry's life. It was a life lived on the open road; a life of freedom, travelling wherever they wanted, camping in woods, watching the sun rise.

"It must be great to travel wherever you want, sell your crafts, meet up with friends at festivals. Everything changing. Not stuck on the same beat-up estate, seeing the same people every day. You'd meet interesting people, people in charge of their own lives," Ravenna enthused.

But Molly didn't share her enthusiasm. She'd been trying to get on with some work whilst Ravenna chattered. Now her face puckered with distaste as she replied, "Yeah, people who don't know where the next penny is coming from and who're constantly being thrown off farmers' land and clobbered by police."

"You're just saying that 'cos you know you couldn't do it. You're too middle-class," Ravenna teased.

"And you are totally unrealistic," Molly replied, as she turned over the page in her textbook and settled down to read.

Ravenna took the hint and quietened down for a while but she didn't feel like working today, she just carried on biting the end of her pen and smiling dreamily. She was inside a bubble of happiness, floating away from the school, away from her family, away from the estate and out over the countryside in the yellow van with dolphins swimming on the side and Beth smiling at her.

Only a sharp comment from the teacher broke Ravenna's dream and reminded her that she should be working.

For a few minutes she scribbled furiously alongside Molly, but it wasn't long before Ravenna's pen skittered to a halt and she was back to her thoughts of Beth.

She propped her elbow on the table, rested her chin in a cupped hand and whispered to Molly, "I bet she's as excited as I am now that she's found me. I wonder if I'm what she expected. Do you think she was disappointed?"

Molly lifted her head for a moment and looked anxiously at Ravenna.

"No, of course she wasn't disappointed, she'd have loved you. But don't you think you might be getting a bit carried away by this? I mean, Beth might..."

But Ravenna wasn't listening. All lesson she was suspended in her bubble and even the thought that next lesson was geography with Dustin couldn't burst it.

And amazingly, when she entered the geography classroom, it was as if Ravenna was hidden inside that bubble and could not be seen. Dustin barely glanced at her as she walked to her seat and when she'd settled down he ignored her. Throughout the lesson he behaved impeccably, intent on his project, never once indulging in his usual sport of teacher-baiting.

Ravenna, determined to ignore Dustin and busy with her thoughts, didn't register his saintly behaviour and was surprised when Molly suddenly said to her, "Hey, Raven, better be careful. If Dustin's behaving this well to impress you then people will want to announce your engagement."

Ravenna stared at her in horror and disbelief whilst Molly giggled and added, "Good God! What a thought."

"Moll, what on earth are you on about?" Ravenna asked.

But she didn't have time to hear the reply. Behind her someone bent to whisper in her ear. It was Dustin, having slunk round the back of her chair on the pretext of borrowing coloured pencils.

"After school, I'll see you in the library. OK?"

Ravenna gave a loud gasp of surprise, causing heads to turn and smirking faces to swivel towards her. Her bubble went pop as she felt Dustin's breath warm on her hair.

She was angry. How dare he approach her after the incident in the science lab! Hadn't she made it obvious that she didn't want anything to do with him? Ravenna struggled to control her temper. She didn't want to argue with him here in the classroom in front of everybody and give the gossips more ammunition. So she gave the slightest of nods and a quick "OK" to agree to his request. That would keep him quiet, but she had to square it with Molly whose eyes were blinking like some extraterrestrial being.

"It's all right. I've no intention of meeting him. Just buying time," Ravenna whispered.

As he slipped quietly back to his seat Ravenna was already planning how to avoid him and longing for the lesson to end. As soon as the bell went she would head for home, thinking about Beth all the way. She'd run and leap and dance in celebration. She'd found a mother, a real mother – young and kind and talented. She wasn't common, she wasn't a slag, she was beautiful and – Ravenna shuddered with excitement – I look like her!

Five minutes before the bell, Ravenna could contain herself no longer. She rose and went to the front of the classroom to talk to Miss Spriggs.

"Can I go home, Miss Spriggs? I don't feel well," she whispered.

Miss Spriggs regarded her thoughtfully, noting Ravenna's flushed face and glittering eyes.

"All right. The bell's about to go anyway. You haven't been yourself all lesson."

Avoiding Molly's eyes, Ravenna collected her things and left the classroom with a triumphant smile. Then she sped out of the side entrance, down the path, past the main drive and was almost into town before the final school bell rang.

Only as she reached the first of the shops did she slow down. She turned into an alleyway which led to a fenced footpath. This was the first part of a long, muddy path that eventually wound down to the back of the estate but Ravenna didn't care how long it took to get home as long as she was alone.

In high spirits she ran along the first part of the path, leaping puddles despite the heavy school bag banging against her back. Looking around she checked to see if anyone was near and, seeing the path was empty, she twirled around, head thrown back, her toes pointing, her hands spiralling from earth to sky.

As she danced she thought of Beth, whom she knew was waiting for her, waiting to see her again. If she'd found her once then she'd find her again and next time they met,

Ravenna knew they'd hug and kiss and talk and she would find the answers to questions that had for so long been burning a hole inside her. It would be like coming home. She'd belong, really belong to someone and she'd never let Beth go again.

Of course, she wouldn't leave Maddock, not right away – it wouldn't be fair to Kirsty – but she'd see Beth, they'd keep in touch, and when the time was right she'd leave the estate and make a home with Beth – a real home.

And Beth would help her to be strong. She wouldn't give in to handsome dorks like Dustin. She'd believe in herself and she wouldn't make bad decisions. Dustin had really shown himself up in the science lab today. No use thinking love could transform him. For a few moments at the school dance he'd been tender and charming, but underneath he was the yob she'd always known.

Ravenna thought of him now, waiting for her in the library, and wondered how long it would take to sink into his vain brain that she wasn't going to turn up. He'd get angry . . . very angry. Ravenna smiled but the smile faded as she remembered the strength of that anger directed towards the boy who'd interrupted them in the science lab. She'd have to be careful.

Pausing for a moment, Ravenna hitched her bag on to her other shoulder and walked on, but she didn't feel as elated now. Thinking of Dustin had tainted her happiness. She was hungry too. She remembered she had skipped lunch and stopped to forage in her bag for an apple she thought might be in there. She found no food except a sticky sherbert lemon.

Ravenna wandered on, sucking at the sour lemon. The

spring had gone from her step now and doubts began to poke holes in her theories about Beth. Tortured questions began to creep into her mind. Why hadn't Beth told her who she was?

Ravenna tried to understand Beth's motives, to put herself in Beth's place. After all, she argued, Beth couldn't just walk up to her daughter after all these years and announce, "I'm your mother."

Trailing home more slowly now, Ravenna thought of Beth as a schoolgirl, all those years ago, walking home from school just as she was now but knowing she was pregnant, wondering what to do. Of course, nowadays there was abortion but ... the thought of this hit Ravenna like a lump of ice. *I wouldn't be here. I'd never have been born,* a voice inside her cried.

Ravenna wondered what it had been like for Beth, going through with the pregnancy, having to leave school, having to give up the baby that had been inside her for nine months. She'd try to forget, try to make a success of her life to compensate but the pain would always be there. Eventually she'd have to find that baby again, see how she'd grown up. That's why Beth had come looking for her. But of course, Beth was careful; sensitive. She'd think Ravenna might not want to meet her and her visit might hurt Ravenna's adopted parents. So, Beth had had to contrive a chance meeting.

Behind her, Ravenna could hear voices. Some of the estate lads used this path to walk home so that they could save their bus fare. She quickened her pace again, walking as fast as possible over the grassy path which was punctuated by muddy swamps. She side-stepped on to a grassy hummock and leapt to a heap of stones. They crumbled under her weight and her shoe sunk into slime. If she stopped to wipe it off, the boys would catch up and she didn't want to be subjected to more comments about her and Dustin, so she limped on, accompanied by loud sucking noises.

Her feet slopped out a rhythm – damn Dustin – slurp, damn Dustin – squelch.

But then a thought came into her head that made her break her slippery stride. What if Beth had come to find her, just to look at her and then, having satisfied her curiosity, gone away again – for ever? As this thought took hold, all Ravenna's happiness evaporated and she was hit by an overwhelming sense of sadness.

The boys were close behind now, she could hear shouts but she didn't care. She felt unbearably lonely; the wind was blowing her hair over her face, her hands were cold and her feet were filthy.

Niggling doubts became convictions. Ravenna realized that all afternoon she'd let her imagination run riot but now she began to question everything. How could Beth have known she would be at the car-boot sale that day or that Ravenna would go to her stall? And how old was Beth? My real mother will be thirty-one or -two and Beth looked older than that. Or had she? When Ravenna first saw her bending over her painting she'd thought Beth was a teenager, then when she'd raised her head, she was beautiful but older than she'd expected – about thirty-five maybe. But Ravenna also remembered Beth's shining face when she'd placed the shawl around her shoulders. Then she'd looked so young, barely twenty.

Her head was whirling with possibilities and doubts. She must see Beth again. Must know if she was her mother, but how? Beth had said "another time maybe", but that wasn't certain enough. Ravenna decided she must search for her. Dance festivals, car-boot sales – from now on she'd become as eager a bargain hunter as Ian or Sheila. If Beth didn't come to her – then she would find Beth.

When Ravenna arrived home from school Sheila was sitting at the kitchen table puffing on a cigarette whilst Kirsty pummelled play-dough. Sheila didn't look up as Ravenna entered but was concentrating on the folded newspaper in front of her.

"What's a cleansing agent beginning with s – four letters?" she asked.

"Soap," Ravenna replied, as she pulled off a piece of play-dough and started to roll a snake.

Sheila penned in the four letters. "It fits," she announced triumphantly.

"Course it does. I'm a genius," Ravenna shrugged.

Sheila coughed.

"You shouldn't smoke in front of Kirsty."

Sheila threw down the newspaper and pen. "She doesn't mind, do you, Kirsty? Keeps your mum happy, doesn't it?"

Kirsty picked up the snake Ravenna had made and put it to her lips, puckering them and blowing.

Sheila giggled but Ravenna didn't find it funny.

"It's a filthy habit," she said. She was annoyed that Sheila hadn't made any real attempt to give up. I bet Beth doesn't smoke, she thought. She wouldn't be so stupid.

On the way home from school, she'd made up her mind to ask Sheila about her adoption, get her to tell everything she knew about her real mother, but she could see the questions would have to wait. The water had hardly boiled for the tea, when Brett burst in.

"Just in time, *Blue Peter*'s on in a minute," Sheila smiled at him.

Brett grabbed a biscuit before scuttling off into the sitting-room and Ravenna knew Sheila would follow.

"I'll bring you some tea in a minute," Ravenna said as Sheila rose and ambled towards the sitting-room. "Don't forget these," Ravenna shouted after her, scooping up the cigarettes and ash-tray and handing them over. "Don't want Ian to think you've been having a crafty drag, do we?"

Ravenna knew there was no chance of talking to Mum in private for ages now. She and Brett would be glued to *Blue Peter* – with double-sided sticky-backed tape. Mind you, she had to give Mum her due: the *Thunderbird* space station she and Brett had made just before Christmas had looked really professional. But after *Blue Peter* it was *Byker Grove*, then there was *Neighbours*, a quiz show, *Coronation Street*, Kirsty's bedtime and homework. It could be hours before Ravenna could speak to Mum.

And it was. Two and a half hours later, Ravenna lay on her bed, her maths book open, hoping Kirsty would settle so she could finish her homework and have a talk with Sheila. It was difficult to concentrate on the maths because Kirsty was doing her usual night-time trick of banging her head against the cot bars. She'd always had this most bizarre way of getting to sleep, banging her head rhythmically – sometimes accompanied by loud humming. She was too big to sleep in a cot now but Mum said she wasn't moving her into a bed until they could afford a new one. Bunk beds had been suggested until Ravenna had said, "Over my dead body."

At nine o'clock Ravenna went downstairs, hoping Mum would have switched off the TV because it was news time. Ian was cleaning a set of spark plugs on the kitchen table. He smiled up at her.

"Got your homework done?" he asked.

Ravenna nodded and thought for a moment of asking Ian about her adoption. He must know – surely he and Sheila had talked about it – but she guessed he'd tell her to ask Sheila. He was very loyal.

Sheila hadn't moved from the sofa since teatime, her legs were tucked up underneath her and her eyes were still glued.

"When does this finish?" Ravenna asked.

"Sssh!"

"I only asked when it finished," Ravenna protested.

"Another half hour," Mum replied, her eyes flickering momentarily to the clock then back to the screen.

Ravenna closed the door and sighed. She'd have to wait until Mum came up to bed. She might as well go back to her room.

At least Kirsty had gone to sleep. Ravenna listened for a moment to her regular breathing then crossed to the dressing-table. She opened a drawer and delved beneath the sweaters and T-shirts, feeling for the smooth silk of the shawl. Her fingers found it and gently she drew it out and held it in front of her. The shawl unfolded, rippling and cascading down-wards like an iridescent waterfall. She lifted it high above her head, then stepped back and turned round. The shawl swirled gently, shimmering in the soft glow of the bedside lamp, casting its glamour around the room.

Ravenna laid it on the bed, smoothing the creases and tassels, watching the birds and flowers rise in dark relief until they floated above a sea of silk. She lifted a fragment to her face, wondering if the material carried Beth's scent. Yes, it was faintly perfumed – the smell reminded her of bluebells in spring woods. She gathered more of the silk to her face and breathed deeply, thinking of Beth, and she saw her clearly as if she was in the room. It was Beth as a young girl, holding a baby wrapped in the silky rose-coloured shawl, her dark hair sweeping the baby's head. She was holding the baby she knew she had to give away. Ravenna closed her eyes and felt a deep thud in her chest as if her heart had stopped.

She trembled and let the shawl fall back on to the bed. Then she stood up, took a deep breath and shook her head. Crikey, what was happening to her? She was seeing ghosts now. She put her hands to her eyes and rubbed them, stooped to take off her shoes, her tights, her skirt and the rest of her school uniform. Shivering slightly she bent to gather the shawl, pulling it round her, draping it over her bare arms and shoulders.

In the mirror she saw herself, aflame with colour, the beads dazzling as they reflected the light. Then the colour and lights fused as Ravenna lifted her arms and spun, lightly, delicately, gliding and turning in the glow of the lamp like a darting insect, the shawl fluttering, beating like glossy wings.

Carefully avoiding Kirsty's cot, Ravenna dipped and swayed, her neck arching, arms swooping, fingers rippling, the shawl drifting behind her. She danced as pictures whirled inside her head. She saw Beth holding a baby, then she set the baby down and Beth was dancing too – dancing with her.

Ravenna lost all sense of place. Her bedroom seemed to expand, the furniture and walls pushed back by her gliding arms. She was creating space, filling it with weaving patterns. But a knock on the door froze her in mid-flight, then sent her diving into her bed, bundling the shawl and herself under her duvet.

"What's going on?" Sheila peered curiously around the door.

Ravenna, quivering under her duvet and panting slightly, didn't reply. She felt as guilty as if she'd been caught in bed with a boy.

"I've seen you in the nuddy before, you know. No need to hide from me."

Ravenna felt the cool swathes of the shawl against her legs as she reached for her nightshirt.

"I was just getting into bed," she said.

Sheila snorted. "Well, you were making enough noise about it. I don't know how Kirsty can sleep."

"Thought you were watching TV," Ravenna said, pulling the nightshirt over her head.

"Wasn't much good. It kept shifting from one place to another, first England, then Italy, I couldn't keep track."

"Mum..." Ravenna began, as she wriggled the nightie downwards. "I want to talk."

Mum, still half-hidden behind the door, now plunged forward into the room.

"I thought there was something wrong. You've been looking peaky lately. It's not school, is it?"

"No, everything at school's fine."

Ravenna paused. Now was the time to ask all those questions she'd been storing up, but she knew she had to be ultra careful where Mum and adoption were concerned.

"Well, spit it out," Mum encouraged, plumping herself down on the bed. "It's not boys, is it?"

Ravenna laughed. "I haven't even got a boyfriend, Mum."

"I know. I think that's part of the problem. A girl like you should be having boys calling for her every night, not moping about and studying all the time. You'll ruin your eyes. You'd be better going out, enjoying yourself."

"It's not boys, Mum... I like studying, I don't mind it. Anyway, most of the boys are..."

Ravenna stopped. This wasn't what she wanted to talk about. She wondered how to broach the subject of adoption whilst Mum clucked on.

"Nobody good enough for you, how do you know if you don't try, might be nice enough if you get to know them but you never give them a chance. Nobody will want you if you —"

Ravenna cut in. "Mum, I was thinking. If I did want to marry somebody – I mean, eventually – and if I had kids I'd have to know about my family history, wouldn't I? I mean, I wouldn't know if my mum or dad had any terrible diseases in their families, would I? We were watching this film in science about genes and they were showing you how haemophilia is passed on by the mother but only boys get it. Well, I wouldn't know, would I?"

Mum sighed. "You've asked me about this before,

Ravenna, and I've told you, there's nothing life-threatening in your background."

Ravenna sighed too. She knew this was going to be hard work.

"I haven't asked you for ages, Mum. You're my mum and I love you but sometimes I can't help wondering, thinking about . ."

"Well, thinking never did anybody any good," Sheila replied curtly.

Ravenna knew that Sheila was ready to walk out and somehow she had to delay her.

She couldn't think of anything subtle so out it came, clumsy but to the point. "Does my mum ever write to you? Ask how I am?" she blurted out.

Sheila got to her feet. "If any strange letters came here, you'd see them, wouldn't you? We only ever get bills, circulars and birthday cards," she rapped, looking down at Ravenna with annoyance. And before Ravenna could say anything else she continued, "No, she doesn't write. I don't know where she is neither. She used to send birthday cards. Phil knew more about it than me. He kept in touch with her for a while. Sent reports about you and he saved the birthday cards, but when he died and we moved, a lot of things disappeared."

"I wish I had those cards," Ravenna said longingly.

"Yes, well, no doubt you wish she'd kept you too."

Ravenna saw Sheila's face tighten and her lips draw in to a thin line. She reached out and took Sheila's podgy, freckled hand in hers.

"No, I don't. You're my mum, always will be. My real

mum because you're the one that's looked after me. It's just . . . well, will you tell me what you can remember about when you got me?"

She smiled at Sheila encouragingly and squeezed her hand.

Sheila, pacified for the moment, sat down again.

"There's not much to tell. They didn't give you much information then. . . I'm sure I've told you before anyway. Your mum was a schoolgirl, fifteen. Nice family. Wales they came from, but they were living near here. They were respectable, father was a clerk of some sort, not common, but they couldn't keep you. The girl was clever, wanted to go to university and her mum was ill." Sheila scratched her nose and coughed. "Probably with all the worry, I shouldn't wonder."

Ravenna lay back on her pillows. It hurt her to talk about Beth now that she knew her. "Where did she live?" she managed to ask, her voice cracked and thin.

"Near Stenfield but they moved away. Back to Wales I think, but the cards for you came from all over the place, then they stopped."

Ravenna leaned forward. Her voice was urgent now but scored with sadness. "But Mum, we moved. She could have still been writing, wanting to know how I was."

Sheila folded her hands and looked away. "You're too full of imaginings, Ravenna. Life goes on, you know. She'll be over thirty now, married likely as not, with a family of her own. People don't want unhappy memories haunting them."

Sheila gave Ravenna a sharp look, got up from the bed and turned away.

Ravenna knew that once Sheila went through the door the subject of adoption would be closed.

"What did she look like?" she desperately addressed Sheila's back.

Sheila stopped and turned towards Ravenna again. "I've told you I only saw her the once . . . and it wasn't the best of circumstances. She was tall like you and dark-haired. You look like her, I suppose."

"Was she upset?"

"Of course she was upset. She'd be pretty unusual if she wasn't, wouldn't she? Giving her baby up for adoption."

Sheila had had enough and turned to the cot, tucking in Kirsty's blankets and muttering something about disturbing this baby. Ravenna knew that in another moment she would walk out of the room. She had to say something else to detain her.

"Was she a dancer?" Ravenna blurted out more loudly than she'd intended.

Sheila chuckled, her shoulders shaking. "You come up with some things, Ravenna! She was a schoolgirl. An ordinary girl that got herself into trouble. I don't know, she might have been keen on dancing but she wasn't Margot Fonteyn or Madonna and it won't do you any good to imagine she was. You want to think about your future, make a success of your own life and never mind about what's past."

And with that, Sheila, still chuckling, stooped to kiss Kirsty and walked to the door.

"Sleep tight and be thankful for what you've got," she said as she went out.

Ravenna collapsed back against the pillows. She hadn't

handled that very well. She knew no more than she had done before, although Sheila had repeated that her mother was Welsh.

Ravenna remembered Beth's voice. "We're off to the village. There's a dance festival. Want to come?" Each phrase spoken like music trilling up and down. Definitely Welsh.

Her heart thumped against the shawl and she hugged it to her. She had a place to belong to, an ancient land of myths, of dragons, Druids, Merlin and Morgan le Fay, a land of green valleys and golden beaches – she'd been there on holiday.

This last thought sobered her. There were a lot of people who spoke with Welsh accents. Sheila was probably right – she'd been letting her imagination run riot. There could be dozens of women who spoke with a Welsh accent, had long dark hair and almond eyes. Her mother was probably in another part of the country, living her own life with her own family. Whatever is the matter with me? Ravenna thought. I meet a stranger and just because she has a Welsh accent and is kind enough to give me a shawl, I think she's my mother. Crazy.

Ravenna slid down in the bed. She felt tired, her head hot and confused with thoughts of Beth, Sheila and Dustin. The best thing she could do was try to sleep and finish her homework in the morning. But as she turned on to her side, Ravenna felt the beads of the shawl prick her thigh and she drew it out from under the duvet. For a moment she held it spread in front of her, watching it transform her bed into a magic carpet. But that's just what I've been doing, she thought, riding on a magic carpet of fantasy. Quickly she slipped out of bed and bundled the shawl back into the drawer. She closed it and shut all her fantasies away.

It wasn't so easy to rid herself of the images that dominated her dreams, however.

9.

Rachael and Molly were late. Ravenna waited for them in the school entrance hall whilst people marched past her purposefully, on their way to evening classes. Car maintenance, square dancing, flower arranging, languages of every hue – they were listed on the notice-board opposite. People brushed past her with sports bags, carrier bags, bunches of flowers, folders and briefcases. She was the only stationary person. Where were Rachael and Molly? And why had she worn this bright pink T-shirt over her leggings? It was so conspicuous; she looked like a giant strawberry ice-cream cone.

Sighing, Ravenna looked at her watch for the third time and decided to give up. She turned to go just as Rachael burst through the entrance doors in front of her.

"Hi! Sorry, missed the bus. We'd better hurry or they'll be starting."

"I've been standing here for half an hour," Ravenna replied, wheeling away from her and striding through the now empty hallway. "And Moll isn't here either."

Rachael ran to keep up with her. "More trouble at mill maybe."

"Don't think so. She told me today they'd won a big new order. Perhaps she's gone out celebrating but..." Her voice trailed off doubtfully as they crossed the floor of the main hall.

Rachael was thinking the same. "It's not like Moll to let us down."

Ravenna didn't reply but hurried on ahead, vaulting up on to the stage to take a short cut through to the gym.

"Hope this is going to be OK," Rachael said when she caught up.

Ravenna smiled. "It'll be a cinch. I've seen it all on TV. Hand on the collar, arm up the back and flip! They're on the ground."

"Oh, yeah, who are you kidding? I can tell you from great experience that anything that looks easy . . . isn't. Remember the wind surfing?"

Ravenna giggled as she paused outside the doors of the gym to remove her shoes.

"OK. Here goes," she said, straightening up and flicking back her hair. "Let's sock it to 'em. Geronimo!"

As Ravenna stepped inside, the door thumped back against the wall and her voice echoed around the hushed gymnasium. Instead of thudding bodies and cartwheeling screams, Ravenna was faced with a large block of silence. Around two padded mats, kneeling girls looked up startled, as if Ravenna had interrupted their prayers.

Ravenna flushed and wondered for a moment if she was in the right class, but then a slim black woman with cropped hair stood up and padded barefoot towards her.

"Hallo," she said quietly. "Nice to see you. I'm Selina." She asked for their names and gave them a warm smile. "Don't worry, we're not a religious order, we always start with meditation. It helps concentrate the mind." She gestured towards the mats and led the way to a space. "Come and join us."

Ravenna and Rachael knelt with the rest but, having come

in at the middle, Ravenna found her thoughts turning back to Molly. Something dreadful could have happened: her dad, he'd been drinking a lot or . . . maybe she was ill.

The silence continued but Ravenna couldn't find peace. She looked at the girls opposite and was surprised to see some of them weren't girls at all but women, some of them as old as her mum. And then she spotted Faye Mellins. Oh, trust her to be here. What did she need with arm-locks when she'd got her tongue?

The silence was broken by Selina telling them carefully and quietly that this course was not a martial art. It did not follow any Oriental philosophy but was designed purely and simply to help the students defend themselves against would-be attackers. After ten weeks they should have learnt techniques which would equip them to deal with assailants, and most importantly they would develop the confidence to use them.

"The first few seconds when you are under attack, when most people panic, are vital," Selina said. "If you put your learned techniques into operation in those first few seconds, then you'll have a good chance of getting away."

Selina positively glowed with confidence as she spoke but she did look rather small and slight, Ravenna thought. There was no doubting her strength and determination though. She chose a big, heavy girl to be her attacker and with a nifty throw despatched her to the floor.

"It is possible with practice to use the strength of an opponent to your advantage," Selina explained, helping the girl to her feet.

Ravenna watched with amazement. This is for me, she thought, imagining Dustin sprawling in the mud.

"Right, now it's your turn," Selina said. "First we'll concentrate on the weak spots, starting with one we all know. Bring your knee up like this, hard into the scrotum, or grab and pull."

Ravenna gritted her teeth as she jerked her knee upwards.

"Don't think about their pain, think about your escape," Selina said. "You've got to be ruthless – it's either you or them and *you* want to survive."

Ravenna had no problem in conjuring up enough aggression as she remembered Dustin at his most neanderthal in the science lab, but the next instruction made her a little squeamish.

"Blind them," Selina said, demonstrating how to poke at the eyes.

Ravenna took a deep breath, planted her feet firmly and flinched only slightly as she stabbed two rigid fingers into an imagined eye. Swallowing hard, she paused and was about to repeat the move when a small, dumpy, middle-aged woman with doe eyes lunged at her with all the savagery of a pit-bull terrier.

The woman laughed. "Nearly had you there!" she exclaimed.

Ravenna couldn't help laughing, partly with relief that she'd managed to dodge out of the way, but also because she was enjoying herself.

The stomach was the next target. "Wind them," Selina instructed. After practising this move with fist and elbow, Ravenna slotted in between Rachael and the dumpy woman in a line at one end of the gym. Now the idea was to try the

DON'T FORGET TO DANCE

moves in sequence, prodding and kicking their way towards an opposite line of women at the other end of the gym.

As they advanced towards one another, groaning and stamping, the air crackled with the release of violent energy. When the women halted a few metres apart, Ravenna surveyed the flushed faces opposite. They were positively beaming at the thought of winding, blinding or crippling their attackers.

When Selina called for them to find partners, Ravenna looked around for Rachael but saw she had been grabbed by a woman in a green shellsuit. Rather embarrassingly Ravenna seemed to be the only one left without a partner until Selina came towards her leading . . . Faye.

"Right. Now I want you to try out these moves on a partner. Of course, you'll have to stop some moves a few inches short of the target. We don't want anyone getting hurt. . ."

Ravenna and Faye faced each other, their eyes sparking with a mutual dislike. This was the next best thing to tackling Dustin, Ravenna thought. She gritted her teeth as her fingers shot forward, splayed and ready to poke into the whites of Faye's eyes. But Faye didn't flinch and Ravenna found her fingers frozen millimetres from the staring eyes as if stopped by a natural force. Faye grinned – now it was her turn. Ravenna drew in a breath and stood stone still as curved fingers clawed towards her. She held her breath as a talon big as a vulture's filled her vision. Faye held it there a moment, rigid and menacing, then casually let it drop. Ravenna breathed out and found herself grinning with relief. And to her amazement, Faye was grinning back at her.

At the end of the session Ravenna was hot and sweaty and

gladly joined in the relaxation exercises before going home. She lay on a mat clenching and unclenching muscles she didn't know she had and trying to empty her mind. But where there was supposed to be space, Ravenna saw Faye grinning or Beth smiling or Molly crying. And then her mind turned reluctantly to Dustin. He'd been absent from school for the past two days – that had been a relief. When she didn't see him it was easier to remember just how despicable he was. Just let Dustin Harrows try lifting me off my feet again! she thought. Next time I'll be ready for him.

In the silence of the gym, Selina said quietly, "You all did really well tonight. Now I want you to get up in your own time, leave when you're ready and don't forget – it's a jungle out there but . . . there are some nice monkeys."

Ravenna smiled and lay for a moment longer. She was still trying to obey instructions and relax but she couldn't help wondering what had happened to prevent Molly from coming to the class and hoping it was nothing dreadful.

Behind her closed eyes, Ravenna saw Molly as she had looked at school that day, pinched by worry. Then she saw Beth's face clearly, smiling at her as if beckoning to her. She smiled too and at last relaxed, flattening her back against the padded mat, her head lolling to one side until she could hear people around her rolling over and shuffling to their feet. When Ravenna rose she saw Rachael was busy talking to Selina. She went over to them. "I'm going. I've realized if I rush I might just make the twenty-to bus, otherwise I'll have to walk or wait half an hour."

"Did you enjoy the lesson?" Selina asked.

"Yes," Ravenna said as she hurried away. "Thanks," she

yelled back over her shoulder, hoping they didn't think her rude.

Classrooms were emptying as Ravenna rushed out of the hall. African music was pouring out of one classroom, and as Ravenna passed she glanced into the room and saw bodies shifting and bobbing to the pulsing beat. She didn't have time to stop and watch but the music followed her down the corridor, her feet taking up the rhythm as she pounded towards the main doors.

Once outside she began to run and was about halfway down the drive when a motor bike roared past her, driving so close that she felt a rush of cold air on her face and her hair was whipped sideways in its slipstream.

"Idiot!" Ravenna yelled.

The driver screeched to a halt just ahead of her but Ravenna didn't stop running. She wasn't going to be frightened into missing her bus by some stupid maniac on a motor bike. As she closed on the bike, the anonymous helmet skewed round and shouted, "Want a lift?"

"Not with you, I don't," Ravenna shouted back as she swerved around it.

"Bet you don't know who it is," the black helmet challenged her. But as it spoke Ravenna realized that she did know. She should have recognized that voice, that physique, at once. It was Dustin and he'd got himself a motor bike.

She carried on running and was breathing heavily as she saw in the distance the headlights of the bus sweeping towards the bus stop. Two people were waiting and Ravenna shouted to them to hold the bus but her cry was lost in the revving of Dustin's bike. He drove after her, passed her again, weaving in front of her, making her halt momentarily, then he carried on to the bottom of the drive and followed the now departing bus.

Ravenna stood and cursed him. That stupid nerd with his showing-off had made her miss the bus. She stood wondering what to do, whether to return to school and find Rachael or to carry on and walk home. Cars from the school car park were passing her now and she wondered if anyone was going her way. Before she could make any decision, however, a blinding light blazed into her eyes. The motor cycle was back, driving straight at her, and Ravenna was caught, frozen like a rabbit in an arc of light. She struggled to hold on to her nerves as the bike stopped inches from her feet.

"You'll kill somebody if you're not careful," she rasped.

A leather-clad arm reached out but Ravenna dodged around it, walking blindly on, hoping Dustin wouldn't follow her and wondering what to do if he did. She couldn't knee him in the groin when he was on a motor bike and his eyes were protected by his visor.

Behind her she could hear Dustin turning and revving the bike. Why hadn't tonight's lesson included how to unseat and exterminate motor cyclists? Her mind grabbed at possibilities – a nylon thread stretched across the drive? No time. A brick thrown at his fuel tank? No bricks handy. She couldn't even see a big stone.

Ravenna carried on walking, waiting for Dustin to catch up, but now she was out on to the main road and the sound of his engine was lost to her, drowned out by passing cars and lorries. She wondered what he was doing but wouldn't look back.

She'd nearly reached the shops before Dustin flashed past her again, the engine making a high-pitched whine like a thousand angry bees. Daredevil Dustin! Just like him to want something hot and throbbing between his thighs – pity it's only 50cc, she scoffed.

He stopped just ahead of her. Well, let him play his silly games, I'm not going to run away, she thought and walked on slowly, deliberately. By the time she reached him he had removed his helmet and as she passed, his face was turned towards her. In the glow of the street lamp she saw he was smiling.

"I wanna talk to you," he called out as she passed him.

Ravenna made a quick decision. She knew she had to try and settle this thing and it might as well be now. She stopped and turned around.

"I've got nothing to say to you. Just keep away from me," she told him loudly and clearly.

Dustin switched off his engine and scooted his bike up close to her. "You don't mean that," he said softly, so softly Ravenna almost didn't hear it.

His smile faded and he looked at her seriously as he said, "I like you, Ravenna, and I thought you liked me. Why didn't you come to the library? I waited ages for you."

He reached for her hand but she drew away. She heard him sigh and when she looked at him again he was huddled over his motor bike, his hair falling forward on to his cheeks. Ravenna felt a stab of sympathy for him – a mighty fallen warrior clad in black leather armour on his shiny steed. But then she was instantly cross with herself for being so fanciful and soft. Damn it. She wasn't going to feel sorry for him. He'd upset her too much.

"I don't like you," she said resolutely. "I don't like the things you say or the things you do. I don't like your friends, your attitudes, the way you've been talking about Molly and ... about me."

As she delivered this speech, Dustin lifted his head, looking at her first with disbelief then, she thought, with guilt.

He tried to defend himself. "Hold it, wait a minute. I get the picture. You think I'm the one who's been spreading lies about us. It wasn't me, it was Malc and Kenny. You think because I hang around with them that I'm like them ... well, I'm not."

Ravenna stood her ground. "No, you're not like them," she said, staring straight into his eyes. "You're worse."

Dustin flinched and wrapped his arms tightly around his shiny new helmet, hugging it to his chest. Then he looked up at Ravenna with pleading eyes. "And there's nothing I can do that will change your mind?" he asked.

"No," Ravenna replied triumphantly, on the point of walking away.

"You haven't given me a chance," Dustin protested.

Ravenna sniffed. "I don't need to, I know what you're like," she pronounced, but he looked so downcast that she found herself thinking *perhaps he really loves me*. For a moment there was silence between them, then Ravenna tossed her head and spoke, her words stabbing the air, sharp with anger. "You're a racist and a bully."

"Prove it," Dustin challenged.

The familiar belligerent expression now smeared Dustin's

face and Ravenna glared down at him. He was easier to deal with like this.

"I don't have to. Everybody knows it. Last week, in drama, you made out that all Asians are grasping landlords and you're always on about immigrants. You never talk to any of the Asian kids in school but you're against them."

"I'm talking to you, aren't I?"

"What?"

Dustin smiled slyly. "Faye told me – you're adopted."

Ravenna took a step back. "So – what's new about that?"

"Well, you're a Paki, aren't you?"

Ravenna stared at him, dumbstruck.

"I knew when I kissed you. I could smell it. That's why you're always defending them."

Dustin was grinning victoriously as if he'd won some contest. "See, I'm not racist. I don't mind. I like you."

Ravenna stood gazing at him blankly until she found her voice.

"What! You think I'm Asian?" she asked incredulously.

Dustin shrugged his shoulders. "Well, Faye's mum said you are but I knew it anyway. I can tell."

"Well, you're wrong. My mother came from Wales. I'm Welsh."

"Maybe. But everybody's got two parents. It was your father then, he was a Paki," Dustin sneered.

Ravenna saw him smirking, watched him rub the back of his glove across his mouth, saw him drop his hand back on his helmet. The gathering darkness seemed to close in around her and she had to put her hand on the motor cycle handlebars to steady herself.

She heard Dustin laugh and she wanted to hit him. Knock those stupid grinning teeth down the back of his throat. She swallowed hard, tears pricking at her eyes. She let go of the motor bike and Dustin grasped her arm.

Ravenna looked down at his black leather hand around her sleeve. Who am I? she thought. Then she lunged at his face.

10.

Dustin's words set off an earthquake inside her. Feelings that were long buried began to bubble and rise until they threatened to crack her open. And Ravenna felt she'd burst if she didn't get away.

So she ran – hair flying, arms pumping, mouth open – away from Dustin. In front of her she saw Beth's face, her cheek slashed by a deep crescent scar. Behind her she heard Dustin shouting, "Bitch, stupid Paki bitch!"

Oh God, he was so crass, so ignorant! How could she have ever let him kiss her? He was despicable. She could still hear him shouting, "Paki, Paki!" What a pea-brain. He didn't even understand it wasn't an insult. She'd be proud if her father came from Pakistan. That didn't upset her. It was something else that was so painful: dim and distant memories, sharp and barbed, a memory that she couldn't quite get hold of. She was young, eight or nine, her jeans had a sticker on the knee, her hair was in a plait. She was frightened, upset. She'd climbed a tree, and below her some kids were shouting up at her, shouting something horrible, and she hid her face against a branch and she cried.

She had stayed up that tree for a long time, sitting straddled over the rough bark until her legs and arms ached from hanging on. She couldn't remember what the kids were shouting but she could remember running home and Sheila telling her not to be so sensitive.

Tears trickled down her face. Why hadn't Sheila told her

everything she knew about her parents? It hurt so much to think that Dustin and Faye and probably half the town knew things about her past that she didn't. She wanted to run to Beth, to be held and protected and loved. To be told that she belonged and Beth would never let her go again.

Stumbling as she ran over a crack in the lamp-lit pavement, Ravenna expected that any moment she'd hear Dustin's motor bike revving behind her. She was running in the wrong direction back down the dark river of tarmac but she didn't care. She ran recklessly, gasping and panting, only stopping when she was dazzled by a violent light. Headlights glared. A car swerved and pulled in to the kerb.

A car door opened and a figure approached her, saying something in a gentle soothing voice. A strong arm wrapped around her and steered her into the back seat of a car. Ravenna knew it was Selina's voice but all she could hear was the sound of her own crying. Tears were spilling down her cheeks, splashing on to her hands.

Then Selina's voice became clearer. She was repeating softly but insistently, "Are you all right? What happened?"

It was some moments before Ravenna could speak. "I'm OK," she managed to say, sniffing and breathing out in huge gasps.

Selina handed her a tissue and Ravenna mopped at her face.

"Are you sure you're all right?" Selina asked. "You looked as if you were running away from something or ... somebody."

Ravenna shivered. "I just wanted to run. I had to ... but ... it's OK. Nothing terrible happened."

"Well, you looked pretty desperate. I'm glad we came along," Selina said firmly.

Ravenna sat back in her seat, sniffed, blew her nose and tried to stop sobbing. She felt embarrassed now. Selina must have thought she'd been attacked when she saw her running like that, fleeing like a mad dog, eyes wild, tongue lolling, almost frothing at the mouth.

She shivered and was thankful for Selina's arm around her and her closeness. Then she became aware of another presence in the car as Mr Barstow's deep voice came from the driver's seat.

"Harrows hasn't been bothering you, has he? I saw him hanging around tonight."

Ravenna tried to speak evenly. "He didn't do anything, he just said something that upset me."

Mr Barstow turned round, his large head framed between the two front seats. "Oh, I can imagine. He's good at that – but don't let him upset you, he's not worth it."

Ravenna frowned. Mr Barstow had seen them together in the science lab and now this.

"He's not my boyfriend or anything. I can't stand him," she said sharply. "He just followed me on his stupid motor bike."

"Oh yes, I saw he'd got himself a suicide machine."

Selina patted Ravenna's arm. "Well, don't worry, we'll get you home safely. Where do you live?"

"On the estate. Derwent Avenue," Ravenna mumbled; she always hated having to admit to her address.

"Used to live there myself," Mr Barstow said cheerily. "In the next street."

"You did?" Ravenna asked with surprise.

"When I was a kid. Amberly Crescent," he informed her as he started the engine.

Selina handed Ravenna her seat-belt clip and she sat in silence as she fastened it securely. She was grateful for the security and the lift but wished she hadn't fled from Dustin, let him see how he'd upset her. He was bound to stir up more trouble for her now, he and his mates and Faye Mellins. She wished she'd given Faye a hammering when she'd had the opportunity.

The car moved off, Ravenna assuring Selina once again that she was fine, but when she leaned against the window she felt choked with anger. Closing her eyes she conjured a bright image of Beth dancing with a baby in her arms, but instantly Beth's gauzy dress began to shimmer and fade and was replaced by an oversized head of Dustin laughing, his mouth open, his eyes glinting like a cat's, his teeth gleaming like piano keys.

Ravenna shook her head to try to stop the pictures and Selina squeezed her arm.

"We're almost home. Don't let Dustin get to you," she said gently.

The car slowed as they turned into Derwent Street and Ravenna directed them to her house.

"Do you want me to come in with you?" Selina asked.

"No, I'll be all right," Ravenna answered as she fumbled for the door handle.

"Promise you'll come to the class next week," Selina asked. "We'll give you a lift home, won't we, John?"

Ravenna was surprised at the use of Mr Barstow's Christian

name but of course, if Selina was his friend she was hardly likely to call him Mr Barstow, was she?

"No problem. We have to come in this direction anyway," John Barstow reassured her. Then he added, "Look, will you come and see me tomorrow at school – lunchtime?"

"Yes, I will... I'll come to the class and see you tomorrow. Thanks," Ravenna said as she climbed out of the car.

Ian was in the kitchen sorting lead soldiers when Ravenna entered.

"You all right?" he asked, glancing up at her tear-stained face.

"Yeah, just got a bit of a knock in the class. The instructor brought me home. Think I'll go and have a bath or my bones'll seize up. Any hot water?"

"Should be plenty. Have a good soak. Kirsty's fast asleep, I just checked."

Relieved to hear this, Ravenna went quietly upstairs, turned on the bath taps then went into her bedroom. She undressed in the soft glow of the bedside lamp, put on her dressing-gown and crossed to the dressing-table. She stared at her face, then pulled the dressing-gown down to expose her shoulders. The image that stared back at her looked familiar. What had she expected – that her skin would have suddenly turned several shades darker? She turned her head sideways, trying to examine her profile. Her nose did seem to have become more pronounced over this past year but what did that prove? She could be Italian, Jewish, Arabic – many races had prominent noses, so did many British people.

She turned full-face to the mirror again, looked at her dark hair and eyes and tilted her head to the light, tracing her cheek-bones with long, delicate fingers. The fingers quivered as she thought of belonging to an Eastern culture. She felt a sudden thrill of excitement as images invaded her eyes: the Taj Mahal, tigers, elephants, crowded bazaars, jungles, rolling plains. She smiled as she remembered how she'd always loved the smell of spices and the feel of the sun warming her body.

Crossing to her bed, she lay on her back, flexing her fingers and circling her hands as the Bengali dancers had done. Then she rolled on to her side and laughed at herself. You stupid romantic idiot! she scoffed. Even if your parents were of Asian descent, they probably lived all their lives in Bradford or Derby. But she liked the fantasy.

She thought of Beth in the arms of a dark, smiling lover, a young Indian boy who wanted to marry her but was prevented from doing so by his family. Her insides snaked with excitement as she thought of the passion and anguish of two young lovers divided by their cultures.

Getting down from the bed she crossed to the mirror again. Her eyes were deep, dark pools and her hair an inky river. Reaching for her make-up bag, Ravenna extracted a dark pencil and with the soft lead lined her eyes, drawing black fish shapes. Then she took a bright red lipstick and painted a vibrant circle between her eyebrows. Bending down she opened a drawer and pulled out the shawl, which she draped carefully over her head. Then stepping back she looked at herself and was dazzled ... gazing back at her was an Indian princess.

She stared at her reflection, stunned by the transformation, suddenly unnerved and confused. Moving quietly, so as not to wake Kirsty, she stepped away from the mirror, lifted the shawl from her head, draped it over her shoulders and began to dance. Slowly, elegantly, her shadow flitted across the walls, her fingers splayed and fluttered like dark birds, she bobbed like a shadow puppet until she forgot her worries, her fear, her anger and her sadness. She danced into a space where it didn't matter who she was or where she came from. All that mattered was the joy of movement. She drifted through that space until she dropped as if felled by a stone and lay on her bed with silent tears running down her cheeks. She lay until she heard a sharp shout from the bathroom and a tap on the bedroom door.

"Ravenna, what the heck are you doing?"

Ravenna leapt up and rushed on to the landing to face an angry Ian.

"You left the bath running. It's overflowing! It's a good job I came up or it would have been through the ceiling."

"Oh God, I'm sorry, Ian."

His anger faded quickly as he examined Ravenna's woeful face with the large red circle between her brows. "You practising for something?" he asked.

Ravenna had forgotten the lipsticked spot.

"I dozed off."

"Oh, a sleeping part, is it?" Ian enquired, with an amused look on his face. "Anything I can help with?"

Ravenna shook her head. "No, I'm fine, just a bit tired. That class really knocked me out. Sorry."

"Well, you'd better have your bath, then. There's plenty of water. . . I should wash your face if it's still hot."

Ravenna was putting on her nightshirt when she heard the

outside door bang and knew Sheila must be home from bingo. Grabbing her dressing-gown Ravenna ran to inspect her face, making sure all traces of the make-up had disappeared, and then hurried downstairs. Her head was full of questions – if only Sheila was in the mood.

By the time Ravenna poked her head round the sitting-room door Sheila was already in position on the couch in front of the TV. For once, Ian was sitting next to her but, as usual, the television was monopolizing the conversation.

"Hi, Mum. Did you win?" Ravenna asked, as she dusted crumbs from an armchair and sat down.

"Not a bloomin' thing. Don't know why I bother."

Ravenna smiled. She knew Sheila was hooked on the excitement – it didn't really matter whether she won or not, she'd keep going.

Sheila yawned and sighed. "You can talk to me. I'm not really watching anything. Tell me about your class."

Ravenna didn't want to talk about the class but she began to explain what they'd done whilst madly searching for a way to ask her burning questions. She tried to make her account of the class as lively and funny as possible to win Sheila's attention, because nobody had moved to switch off the TV and Sheila was intently watching a doctor stitch the head of a drunken man.

"He was better in that other series," Sheila interrupted Ravenna. "You know, that one set in Australia," and she became absorbed in trying to recall the name of the earlier series.

Ravenna never could understand Mum's fascination with hospital dramas and soaps. All she had to do was go out the front door and she could find all the real-life drama she wanted. Drug dealing, child abuse, rape, theft – it all went on on their estate and featured heavily every week in the local paper.

"Mum, I was telling you about the class," Ravenna protested, but Sheila was busy going through all the hospital series she'd ever seen.

An advertisement for sanitary towels with wings replaced the programme and Ian said he'd make a cup of tea. As he left, Ravenna seized the chance to talk.

"Mum, did you know Faye's mum when. . ."

But Sheila interrupted her. "Are you all right?" she asked. "Ian said you looked as if you'd been crying when you came in."

"I'm fine," Ravenna answered irritably. "I just got winded when we were doing some exercises. I enjoyed the class, it was good."

"Well, if it's that violent I don't see how it's doing you any good. You're supposed to be learning how to defend yourself, not getting knocked out."

"We did learn how to defend ourselves – it was just an accident, that's all. But afterwards I saw. . ."

"What did they teach you then?" Sheila cut in.

"Oh, just how to maim, blind and castrate any man that pounces on me," Ravenna answered shortly.

Sheila chuckled. "Let's hope he's not just asking for a light, then," she said, as she rummaged under the cushion for her cigarettes. She found the packet and flipped open the top. "Last one," she said with a wink as she removed it and lodged it between her fingers.

Ravenna was gripped by frustration but she knew it was no use. She could see Sheila was in no mood for serious discussion. "Mum, I thought you were giving up," Ravenna protested.

"I am, after this one," Sheila replied, lighting up and inhaling deeply.

Ravenna put on her most superior look. "You've got no will power. If you die, I won't stay at home to look after Brett and Kirsty."

"Don't worry, Miss High and Mighty, I won't expect you to and I am giving up," Sheila said angrily. "It takes time, that's all." Then she added, with a pleading note, "I need them, Vernie."

Ravenna sighed. Somehow all her burning questions had disappeared into a puff of smoke. There was silence between them. Ravenna looked at Sheila in her too-tight stretch skirt and cardigan, her bare mottled legs splayed over the Dralon couch and her bunny slippers. She was fond of her and wished she wouldn't smoke – it was bad for her.

Sheila flicked the ash from her cigarette into the empty packet. "What time did you get in?" she asked.

"The teacher gave me a lift home," Ravenna told her.

"Oh, that's nice. I don't like you being out at night. You never know what can happen."

"You do, Mum. You see it all on the telly," Ravenna replied.

"Yes, well, you want to be careful."

"That's why I'm going to the classes. They're not just for young people though, you know. Why don't you come?

Walking back from the bus after bingo, you could get attacked. There were some people your age at the class."

"Oh, I'm sure I'd look well kicking up my legs. If anybody came after me they'd want their eyes examining." Sheila took another drag then added, chuckling, "I'd just give in."

"Mum, it's serious, it's not. . ."

But Ravenna didn't get a chance to voice her frustration because Ian came in with a tray and glared at his wife. "Sheila, you're supposed to have given those up," he rapped.

"I have, it's my last one. Look." She held out the empty packet as if it proved something.

"That just means you've smoked all the rest," Ian said.

"Oh, stop getting at me," Sheila answered, closing her eyes and pushing herself further into the corner of the sofa.

Ian poured the tea and passed it round. Ravenna looked at Sheila's podgy fingers as she grasped the saucer, at her round pink-cheeked face and blonde fluffy hair.

"Mum, do you think I look foreign?" Ravenna asked.

Sheila's eyes flickered curiously at Ravenna through the haze of smoke, but then immediately returned to the TV screen. She was puffing away now as if the cigarette was indeed her last.

"What do you want to know that for?" she asked sharply.

Ravenna could see she'd annoyed her and knew she'd get no further.

"Oh, nothing. Somebody just said I looked like Cher," Ravenna smiled.

"Can't be bad then, can it?" Ian chuckled.

Ravenna picked up her cup of tea. "I'll take mine up with me. Good night."

In her bedroom Ravenna lay for a long time without sleeping. She wanted the clues to her past that other people held. She needed to trace Beth – she had to know her story or she'd never feel whole again.

1 1 .

The moment Ravenna entered the tutor room, a strident, discordant wailing sound split the air, stretching around the room like chewing-gum until it snapped into a few bars of something that approximated to Indian music.

Ravenna's eyes swivelled towards the noise but darted away as it ceased and the singer began to speak.

"Lo, our Arabian princess. What blessed magic carpet has brought you to us this morning, your majesty?"

Unmistakably Dustin. Arrogant, crass, but sharp and cutting as ever and amusing to some.

Snorting laughter followed his remark. He was surrounded by his mates, holding court, enjoying his favourite pastime – a joke at someone else's expense.

As Ravenna made her way over to where Rachael was sitting there was more giggling, and out of the corner of her eye she saw Dustin giving a low theatrical bow.

He spoke again, sneering from his corner. "It's so good of you to honour us with your presence. Have you come to inspect our education system? It's not all it might be but remember your subjects do use it for nothing."

Ravenna heard the sniggers and felt everybody's eyes on her as she sat down. She couldn't let him get away with this.

Forcing herself to look unruffled but thinking fast, she leaned back in her chair, crossed her legs and flicked back a strand of hair.

Dustin began to sing his wailing raga again. She turned and

gave him a hard, challenging stare, noting with a small flicker of triumph that there was an angry red line down the side of his face. Her nails had left their mark.

She turned back to face Rachael, smiled and said, loudly, "Saw the police down the office just now. They're looking for a stolen bike, a motor bike. Wanted to know if anybody at school had just acquired one. Baker was leading them this way – can't think why."

In the brief silence which followed there seemed to be a communal intake of breath. Ravenna turned to look again in Dustin's direction, her smile becoming broader as she saw her words had had their desired effect.

Dustin's shoulders hunched, he drew his head in, then it bobbed up and forward. For a moment he preened and peered about him like a cockerel looking for a fight.

"Well, it's nothing to do with me. I bought my bike new from Hassops. My mam can vouch for that and I've got the receipt to prove it."

"Oh yeah, thought you'd found the money a bit quick," Malc Orridge chuckled.

"It was for my birthday. Mum's been... Shut your mouth," Dustin warned as he shot forward out of the classroom.

Ravenna grinned. Inspiration had come to her not by magic carpet but via two wheels – she'd worked out where Dustin's weak spot lay.

"Do you really think he stole it?" Rachael asked.

Ravenna laughed. "I doubt it. I didn't see any police. But stands to reason, doesn't it? Anybody whose dad's in prison isn't going to like 'em."

"Nice one. I've never seen him look so worried," Rachael chuckled. She flipped a piece of gum out of her mouth and into a waste bin in two well-practised moves. Then she frowned as she asked, "What's with him and this Indian music?"

"Oh, he's decided one of my parents was from India or Pakistan or Bangladesh or Bradford. Thinks I look foreign . . . Asian," Ravenna answered, trying to sound nonchalant.

"I thought you were Welsh."

"I could be anything. Welsh, French, Indian. What do I look like?"

Rachael raised her eyebrows. "Now there's a tempting question," she said as she unwrapped and popped a new piece of gum into her mouth. "Unfortunately I can't think of anything witty to say, and anyway you're so bloody gorgeous that it's not worth it."

"Yes, but do I look foreign?" Ravenna asked.

Rachael's jaws set to work on the problem. Her pronouncement after a few moments of mastication was, "Yeah, foreign like Jewish, Arabic, Indian, Italian, native American, the French assistant who taught us in year two and this Polish woman who does my mum's hair."

"Oh, you're a big help," Ravenna countered.

Rachael blew a bubble and let it pop before saying, "Dustin's hung-up about immigrants, take no notice. He's just trying to annoy you."

Ravenna sighed, wound a few strands of her dark hair around her fingers and looked at the silky black threads.

"Have you seen Moll?" Rachael asked.

"No. She's usually here by now."

"Something's up," said Rachael, picking up her bag as the bell sounded.

"If she doesn't turn up I'll ring her at break," Ravenna promised.

After what seemed like a very long history lesson, where Ravenna divided her thoughts between Molly, Beth and the Vietnam war, Ravenna rushed out of the classroom and down to the phone at the end of the long corridor.

She had to move fast, skirting round clusters of pupils spilling out of doorways and barging through slow-moving huddles of friends. If she didn't get there quickly there would be a queue of desperate people eager to beg Mum to bring in forgotten gym kit or bus money or to pledge undying love to Mike the mechanic.

Pushing through an even bigger crowd around the tuck shop counter, Ravenna saw someone had beaten her to the phone. Damn! Judging by their size, they were a year seven or eight pupil though, so hopefully it was a lost bus pass rather than a lost boyfriend.

Ravenna planted herself squarely behind the girl so that no one could get in between them.

"I didn't know it was Friday," the girl was saying. "But Mum ... please. I'll get into trouble."

Ravenna hoped Mum would give in quickly. Behind her other girls were rattling their money.

"Great!" the girl shouted, triumphantly slamming down the receiver.

Ravenna darted forward, slotted in a coin and punched in Molly's number.

After only two rings the receiver at the other end was picked up. It wasn't Molly's voice, however, but her mother's.

"Hallo. Hilary Morgan here." Her words were curt and clipped.

"Hallo. It's Ravenna. Can I talk to Molly?"

Ravenna expected Hilary's tone to soften when she knew who was speaking to her but her voice was like ice.

"No, I'm afraid she's too ill to speak to anyone at the moment."

"Oh gosh, what's the matter?"

"Flu," Hilary said, so sharply she made it sound like a fatal disease.

"Could I come and see her after school?"

"No, I'm afraid that won't be possible."

Ravenna heard a click and then the dull empty dialling tone. She looked for a moment at the receiver in her hand, hoping it might crackle into life again. She wanted to say, "Come on, it's me, Molly's best friend." But Hilary hadn't given her a chance. Something was wrong. Even if Molly did have flu it would hardly prevent her from talking on the phone. After all, she had one right next to her bed.

Ravenna didn't have much time for reflection, however. The next moment she was barged by an impatient girl eager to slot her ten pence into the phone. Stepping aside, Ravenna turned to pass through the waiting crowd and walk to her next class.

At lunch time, Ravenna remembered Mr Barstow had asked her to see him. She wandered over to the science labs and found him setting up an experiment. His large figure in dazzling white coat loomed over a web of tubes, jars and pink bubbling liquid. Against the white cloth, his beard looked bushier and redder than usual and Ravenna found herself thinking of mad scientists and abominable snowmen. She wondered how he managed to avoid crushing the small glass test-tube he was holding.

"Ah, Ravenna, glad you could make it," he said, as if they were about to embark on some high-powered research project. Then he turned to the lab assistant who was helping him. "Could you finish this for me? I want to see Ravenna about her work."

The lab assistant said she could manage and Mr Barstow led Ravenna over to his office.

"I've had a look at your project. Excellent. Ought to get you an 'A'," he said, lifting files and papers, searching underneath them with his big meaty hands until he found Ravenna's folder.

"I hope you're thinking in terms of A-levels and university?" he said.

"I suppose so," Ravenna replied. She didn't feel certain of anything at the moment.

She looked at Mr Barstow and then at the folder. He seemed about to open it but then set it down, put his hands on top of it and leaned towards her.

"You're perfectly capable of it. I want you to know that."

Under his intense gaze, Ravenna stammered an embarrassed "Thank you". Then she shifted from one foot to another as he stood looking at her, a slightly puzzled expression on his face.

"I know it's not always easy when your friends might be

planning other things. How would your parents feel about you going to university?"

Ravenna stared at him. She heard what he said but for a moment she didn't understand; couldn't decipher his words. She had a feeling of distance, of his light blue eyes zooming in and out at her like a camera lens. Then she spoke, clearly and firmly.

"I don't know who my parents are . . . I'm adopted."

She saw the skin around Mr Barstow's eyes crinkle. He frowned slightly as if trying to remember whether he had known this.

"Oh, I see," he said slowly.

"When I was a baby. I was an accident . . . or," Ravenna snorted, "more like a natural disaster. My mum was a schoolgirl."

Mr Barstow smiled sympathetically. "Well, that's bad luck but you can look at it two ways. It was unfortunate for your real mother but very fortunate for your adopted mother. She must have wanted a child very much."

"Yes, she did." Ravenna paused. "Except that later she had two of her own."

"And now you feel left out?" he asked.

Lowering her eyes, Ravenna slowly nodded her head in agreement. "They're not my real family. I don't belong."

"I can imagine it's tough but people don't always get on with their real families, you know. I used to wish I had been adopted."

The last statement was made almost lightly but Ravenna could hear the bitterness behind the words and before she had time to stop herself, she asked, "Why?"

John Barstow's hand went to his beard, giving it a nervous tug before replying. "I wasn't the sort of child my father wanted. He couldn't stand anybody studying. They're getting above themselves, he used to say, if anybody from the estate wanted to go to college or, God forbid, university. Time wasters, he used to call them."

"But you went, didn't you?" Ravenna asked.

"Yes, after a hell of a battle. Not at first. First I was an electrician. He approved of that, working with your hands, you see, but well..." He folded his hands on the table between them. "I'm sure times have changed but I just wanted to say that if you want to go to university, go for it, don't get distracted, will you? It's worth it. I know it's no guarantee of a job nowadays but it opens doors."

Ravenna looked at the bearded, softly spoken man, and felt the kindness in his voice.

"It's a bit hard to think beyond GCSEs at the moment," she said quietly.

"Yes, of course, I know, one thing at a time. I just don't want you to sell yourself short. Have you had any more trouble from Harrows this morning?"

"I can handle him. I just let him get to me last night," Ravenna replied, reddening.

"Well, I don't want to ask you what it was about. But he's not your type, is he?"

For a moment, Ravenna was angry. Did he still think she was going out with Dustin? Did everybody still think that just because of one stupid kiss?

"I don't want anything to do with Dustin Harrows. I can't stand him," she almost shouted. Then she collected herself and added in a softer but resolute voice, "Anyway, I can deal with him."

Mr Barstow nodded. "Well, give me a shout if you need any support."

"Thanks," Ravenna said. She knew he meant to be kind but she'd got more important things on her mind than Dustin Harrows.

"Oh, one other thing," Mr Barstow said. "I hear you like dancing?"

"Er . . . yes," Ravenna replied, surprised.

"Well, a friend of mine is looking for some dancers for a special project. I thought you might be interested."

"I would, usually, but I've got too much school work at the moment."

"Ah, but this will be in the summer holidays. Just the thing to keep you busy – unless you're going away, of course."

"I doubt it," Ravenna said wryly. "What sort of dancing is it?"

"A mixture. Ballet, jazz, African. The teacher's really good, used to be quite well known . . . innovative. She gave a one-off session at school last night. Pity it clashed with the self-defence – you'd have enjoyed it."

Ravenna suppressed a grin. So that's what Mr Barstow was doing at school last night – dancing. She looked at his broad frame – not ballet surely?

"Well, if you're interested, why don't you come along to the next session?"

"I'm not sure," Ravenna said doubtfully.

"It was a shame, we got very few young people last night. We should have advertised it more but Beth said. . ."

Ravenna leapt in before he could finish. "Beth?"

As she spoke she swayed slightly, leaning against a stool which tipped and fell to the ground with a clatter. For a moment she gaped, open-mouthed, at Mr Barstow. Then again she whispered, "Beth?"

"Yes, my friend, Beth Owen. She and her partner, Harry, have just come to live behind Atkinson's antique shop. Anyway, if you're interested I'll..."

"Do they drive a yellow van with dolphins painted on it?"

John Barstow laughed. "That's Beth and Harry," he said. "Do you know them?"

"No, not really," Ravenna said quietly. "I just met them once."

She could hardly breathe. She held on to the edge of the table, her hands tingling. She'd known it all along – Beth, her mum, was a dancer.

Mr Barstow looked at his wrist-watch. "Oh damn, I've got to rush, got a meeting, sorry, remember what I've said, won't you, about your future?"

Remember? Ravenna stood staring after him as he hurried away.

After school, Ravenna ran straight to Atkinson's antique shop. A quick enquiry to the shop owner led her outside again, round to a cottage built on to the back of the shop. Breathless and sweaty, her cheeks flushed, and with long strands of hair hanging over her eyes, Ravenna stood in front of Beth and Harry's door.

She hesitated before knocking, looping back the stray strands of hair, then bunching her hair together she lifted it on top of her crown so that her neck was bare. She turned her head gently to catch the breeze then blew a stream of air up towards her forehead, hoping to cool and calm herself. It was no good, however. Her heart was pounding, her stomach tossing like a ship on rough seas and her legs trembling as if on deck. She didn't want to meet Beth like this.

Three times she walked away from the door and back into the street. Three times she raised her hand to knock but her fist tightened and froze in mid-air. She hadn't thought enough about what she was going to say. She looked a mess. Beth might not want to see her.

Finally, after plodding up and down the street, planning what to say, she plucked up courage, knocked firmly and waited with banging heart – waited and waited but nobody came. Beth and Harry were out.

For a while she sat dejectedly on a low window ledge hoping they'd return, but eventually she gave up and hurried home disappointed. A promise to Mum that she would babysit meant she'd already be in trouble for arriving late.

After Mum and Ian went out, the usual routine of food preparation, washing-up, nappy changing, baths and bedtime stories prevented Ravenna from brooding. Brett was in monster mood after playing with two older friends in the garden and Kirsty was her usual ebullient self. It wasn't until they were asleep that Ravenna could indulge herself, let the excitement bubble up, imagine what Beth might have said. "I've never stopped searching for you from the day I gave you away," she would say as Ravenna hugged her and they both cried delicious tears.

But the joyful picture soon faded. The house was so silent

now that it seemed eerie and Ravenna began to think it a bad omen that Beth was out when she called. She turned to her homework but couldn't concentrate. She roamed the house making cups of coffee she didn't drink and switching on TV programmes she didn't watch. Finally she lay on the sofa in a mindless kind of stupor only to rouse when the phone rang.

"Ravenna, it's me. Mum wouldn't let me speak to you earlier."

Molly's voice sounded strained, over-bright and brittle.

"Your mum said you had flu."

"She would."

"Well, are you ill?" Ravenna asked.

"No, not really."

"What's the matter then? What's happening?"

Ravenna could tell it was difficult for Molly to answer. She heard her sigh and make swallowing noises but the reply didn't come.

"Why weren't you at school?" Ravenna tried, but still no reply.

It was useless over the phone, Ravenna thought. If she could see Molly then she'd winkle the problem out of her.

"Moll, why don't you come round? I'm on my own," Ravenna suggested.

There was sharp intake of breath at the other end of the phone, followed by a sob.

"I can't, it's terrible. Everything's dreadful. Mum's gone to get Dad from the police station. She says I'm not to talk to anybody, she won't let me go out."

"Why? What's wrong?"

Molly's voice was punctuated by sniffs. "I can't tell you

over the phone. Come round tomorrow afternoon. Don't come to the door, wait at the back of the garage about half two and I'll try and slip out."

Ravenna heard a strident voice in the background and Molly said quickly, "I've got to go now."

"All right, Moll, I'll be there," Ravenna assured her.

At ten Ravenna went to bed but sleep proved impossible. She lay wondering what had happened to Molly's dad, why the police were involved and what was so dreadful that Molly couldn't tell her over the phone. Her thoughts didn't stay long with Molly, however – it was Beth who filled them.

In the darkness she picked over every detail from her brief meeting with Beth and Harry, although, strangely, Beth's face eluded her now, like a reflection on water, rippling and dissolving.

Irritably, she tossed and turned, feeling as tense as the coiled mattress springs underneath her. Finally, giving up the idea of sleep, she sat up and switched on the bedside lamp. Time for diversionary tactics, she decided, reaching for a book. But instead of her bedtime novel, her hands grasped at a school copy of *Romeo and Juliet*. Oh great! A little light relief. Juliet – now, there was a girl with a problem. Ravenna flipped open the pages.

"I have a faint, cold fear thrills through my veins
That almost freezes up the heat of life."

Juliet had courage – drinking that potion not knowing if she would wake up and if she did to be surrounded by skulls and rotting bodies. And all I need is a bit of courage to go and see Beth tomorrow, Ravenna thought. After all, I only want to ask her a question. I mean, it's not a matter of life or death. But at the thought of asking that question, Ravenna's blood froze and a cold shudder shook her so that she snuggled down into her pillow and pulled the duvet up around her neck.

Sleep came at last but it was in dreams filled with tormented images: skeletons on motor bikes riding at her with flashing daggers, madonnas cradling dead babies. It was horrific. But by dawn the figures faded away and she slept for a few sweet hours before waking to a bright spring day.

12.

It took nearly half an hour to walk through the estate and up the footpath into Maddock's High Street. Trying to hurry, Ravenna regretted having chosen to wear a long flowered skirt and heeled shoes – if she'd worn jeans she could have run. It would be dreadful to arrive at Beth's only to find her out again.

The High Street was already busy with Saturday morning shoppers and traffic. Dodging pushchairs and trolleys Ravenna hurried towards the pedestrian crossing opposite the antique shop. All the way along she looked for the van with dolphins and rainbows swirling around its sides but could see nothing so colourful amongst the parked cars.

At the crossing she stood poised, waiting impatiently. A woman loaded with plastic bags joined her and when the cars halted they stepped out together. Ravenna with her longer stride was the first to reach the middle of the road but as she did so, a motor bike streaked round the cars and shot in front of her. Ravenna jumped back and banged into the woman's shopping which fell from her grasp, apples and cans rolling.

"Idiot!" Ravenna yelled into the trail of fumes. She'd recognized the studded black leather jacket and torn jeans.

She helped the woman retrieve the dinted cans and bruised apples whilst she cursed Dustin under her breath. If he carried on like that he'd splatter somebody.

"You know him, do you? Friend of yours, is he?" the woman asked.

"Yes, I do and no, he isn't," Ravenna replied fiercely, handing over a tin of cat food.

Burning with anger, Ravenna stood in front of the antique shop. Damn Dustin. It was nerve-racking enough wondering what she should say to Beth without being nearly killed on the way. She tried to calm herself, putting her forehead to the cool glass of the shop window and breathing in and out as deeply and evenly as she could.

For a few seconds she closed her eyes, trying to shut out everything. The window reverberated with the throbbing traffic and her trembling body seemed a part of it. She swallowed, clenched and unclenched her hands but couldn't get her nerves under control.

The hiss of brakes from a heavy lorry startled her and she opened her eyes. She felt jumpy as if every nerve in her body was a firework waiting to go off. With thumping heart, she looked at her murky reflection in the window of the antique shop.

"I mustn't hope for too much," she told herself.

Her words had no effect on her body however; she felt so excited that she could hardly walk from the shop to the alleyway beside it.

The alley opened into a courtyard filled with plants. Ravenna remembered them from yesterday but had there been so many? Spilling over every available ledge and window-sill, foliage lurked, oozing from pots on a wrought-iron fire escape, cascading down drainpipes. A sink full of purple pansies stood under the large green window where Ravenna had waited yesterday. Tubs of yellow pansies clustered around an old iron water-pump and a treadle sewing machine stood in the midst of more flowers. Ravenna surveyed it all and smiled, her nervousness losing its edge as she imagined Beth bending over the tubs, lovingly planting pansies. Heart's-ease, Ian called them.

This time Ravenna was resolute. She stepped up to the door and knocked twice. She listened and waited, biting her lip, her feet tapping and twitching. She thought she heard a sound from inside but the door didn't open. She stared at it desperately, willing Beth to be on the other side.

Her hand was poised to knock again when a loud bang from inside sent her reeling backwards. Ravenna caught her breath and steadied herself as the door knob turned. The door opened a crack, then was dragged inwards with a loud scouring sound. It stuck, juddered and someone complained quietly to it. It was Beth.

The face Ravenna had imagined so many times was there, all pieced together: the shining sea-green eyes, the tawny skin and the pale scar that disappeared under high cheek-bones as the mouth widened to a half moon.

"Hallo. Sorry it took me a while, I knocked a pot over. I'm baking," Beth said, smiling warmly.

Ravenna could only stare as Beth's face seemed to grow more vivid by the second, becoming magnified, distorted, the eyes, the hair, the clothes liquefying into a blurred and shimmering vision.

"I came about the dancing," Ravenna stammered.

Beth nodded, her silvery earrings of moons and stars jangling.

"John said you might call."

Her voice was warm and welcoming. She tossed back her

silky hair; her skin and eyes glowed, reflecting the sunlight streaking the courtyard. She was wearing a red blouse and long skirt of rich dark colours. Everything about her seemed so vibrant and magical that Ravenna wanted to reach out and touch her and ask the unspoken question right away: are you my mother? Are you my mother?

The words were repeating themselves inside her head but Beth had gone, turned and disappeared inside, bidding Ravenna to follow.

The room was a little dark at first after the bright sunshine outside and Ravenna hovered near the doorway, confused. She was in a small kitchen which was filled by a huge table. As her eyes got used to the light she saw the table was covered with scattered flour, a rolling pin, pastry cutters, books and papers. Around the kitchen there was the same profusion of plants as outside.

"Leave the door open. We'll let the sunshine in now I've finished baking. I'll just pop these in the oven," Beth said, lifting a tray of doughy rounds. "Sit down, I'll be with you in a minute."

Beth was all energy and action, putting baking trays into the oven, filling the kettle and placing it on an old gas stove, then leaning over the table to mop up flour with graceful sweeping movements.

And all the time she talked quietly to herself, commenting on her actions, "I'll just wipe this ... put this in here ... this goes here ... wash this. Could you put this on that shelf for me?"

Ravenna took the green glazed pottery jug from Beth and with trembling fingers placed it on the pine shelf behind her.

She was happy to do Beth's bidding. Then she removed a heavy book from a chair, carefully placed it in a clear space on the table and sat down, glad to rest her wobbly legs. She wanted Beth's attention but was also glad of a few moments to collect herself. She sat gripping her knees, trying to quell the trembling and the questions that were boiling inside her brain. Is she going to tell me? When she sits down is she going to say, I've been looking for you? Does she know who I am?

Beth was at the sink now washing her hands, calling to Ravenna over her shoulder.

"I'm glad you came. We didn't get many young people at the workshop the other night. I strongly believe everybody can dance but we were a bit short on youth and grace."

Ravenna heard Beth's throaty chuckle and saw her long narrow back and shoulders shake.

"I'm not a trained dancer," Ravenna said.

"That's all right. I am," Beth replied turning to face Ravenna.

For a moment Ravenna couldn't speak. Her throat went desert dry. There seemed to be so much meaning in those two words – I am. She stared at Beth, wondering if she would say something now. But Beth didn't speak. She just stood, head tilted slightly to one side, her dark hair falling over one shoulder; she was drying her hands slowly, meticulously, wiping between each finger and underneath her rings. Then she replaced the towel on a hook and sat down in a tall ladder-backed chair, smoothing her gauzy patchwork skirt.

"The scones will be ready in a minute. You'll stay for some, won't you? Harry will be back soon. He loves scones as long as there's plenty of jam and cream."

Ravenna watched Beth's eyebrows rise and her mouth turn up at one corner into a wry smile as if the scones were a naughty indulgence – a secret she was sharing.

But then Ravenna grew uncomfortable as Beth, sitting straight-backed, carried on smiling but said nothing more. Ravenna looked down at her hands, saw the long slender fingers that were just like Beth's. When she glanced up again Beth's smile was frozen on her face but the joy behind it had gone and the smile seemed to mock her.

Ravenna saw something was wrong but couldn't bring herself to ask what it was. She twisted her fingers together, snaking them round each other, plaiting them.

Finally she broke the silence. "Do you remember? I saw you at the car-boot sale, you gave me the shawl."

Beth's voice seemed to come from a distant place and she spoke slowly and softly. "Yes, I know. Harry said you'd come."

Ravenna squeezed her hands tightly together. Beth's voice sounded so flat and dull now and yet only a few moments ago she'd seemed so happy to see her. Something was wrong. Ravenna felt her body sag like wet putty. She could think of nothing to say and Beth was silent. All the life and joy seemed to have left her and Ravenna's hope was evaporating.

"How long have you lived here?" Ravenna asked hesitantly.

The words seemed to stir Beth. She blinked rapidly, shook her head slightly as if waking from a dream and smiled her bright smile.

"Just a couple of weeks, isn't it? Harry's working up here. He's restoring some paintings at Charnesforth Hall. Tom Dalton, he owns the antique shop, offered us this place whilst the job lasts and Harry is doing a bit of work for him too, now.'

Ravenna heard the springiness of Beth's Welsh accent as she spoke and watched as she flicked back her long hair. Now she seemed relaxed, animated, wanting to talk; the flatness had gone.

"We're just getting sorted out but I planted the yard this week. Makes me feel at home if I've put some plants out. We went over to the market yesterday afternoon. That's the trouble in moving about. I have to keep leaving my plants behind, see. I'd love a house with a garden but it's impossible with Harry's job ... well, unless we spent lots of time apart."

She looked wistful but this changed to a look of determination as if she had to make an effort not to brood and, with her former energy, she rose and said, "Right, the kettle's boiling. What would you like – blackberry, peppermint, orange dew or Earl Grey ... or just ordinary?"

Ravenna's usual tipple was whatever tea bags had ten pence off at the supermarket, but not wanting to appear too conventional, she asked for blackberry and hoped she'd like it. She watched as Beth selected tea bags from the fruity boxes and dunked them in bright mugs.

"I'll just clear this lot away," Beth said as she gathered up a bag of flour, some notepaper and books and redistributed them before wiping the edges of the table. Then she put down some pretty flowered plates, took a block of butter out of the small fridge and carefully placed it on a dish, making criss-cross patterns on the yellow surface.

"They should be ready now," Beth said brightly as she picked up a cloth and stooped to open the oven door.

A drift of warm toasted air wafted towards Ravenna as Beth turned with shining eyes, triumphantly holding a tray of risen golden rounds.

"I've got the measure of this oven now," she beamed. "The last lot were black on the outside and doughy inside but these are just beautiful, I know it. We'll have them when Harry comes. You will stay for a while, won't you?"

"Yes, please," Ravenna said. "I'd like to." As she spoke her eyes met Beth's and they smiled at each other. It was like Ravenna's own eyes beaming back at her. Her heart began to race and her hand trembled as she took the tea from Beth and sipped it.

"Be careful, it's hot," Beth warned. "It really was nice of you to call in," she said breezily. "I'll tell you about the dancing in a minute. But first, just come and look at the new T-shirts I've done. I've just finished them. Come and see if you like them."

Ravenna set down her mug and followed Beth through a narrow doorway into a small white room. The T-shirts were laid out on a large desk which took up practically all the space except for a staircase twisting up to the floor above.

Beth switched on an angle-poise lamp and immediately the hand-painted designs on the T-shirts leapt into life.

"I've based them on Celtic symbols and legends."

"They're lovely, beautiful," Ravenna praised as she looked at the red and gold dragons and the intricate gold lettering.

"I'm glad you like them."

"Oh, I'd love one. The colours are wonderful, the gold on the black and red and that deep blue."

"Yes, it's lovely, isn't it? They're samples for a shop but if you'd like one, I'll do one for you," Beth offered.

"Oh no, I didn't mean . . . I do like them but I didn't mean you to. . ."

"I didn't for one moment think you were asking. I offered. This one's dry. Let's see how it looks."

And she held the shirt in front of Ravenna. Her hands touched Ravenna's shoulders, her hair flowing forward to mingle with Ravenna's own.

They looked steadily at each other and Ravenna felt the question forming in her mouth but was afraid to ask it and looked away.

"It looks lovely on you, doesn't it?" Beth said, smoothing the T-shirt over Ravenna's shoulders and lifting her hair.

Ravenna glanced at her again and saw a shadow flicker across her face, saw her hand drop heavily as she turned to replace the T-shirt on the table. Then Beth sighed deeply and walked back into the kitchen.

Ravenna gazed at the rich colours and thought of Beth caught up in a mythic Welsh land of saints and knights, castles and princes. Leaning over to decipher some lettering, she caught sight of a sheet of paper peeping from underneath the T-shirt. Ravenna pulled at the paper; it was a drawing, a pen and ink sketch, rather dirty and a little smudged, but nevertheless it was a fine, delicate drawing of a little girl dancing. The artist had captured the motion, the strength, the confidence of a small, robust girl. Ravenna gazed at the sketch she was sure Beth had done and then lifted it to reveal another drawing, more detailed and strongly shaded. It was the face of a small child: a child with large, dark, fish-shaped eyes.

Ravenna's breath caught in her throat. Had Beth been imagining the baby daughter she had given away? The daughter
grown into a young girl, graceful and strong, a child with dark
eyes that she had never seen? Was this child herself? Ravenna
stared at the eyes until they dazzled her.

"Are you trying on all my T-shirts?" Beth called.

Startled, Ravenna straightened up and looked away from
the drawings. She felt guilty as if caught reading somebody's
diary and replaced them underneath the T-shirt, and as she
did so heard Beth's joyful cry: "Harry's back."

As Ravenna crossed to the doorway and peered into the
kitchen she saw Harry standing in the doorway busily
unwinding a long stripy scarf from around his neck.

"Hallo. Ravenna, isn't it?" he asked. "It's great to see you
again. Beth hoped you'd call."

"Yes, er . . . oh," was all Ravenna could manage in reply.

Harry looked from Ravenna to Beth and back again.

"Beth really wanted to see you. We thought when John
Barstow described you, that you were the girl at the car-boot
sale. She wanted to ask if. . ." He turned to Beth. "Have you
asked her?"

Beth shook her head. "I was just getting round to it."

Harry beamed at both of them. "Go on then, tell her," he
prompted.

Ravenna looked from Harry to Beth and as she did so, the
room began to blur, the table, chairs, plants, Beth and Harry's
faces all circling her in silence. Then abruptly the motion
stopped and Beth was at the centre. She was standing still,
holding out a plate. Her hands and arms seemed to swim
towards Ravenna, then away again.

Then Beth, speaking clearly and resonantly, broke the spell. "Do you know Charnesforth Hall? Well, Harry's friend has just taken it over. He wants to make it a centre for performing arts. Have open-air concerts in the summer. He's asked me to present some dances on the opening night. So I'm getting a group together. Will you join us?"

13.

Ravenna was stunned; her hopes lay like shattered glass
around her feet. Beth hadn't said she was her mother; she'd
only asked if Ravenna wanted to join her dance group.

Staring helplessly at Beth, Ravenna felt her face tighten and
stiffen, as if daubed with mud that had dried. She was aware
that Beth was waiting for an answer, but when she tried to
speak her mouth didn't respond, only a weak gasp escaped.

She looked down at the table, studying the plate of scones
and the pat of butter until they seemed to glow and pulse like
living things. As Beth moved towards her, she felt herself sway
and her hands reach out, grabbing for something solid, but
her fists closed on air. Then someone's arm was around her,
strong and steadying. She was surprised how easily she floated
forwards, settling lightly on a chair as if she were weightless.
She had the uneasy feeling of not being in the room and yet
being able to see everything with great clarity. A loose thread
hung from a flower embroidered on the tablecloth and a
grease mark peeped from beneath a plate.

Beth's face was in front of her now, only inches away from
her own, and for the first time she noticed there were two tiny
amber flecks in the deep green of one eye. She felt Beth's
hands cover her hands and rub them vigorously.

"I thought you were going to faint there for a moment. It's
so stuffy in here, isn't it? Harry, push the door back. Ravenna
needs some air."

She was aware of Beth's perfume filling her nostrils, pervading them until she imagined a garden full of flowers – roses, honeysuckle, night-scented stock. Harry brought a glass of water. It was as cold as her lips and she shivered as she sipped.

Beth reached up and placed a hand on Ravenna's forehead. "You feel cold. That's strange, it's so hot in here. Perhaps you're feverish ... poor dab."

"No, I'm all right," Ravenna answered. "I just feel a bit light-headed. I should have eaten some breakfast."

But Ravenna didn't feel all right. She was aching with disappointment, thinking, this isn't how it's supposed to be. Beth should have said, "I'm your mother." We would have hugged and cried and then Beth would have added, "I've never been able to forget you. There's never been a day when I haven't looked for you."

Beth held the glass of water to Ravenna's lips again but Ravenna shook her head. "I feel better now. Just lack of food, I expect."

"If it's food you need..." Harry began hopefully, glancing towards the table.

Beth raised her eyebrows. "Trust you to turn any situation to your advantage," she said, trying to sound severe but with a smile hovering at the corners of her mouth.

Harry grinned. "Well look, the colour's coming back to her cheeks. I'll put the kettle on and mash a fresh pot of tea."

"You do that," Beth replied, as she smoothed damp hair away from Ravenna's forehead.

Then she rose from her knees, pulled up a chair to sit close beside Ravenna and rested a hand lightly on her arm. Ravenna was quiet, disappointment still gnawing at her heart.

If Beth had intended to declare that she was her mother, the moment had gone and Ravenna's hopes were slipping away. Molly had been right, her imagination had carried her into the realms of fantasy. Perhaps it was the shawl that had done it, weaving its magic spell. She'd allowed herself to dream, expected too much.

Ravenna lost herself in thoughts, images and questions. She pictured the shawl wrapped around a tiny baby, saw Beth's hands stroking the baby's head, saw Beth's eyes watching her, guarding her. She sat in a trance until she felt Beth patting her arm and realized that she was speaking to her.

"Tell you what, *cariad*, let me go and get you that T-shirt. You shall have it now. I can always paint another."

At first, Beth's words were blurred but gradually sound and meaning filtered through. Beth mustn't give her T-shirts away – they were precious, each one a different design. She must've worked hours, carefully, delicately, designing and drafting. And Ravenna knew they were samples to show to customers. She couldn't accept one as a gift.

Ravenna got up a little unsteadily and followed Beth to the back room to protest. But she only got as far as the doorway, arrested by what she saw.

Beth was standing at the desk holding a T-shirt in one hand and in the other – the sketches of the little girl. She was gazing at the drawings with intense sadness. Ravenna's heart juddered and trembled and she clutched at the door-frame for support. Would Beth say something now? Would she say that she was her mother?

Beth heard Ravenna and turned, her eyes wide, like a startled animal caught in headlights. She looked at Ravenna blankly as if blinded by panic and then quickly turned back to the sketches. For a moment longer she held them, looking at them fiercely, protectively, then she slid them back on to the desk to hide them beneath some folders.

She said nothing. Nothing about mothers or daughters or anything else. She stood silently, head slightly bent, her long hair flowing over her shoulders. Ravenna waited, her hope rekindled for a few moments, but in the swallowing silence it spluttered and went out.

When Beth turned round again, all trace of sadness and anxiety had disappeared. She was smiling, holding out the T-shirt.

"I chose the green one," she said, "to match your eyes."

In a tight whisper, Ravenna thanked her.

"Do you feel up to trying it on?" Beth asked.

Ravenna nodded.

Beth was still smiling, happy to bestow the gift. "Slip it on in here then, if you like. I'll go and see if tea's ready."

As Beth left the room, closing the door behind her, Ravenna held out the T-shirt, looking at the intricate, shining symbols of a culture and a language that was as foreign as Asia and as mysterious as Beth.

When she stepped back into the kitchen wearing the sea-green T-shirt, Beth looked at her proudly. "It looks just lovely on you, doesn't it, Harry?"

Harry looked up. "She's every bit as wonderful as you said she'd be," he said quietly.

Ravenna thought she saw Beth flash him a warning look but the next moment chairs were being pulled up to the table and plates handed round and Ravenna wasn't sure.

Whilst Harry poured the tea, Beth handed round scones and jam and then triumphantly produced a large carton of cream from the fridge.

"You didn't think I'd forgotten, did you?" she teased Harry as she waved the cream in the air. Then turning to Ravenna she said, "Help yourself. We don't do this very often, I want you to understand. All week it's wholemeal bread, spinach and beans."

Harry made a face and Ravenna laughed and reached for a scone. She was hungry. She'd been so busy making breakfast for Kirsty and worrying about coming to see Beth that she'd forgotten to eat. Halving the scone she spread it with butter and jam.

"Have some cream," Harry offered.

Ravenna couldn't quite manage that; her mind and stomach were still churning. But sitting opposite Harry she was distracted from the questions whirling around her brain. She was amused by his enthusiasm for spooning huge dollops of cream on his scones and the expression of contentment his face wore as he munched. Between mouthfuls he told them about an exhibition of local paintings he'd seen that morning.

"There must be a whole colony of artists in this area," he said. "There was so much good stuff. A series of fine pen and ink sketches, one or two excellent still lifes and portraits, and some vibrant abstracts, lovely sense of colour and composition. Many of them as good as anything I've seen in London. Perhaps Maddock is going to be the St Ives of the nineties. It's exciting."

All this was said with a dab of cream on the end of his nose and Ravenna, who had never viewed Maddock as an exciting place, began to giggle.

"It's the cream," she apologized, pointing at his nose and Harry laughed too, wiping it away with a napkin. Ravenna felt her spirits lift, but when she looked at Beth she saw her mouth had tightened and her eyes seemed clouded and dull. She wasn't laughing – she was closed off, nibbling at her scone, delicately, abstractedly. It was as if a quietness had settled on her like someone in church. She was sombre, careful of her movements. Was she unhappy? Ravenna wondered. When Harry spoke to her, her face lit up and when Ravenna had arrived she'd been busy, all nervous energy, but in between Ravenna had seen shadows on her face.

Beth suddenly leaned towards her asking if she wanted more tea and Ravenna, lost in thought, was taken by surprise so that she stuttered and mumbled.

"Still feeling groggy?" Beth queried.

"No, I'm all right. I was just thinking."

"And can I enquire what about?" Beth asked.

"Oh, just that I'm glad I came," Ravenna answered.

Beth responded with one of her bright smiles. "I'm glad too," she said as she picked up the huge red teapot and poured Ravenna another cup of tea.

There was a little frown of concentration on her brow as she poured and Ravenna felt a rush of affection for her. It was hard to believe there was no connection between them, she felt she'd always known Beth. The long curve of her neck, the dark curtain of hair and the full wide mouth were so familiar. It had to mean something.

Beth set down the teapot and reached for the milk jug,

turning her head slightly so that her face caught a shaft of sunlight glancing through the window behind her. For a moment her face was illuminated. The sickle-shaped scar glowed, a taut silver streak across her face. Ravenna wondered what had caused it? And who was the girl in the drawing? Was it Ravenna? If it was, then why hadn't Beth said so by now? And surely a mother would remember the colour of her own daughter's eyes?

"Have another," Harry urged, breaking her thoughts as he offered the plate of scones.

"Thanks," Ravenna replied. "They're very good."

Beth smiled the radiant smile. "They are, aren't they?"

"Now tell us about yourself," Beth asked. "Have you always lived here?"

For a few moments Ravenna was plunged into confusion, questions whirling round her brain. Did Beth know the answer or did she want Ravenna to tell her? Eventually Ravenna managed to say, "I've lived here as far back as I can remember." She almost added, "I'm adopted," but the words stuck.

Beth asked her about the town, school, her family in a matter-of-fact, everyday voice. There was no sense of mystery, no shadow of unpleasant haunting memories. Ravenna told herself she was an idiot. Just because she looks like me I decide she's my long-lost mother. I must be mad.

There was no time for more thought because Beth got up from her chair and said eagerly, "Shall we leave Harry to it? If you can move after all that starch and cholesterol, I'd like you to see my studio."

Ravenna checked her watch. It was just after eleven o'clock.

Good. Molly had said two-thirty, so she had plenty of time. Heaven knows what Sheila would say if she was out all day but Ian would cover for her.

She followed Beth out of the kitchen door, across the bright courtyard and into the back of the antique shop. The door opened into a dim corridor where there was a slightly dank, mouldy smell overlaid with the sweetness of furniture polish. Through a glass partition Ravenna could see the bulky shapes of heavy oak furniture and the shadow of the shop assistant.

There was no time to linger, however. Beth's bright figure glided down the corridor towards a flight of steep, narrow stairs. Ravenna followed, but halfway up the natural light disappeared, and she was plunged momentarily into darkness. Above her she heard the rustle of Beth's skirt. Feeling for a rail or the side wall, she stumbled slightly.

"Stay there. I'll put the light on," Beth shouted.

Ravenna stood still whilst she listened to Beth climb the last steps. Then there was a shuffling sound and suddenly light flooded down the stairs.

Ravenna found Beth standing in a long wide room with a sloping ceiling; hanging fluorescent lights lit a cleanly swept wooden floor.

"Isn't it great!" she enthused. "I wanted you to see it. It used to be a snooker hall, hence the lights – for potting the black," she said with a flourishing sweep of her arms.

There were no shadows on her face now and Ravenna wondered if she'd imagined all that too. Beth's enthusiasm was infectious and Ravenna found herself responding.

"It's brilliant," she agreed, already thinking – what a wonderful space to dance in.

Facing her was a big arched window which took up the whole of the gable end and the space in front of the window stretched towards her – big, inviting ... empty.

"It's perfect, isn't it?" Beth asked. "Tom's agreed to let me have it and he's going to clear away this stuff." She gestured to a pile of picture frames, broken chairs and other bric-à-brac that was heaped in a corner behind them. "I thought I could put some mirrors along that wall and maybe rig up a place to change in that corner."

Ravenna nodded. She could see it all: Beth at work. Teaching, dancing, guiding. She felt a jealous pang as she thought of Beth giving her time to all the pupils and yet why should she? Beth was nothing to her. She was just a friend, hardly even that, yet.

Beth's face was sparkling. She looked truly happy – in her element.

"Listen," she said, "the acoustics are great." And she sang a high trill of clear notes that bounced off the bare walls and up to the ceiling, then she ran over to a cassette player and clicked in a tape. The next moment the room was filled with soaring music: a sombre cello, then rippling violin and piano.

"Come on," Beth said quietly and she kicked off her shoes, stretched her legs and arms and began to dance.

Ravenna watched for a moment. Saw how Beth's body bent to the rhythm, turned and swayed until it became a part of the music, the bright light slipping over the silky red shirt, scorching it pink and shadowing it blood red. Her skirt kicked into frothy bunches then streaked down over an outstretched leg.

For a moment the music died and Beth's head went down,

her hair cascading to the floor. When a flute sounded soft and soulful and the music swelled again Beth looked up and beckoned to Ravenna.

"Join me, it doesn't matter what you do – just dance."

Ravenna pulled off her shoes. The music was faster now; hard edged. Beth whirled away from her, circling the room in blazing pirouettes. Ravenna held out her arms then leapt forward whirling after her. She felt as if she were flying. There was so much space to fill. Then all she was aware of was the music. Beth was a blur, a shifting shape. But the music was strong and powerful, binding it to her with its insurgent beat. She became a Spanish dancer on a burning plain, a native girl jigging under a tropical moon, a limbo dancer, a cajun stomper. Breathless and ecstatic she flashed across the room until the music slowed and poured sleekly as a stalking cat.

Suddenly she was next to Beth. Their arms stretching together, cupping the air, their bodies gliding into the same described curve, the same smooth arc. They faced each other. Ravenna could see beads of sweat glistening on Beth's upper lip and hear her breathing. Beth's hand grasped hers and turned her until she was by her side. Beth's hand was on her shoulder, their feet sliding, legs crossing, stepping in unison as if they'd rehearsed. They dipped and swayed, Ravenna turned under Beth's arm, pulled away then fell against her. Beth caught her as if she weighed nothing and set her lightly on her feet again. Ravenna stood still whilst Beth leapt around her and then as the music became more frenzied they parted and Beth laughed as she went into a wild African dance.

Ravenna followed suit, her head and shoulders dropping, her feet flattening out, pounding and stomping. She was breathless, dripping with sweat but utterly and completely happy. It was exhilarating.

As the music died away, Beth fell on the floor, laughing and panting and Ravenna dropped down next to her.

"Wow! I haven't danced like that for ages. It felt so good," Beth breathed, closing her eyes and throwing back her head.

"You were brilliant," Ravenna gasped. "It was like every dance I've ever seen all mixed up together."

"It was great fun, wasn't it? Not very disciplined, mind, but fun," Beth said, putting great emphasis on the last word.

"I loved it," Ravenna said fervently.

Beth looked at her, smiled broadly and pronounced, "You're a natural."

Ravenna grinned. She was so elated that she wanted to dance all over again.

"Have you had any training?" Beth asked.

"Only a bit at school."

"Well, you've got natural talent. That's a start. I can teach you the rest."

"Really?" Ravenna's eyes sparkled. "That would be great."

"A lot of hard work, mind," Beth warned as she lifted her skirt and used her petticoat to wipe sweat from her brow. "And on one condition," she added, pausing for a moment.

"What's that?"

"That you agree to perform in the summer concert."

"Done," Ravenna said solemnly. Then she lay back on her elbows, glad of a few silent moments to recover her breath. Beside her, Beth stretched her legs, massaged her calves and bent her head down to her knees then rolled up again. Leaning back she lowered herself until she lay flat on the floor.

Ravenna heard her breathing deeply. Above her the fluorescent lights hummed and a telephone rang somewhere below. Then without warning Beth jumped to her feet.

"Come on, no time like the present. I'll show you some basic steps." She looked down at Ravenna's stockinged feet. "Are your feet OK? We'll have to get you some proper shoes."

"My feet are fine but my new T-shirt's a bit sweaty," Ravenna said, holding out her arms and flapping them to create a draught.

"Never mind. All my works of art are guaranteed washable. Right, basic terms – first, second, third … *plié, tendu, glissé, changement, soubresaut…*"

Beth swept across the floor towards the arched window and Ravenna followed, copying every step, her feet gliding naturally into position as if they'd always known what to do.

"Right, now I'm going to call out several terms in succession. See if you can keep up. *Glissade assemblé, pas de chat, pas de bourrée, balancé, balancé, posé temps levé…*"

Beth rapped out the French terms, whilst tapping out a beat with her foot. Ravenna stepped and glided, listening carefully. It was hard work, her muscles were tightening.

"Don't look at your feet. And extend the arms. Finish the gesture – so. Dance!"

Ravenna began to trust her feet and glide more evenly, straightening her back, lifting her head. She held out her arms, curving them gracefully, aware that Beth was watching her with an intense gaze. When the commands ceased, Ravenna danced on, turning and twirling more freely now. But then the tapping stopped – there was no more beat and Ravenna sensed something was wrong. She turned back to

Beth and the commands came again but they were raspy, growing weaker until finally the voice broke. Ravenna hesitated, dropped her arms and slid to a halt. She was directly in front of Beth and could see that she was crying.

Beth bent her head and spoke in sobs. "I'm sorry. I can't..."

Tears were spilling down her cheeks

Ravenna went to her. "What is it?" she asked.

Beth's face crumpled. She shut her eyes tightly, squeezing the flooding tears. "I'm sorry," she stuttered. "I shouldn't have..." She threw back her head and gave a cry of pain that seemed drained from her soul.

Ravenna didn't know what to do. She touched Beth's shoulder but she couldn't reach her. Beth was lost, in some private dreadful place. Tears welled in her own eyes. Only a few moments ago they'd been laughing and dancing. What had gone wrong?

Ravenna heard Harry's firm tread coming up the stairs. Heard him call, saw the smile die on his face as he strode into the room. She stood awkwardly as he gathered Beth into his arms and pulled her to the floor, cradling her in his lap. Ravenna felt she had no place there and stole away.

14.

Saturday shoppers were still crowding the pavements in the High Street as Ravenna walked away from the antique shop and away from Beth. Head down, hands plunged deep inside the pockets of her jacket, elbows tucked in close to her sides, Ravenna skirted around people, not wanting to touch anyone or meet their eyes.

A few moments ago she'd been leaping around Beth's studio, dancing as if she might touch the stars, but now her body felt as heavy and lumpen as a bag of wet turnips. Her ears ached with the sound of Beth's crying and she hated herself for walking away from Beth's grief.

As she trudged towards the end of the shopping parade, she felt like crying herself. All her hopes of a bright new future were gone. Beth had had every opportunity to tell her that she was her mother, but she'd said nothing.

Ravenna stepped into the gutter to avoid some shoppers and noticed two small children, hand in hand, jigging up and down on the pavement. She thought of how she and Beth had danced, fitting together like fingers on one hand, moving in unison.

The memory lifted her despair for a moment and she hopped back on to the pavement, stepping out a little more cheerfully. She remembered how pleased Beth had been to see her when she'd arrived at the cottage, as if she'd been waiting for her to call. And then Harry's words came into her head, "She's just as wonderful as you said she'd be." When she'd heard those words, they'd given her hope. But now she didn't know what to think. It was a statement aching with possibilities. She wished she'd had the courage to ask Beth if she was her mother, then everything would have been settled one way or the other. Now the only certainty was that she couldn't return to visit Beth. She'd seen such pain in her eyes and the sound of Beth's sobs haunted her.

Ravenna's shoulders drooped in misery as she considered that she might never know the truth. She still didn't know who her real mother was and she probably never would.

Out of habit, she turned into the courtyard to take the footpath to the estate but then she remembered her promise to Molly. Two-thirty at the back of the garage at Badger's. It was past two now, but she'd make it if she hurried. She remembered Molly's urgent voice on the telephone yesterday, when Ravenna had invited her over.

"I can't, it's terrible. Everything's dreadful."

Moll had sounded desperate – she needed help, and Ravenna couldn't let her down. Moll had always been there when she needed a friend.

Turning into the road leading to Badger's, Ravenna tried to focus her attention on Molly's problems instead of her own. It was difficult when she felt so miserable, but she had to try. She'd like to talk to Molly about Beth but she knew it wasn't the right time. She wouldn't manage it without crying and Molly had enough problems of her own at the moment. If she couldn't help herself, she might be able to help Moll.

The heavy wrought-iron gate that led into the garden at Badger's swung to with a thunderous clash, the sound echoing like a clanging bell around the still garden. Ravenna glanced nervously at the house, wondering if the noise had alerted the Morgans to her arrival. She knew Molly wanted to keep their meeting a secret.

She stood for a few moments, reaching out a hand to still the shivering metal bars. They felt like her nerves: taut, jangling, vibrating with tension. She sighed. This wasn't going to be easy but for Molly's sake, she had to be calm.

Letting go of the gate, she walked quickly up the driveway, darted behind some thick rhododendron bushes, checked to see if anyone was watching, then skipped past the wide French windows where the drive curved to the garage.

The Morgans' gleaming silver Mercedes, polished as if for a wedding, stood in front of the open garage but the Range Rover was missing.

A narrow path bordered by a beech hedge led to the back of the garage where Molly had arranged to meet her. Here the hedge was tall and she could not see the house or be seen. Ravenna hurried down the path but when she rounded the corner of the garage there was no sign of Molly.

Looking about her Ravenna stood, panting slightly, twitching her fingers, feeling uncomfortable. The gardener might be about. He'd think she was mad – she was too old for hide and seek.

This was the only unkempt area of Badger's – brambles and nettles knotted themselves around an upturned wheelbarrow and a rusty bike was buried in long grass. Around her, the house and grounds were strangely silent; the only sounds were the rustling of dried beech leaves and the flapping of a black polythene sack caught in the hedge.

Stepping gingerly through the nettles Ravenna peered through the hedge so that she could see the side of the house. The tall windows of the sitting-room glowed golden in the afternoon sun and beneath them the flower beds were bright with spring flowers. Everything about the house seemed as usual: the lawns were neat, the curtains drawn tidily, the garden benches exactly placed. There was something so solid and secure about Badger's. There was order, control, everything in its place. It was the only home Molly had known and Ravenna knew how hard it would be for her to leave it.

Sadness made a bitter taste in her mouth and she swallowed hard. If she was honest it wasn't just Molly she was feeling sorry for – Badger's held a lot of her memories too. She and Molly dressing up, tight skirts, high heeled shoes, blue eye-shadow smudged across their foreheads, lipstick smeared across their mouths. Tumbling sleep-overs, midnight feasts, disco dances, tennis matches. Always a warm welcome, the charm and ease of a prosperous family – and an escape from her own raucous one.

There never seemed to be any peace at home – well, not since Brett and Kirsty had come along. It wasn't as if Badger's was a silent place though. One of the big differences between life at Badger's and home was that people talked to one another. Not just "pass the remote control" or "when's the next car-boot?" Hilary and Kelvin Morgan talked about politics, religion, plays they'd been to, films they'd seen, and David talked to her about music and books. Sometimes she'd thought she'd go mad if she didn't have Molly's family.

Now as she stepped back from the hedge, she wondered what would happen to them. She leant against the upturned barrow, spinning the wheel with the palm of her hand, watching it turning, turning. As the wheel slowed she heard a noise from the direction of the house, then heard the crunch of gravel and looked up to see Molly threading her way between the far corner of the garage and hedge.

Molly didn't look her usual self at all. She was rather scruffy in faded jeans and an old sweatshirt. As she came closer, Ravenna saw that her blonde hair, which was usually brushed into a shiny bob, looked lank and there was a pale, strained look on her face as if it had been pummelled and stretched like a piece of dough.

"Hi. You OK?" Ravenna greeted her.

Molly didn't answer but looked at Ravenna with a panic-stricken expression, tears welling in her bright blue eyes. Finally she managed to say, "Thanks for coming, Raven."

"Bit cloak and dagger, isn't it? I feel like a burglar," Ravenna said, trying to lighten the mood.

Molly made a sort of snorting sound that was like laughing and crying mixed together, then she bit her lip and said excitedly, "Oh God, you don't know how good it feels to get out of the house. Mum won't let me speak to anyone. They're trying to keep it quiet but now Dad's gone and got himself arrested so everyone'll be bound to know."

"What? Know what?" Ravenna asked.

Molly sagged as if all the life had been drained out of her. She didn't speak for a moment but hunched her shoulders, folded her arms and breathed in and out through her nose, snorting like a highly strung racehorse. She rocked on her heels as if trying to find her balance, then said, "The share-holders had a meeting yesterday ... the factory's closing."

"Oh, Moll. I'm sorry." Ravenna's response was heartfelt. She knew what the end of the factory meant for Molly, her family and the town.

Molly held on to Ravenna's arm to steady herself and spoke quietly, so quietly that Ravenna had to strain forward to hear her.

"The new order wasn't enough. They're going to announce the closure on Monday. Things are much worse than we thought. Orders haven't been met . . . suppliers haven't been paid . . . liquidators are moving in."

"But your dad can't be arrested for that," Ravenna said.

Molly sighed and her head lolled forward as if the weight of it was too heavy for her neck. "He's been breathalysed," she said. "Last night he went out and didn't come home. Mum was frantic. Then the police rang and said they'd got him."

Ravenna listened with growing sympathy. No wonder Molly had been crying.

"Mum went with David to get him. They wouldn't let him drive home. She's really angry with him . . . said she felt humiliated. Says she can bear to lose the factory, money, even Badger's, but she can't put up with Dad drinking. He's started shouting at her. . . They never used to be like that."

"Oh Moll, it sounds terrible." Ravenna couldn't think of anything else to say. The only spark of comfort was that David was still at home, he'd help calm things down and it sounded as if he was needed. She put a hand on Molly's shoulder in sympathy.

Molly looked up and tried to smile but it came out looking like a bent chip. "Dustin and Co. will have a field day on this one," she said ruefully. "He's probably organizing a lynching party right now."

"Don't... Dustin won't even know yet and when the real story comes out people won't blame your family."

"Dustin will – he hates us."

"Why?" Ravenna asked.

She saw Molly wince and sensed there was something about Dustin that Moll wasn't telling her.

"Why, Moll? What's Dustin got to do with it?" Ravenna asked again.

Molly's bottom lip trembled. She bit down on it, struggling to control her voice. "Mum was one of the magistrates that sent his dad to jail."

"Oh, bloody hell!"

"She was only doing her job," Molly blazed.

"Hold on, Moll. I didn't mean anything. I was just surprised – you never said. I always wondered why he had it in for you."

"I didn't know till yesterday when I was telling Mum how horrible Dustin was to me. Apparently his dad had a string of convictions for receiving and burglary. They had to jail him – he'd used up all his chances."

"Well, it's his fault he got sent down then."

"Yeah, but Dustin doesn't see it like that."

Ravenna kicked at the gravel. "Oh, Moll. What a mess."

Molly shook herself free of Ravenna's arm and laughed, a hollow, empty laugh. "The way Dad's going he could end up in prison as well. He's drinking all the time ... written the bloody car off, could have killed himself ... or somebody else." Her eyes were watery but glinting with anger as she continued, "The press will make a meal out of it. They're like bloody vultures. You know how Mum's always spoken out against drinking and driving. We've already had three reporters on the phone. When they've finished, nobody'll trust Dad again."

She turned away and her shoulders sagged with despair. "I can't fight it. That's part of the problem, I feel so helpless. There's nothing I can do." She pulled a tissue from her jeans pocket and blew her nose, then turned round to face Ravenna and said abruptly, "I'll have to go. Mum'll kill me if she thinks I've told anyone. They're not making the announcement till Monday afternoon."

"Are you coming to school?"

"No. I can't face it and Mum doesn't want me to come back – only to take my exams."

"But you need all the notes from the stuff we're still doing."

"Mum says I can have a tutor for the last few weeks."

"You can't live like hermits."

Molly looked into the distance, as if she could see through the garage wall, then she said flatly, "We might be moving away – to Gram's house."

"What, down to Braymoor – the middle of nowhere? Oh no, that's desperate. You'll hate it."

Molly sighed. "It's sensible. Otherwise, we might be homeless."

A harsh shout from the house sent Molly spinning round as if hit by a bullet. "It's Mum. She's looking for me."

Ravenna had never known Moll to be frightened of her mum. She wondered just how much things in the Morgan household had changed. "Look, I'll wait for a while then I'll come to the house just like I always do."

"Mum won't let you in."

"Wanna bet?"

Molly's smile was genuine this time. "It'd be great to have you there. Everybody's so miserable."

"OK. If I don't get in, it won't be for lack of trying."

Molly disappeared and Ravenna heard voices in the distance before the door closed. She waited a few moments then walked to the front of the garage.

The chrome badges and radiator of the Mercedes shone in the sunlight. How much was this car worth? she wondered – probably about as much as most people's houses. Bending to look inside she inspected the sumptuous leather seats, radio, cassette, CD, telephone – all mod cons; yes, a family could live in there. Takeaway meals behind tinted glass.

She'd never really been jealous of what Molly had – for one thing, Molly had always shared it with her and the Morgans had made her feel like a part of the family. Sometimes she'd pretended Badger's was her home, wished Molly's parents were hers. It was hard to imagine them losing it all.

Straightening up Ravenna ran her finger along the roof ridge and inspected it. Hardly a mite of dust. The gardener must have cleaned and polished it this morning. She leaned forwards and rested her head in her arms on the warm roof; the sun touched her cheek. She couldn't bear to think of everybody she loved at Badger's being unhappy.

She hated the bloody factory and its workers. Hated the stupid newspapers and the police. Hated Dustin. Hated whatever it was that had happened to Beth to make her so miserable. Life was cruel. It was like one big joke. For every good thing that happened there were three bad. If you were happy you couldn't enjoy it because you knew something horrible was about to happen. If you loved someone you'd get frightened about losing them.

Even if she'd found out that Beth wasn't her mother, at least they could have been good friends and the thought of learning to dance was exciting. But now she couldn't go back to see Beth and there was nothing to look forward to. Only exams! And how was she going to cope without Molly?

Last week life had seemed fine. Boring sometimes but uncomplicated. Working hard at school, finishing course work, rehearsing for drama, playing tennis and. . . Tennis. Oh no! The memory hit her like a punch in the stomach. She'd missed tennis practice this morning. She'd been so involved with thinking about Beth and Moll that she'd forgotten. Oh damn! Now she'd be in trouble, probably dropped from the team. What excuse could she give? I went to see a woman I met at a car-boot sale because I thought she was my mother. Mrs Taylor would definitely buy that. Maybe Molly. . . No, she couldn't use Molly's problems as an excuse. That was stooping too low and anyway, she was sworn to secrecy. She'd just have to say she forgot and face the consequences.

Pushing herself away from the car, Ravenna saw her reflection in the car windows, her body squashed, distorted. She glanced along the glossy paintwork to the gleaming bonnet and felt like kicking it.

It was David who opened the door. His body, framed in the hallway, looked square and strong, but the hand curled round the edge of the door was delicate, sensitive. Ravenna wished she could reach out, take his hand in hers and snuggle up to him to find some comfort. She really missed him and if it wasn't for all the factory business she could have told him about Beth.

"Can I come in?" Ravenna asked.

David frowned slightly and looked thoughtful. "I've been given strict orders," he said. "Nobody is to cross the threshold. . . except family." Then he smiled, looked round, stepped forward and whispered dramatically, "But you are family, aren't you?"

Ravenna nodded and David's fingers lightly touched her cheek. "Well, come on in then."

Ravenna felt a thrill of pleasure and smiled at him. David turned and she followed him through the hallway and into the kitchen.

"Ravenna's here," he announced.

It seemed to take a while before anyone reacted to her appearance. There was a hanging silence in the kitchen as if a lot of noise had suddenly stopped and people were motionless. Molly's mum, Hilary, was holding a saucepan in mid-air and Molly held a sieve at arm's length, sieving nothing. It was as if they were posing for a photograph. David, Ravenna noticed, slipped away without another word.

Hilary recovered first and turned to Ravenna. Her face looked puffy and her smile a little forced – but if she didn't want Ravenna there she was determined not to show it.

"Come on in, Ravenna. We're having a late lunch. Nobody's eaten yet. Molly's doing her lovely mushroom sauce for pasta and I'm in charge of pudding."

There was a look of pure shock on Molly's face. She obviously hadn't expected Ravenna to penetrate the house defences, hadn't thought of David letting her in, but she was pleased to see her friend and grinned, almost her old self again. "Great to see you. Help yourself to a drink if you want one. There's Coke and plenty of juice in the fridge."

The camera button had clicked and everything was back to normal. Molly and her mum were cooking, just as she'd often seen them. Had she imagined the heavy silence? Reaching for a can of Coke she shivered as the cold of the fridge hit her face.

"Blasted reporters on the phone again. Why can't they. . .?"

Ravenna turned to face Kelvin Morgan and was shocked by what she saw. His appearance had altered completely. The thick dark hair which before had been lightly speckled with silver looked pewter grey, and his handsome face was red and bloated.

"Hi!" Ravenna said, over-brightly.

"What. . .?" Mr Morgan couldn't finish his sentence, his voice dried and he looked first bewildered then questioningly at his wife.

"Ravenna's here and she's going to stay and have something to eat with us, I think," Hilary Morgan said.

Ravenna nodded. She couldn't take her eyes off Kelvin Morgan's ravaged face. His lovely blue eyes were bloodshot and around them, the skin was crinkled with lines and shadows. For a moment he looked angry but this ebbed away leaving his face blank, devoid of expression. His mouth sagged open and his hands flapped in mid-air.

Ravenna felt as if she had lost her footing and was tumbling down a mountainside. Kelvin Morgan – calm, kind, wise, rock solid – seemed to have crumbled.

His wife went to him, put an arm around him and turned him towards the dining-room. "The food will be ready in a few minutes so set the table, darling. There'll be five of us."

The kitchen was cathedral quiet for a moment after Kelvin had wandered out and Ravenna was aware of Hilary watching her.

"Kelvin's been under a lot of strain at work lately," she said. "Ravenna, dear, would you get the water jug?"

Ravenna turned and reached up to the array of fitted cupboards. She knew where practically everything was in this kitchen. She and Molly had set tables and put away dishes countless times. A cupboard for the water jug and tumblers, a separate cupboard for wine and sherry glasses. The best cut glass in the dining-room.

The thick smooth glass of the water jug was heavy in her hands. Ravenna filled it at the filter tap on the sink. When she turned around, everything in the kitchen was under control. The sauce and pasta were bubbling, Hilary was scraping cream into a bowl and Molly was mixing salad dressing.

Ravenna helped get out some serving dishes and carry the food through to the dining-room. Setting a bowl of pasta down she was comforted to see the table laid as usual. The soft light from the chandelier glinted on the silver cutlery and candlesticks, five gold-edged china plates were set, each accompanied by a snowy white napkin. A platter of fruit brightened the centre – green apples, gold-red mangoes, oranges, lemons, a spiky tufted pineapple.

This had always been one of Ravenna's favourite rooms.

She liked the view of the garden from the French windows, the creamy marble fireplace that held displays of fresh flowers in summer and roasting logs at Christmas time, the family portraits that lined the walls and the paintings of shimmering ships in gold frames with paint so thick it looked as if it had been laid on and sculpted with a knife.

"Right, I think we're ready to eat," Hilary said briskly, coming into the room behind Ravenna and setting down bowls of sauce. She turned to call through to Molly, "Tell David food is ready and . . . oh . . . Kelvin isn't in here either."

Ravenna heard footsteps pounding downstairs and David appeared.

He smiled at Ravenna. "Food – at last – I'm starving."

Ravenna and David sat in their usual places opposite each other and were joined by Molly slipping into her place beside Ravenna.

"Can't find Dad anywhere," she informed them.

Hilary looked anxious and left the room. They heard her running through the house, calling her husband. None of the three left behind made much of an attempt at conversation. David said several times how good the food looked and picked up a fork only to put it down again. Ravenna said the mangoes looked tempting. Molly just stared down at her plate. Then they fell into silence, avoiding each other's eyes. Steam rose from the pasta sauces. Ravenna smelt garlic, mushrooms and herbs.

Suddenly David picked up his fork again. "Well, this is stupid. I don't want mine cold. I'm going to dig in. Come on, help yourselves," he said, piling pasta on to his plate.

Ravenna hesitated. "Shouldn't we wait?"

"It's OK," Molly said.

It was a few minutes before Hilary reappeared. She was flushed and breathless. "Kelvin won't be a few moments," she announced as she sat down at the end of the table.

But Kelvin didn't appear. Molly pushed lettuce leaves around her plate and Hilary picked at a few olives. Even David's pile of pasta didn't diminish by much. The silence was so sharp that it cut through any hope of conversation and the empty chair glowed with vacancy.

Ravenna spooned large clumps of pasta into her mouth. She couldn't bear such a lovely meal to go to waste and she ate ravenously as if trying to make up for the others and stem the tide of misery that was washing around the room. Forks chinked on china and glasses rattled.

Suddenly David began to eat heartily, forcing food down as if trying to eat up the silence. "Delicious pasta," he declared in a loud voice. "Have some more, Venna."

Ravenna was about to reply when she heard Hilary sniff and saw a solitary tear falling down her cheek. It was more than Ravenna could bear. She swallowed her food, put down her fork and said, "I know something is wrong. Will somebody tell me what?"

"It's nothing, Ravenna dear. I'm sorry. Kelvin hasn't been feeling well and I'm a bit upset, that's all."

There was another silence. Ravenna looked at Molly but she had her head down and was pretending to eat.

David fought with another mouthful of pasta, swallowed and said gently to his mother, "Why don't you tell her? She's practically one of the family and anyway, everybody'll know on Monday."

Mrs Morgan made a few stifled choking noises, then blew her nose, wiped away the tears and in a voice tight with control said, "I suppose you're right. There's no point in pretending. We've had some bad news. Things aren't so good at the factory... It's ... closing down."

Ravenna tried to look surprised by the news although she didn't really feel anyone would notice whether she was or not. Nobody was looking at her. "Oh no. I'm really sorry," she said.

Hilary was looking down at her plate, examining the olives. "Kelvin is distraught," she said, and now her voice was beginning to crack with tension. "It isn't his fault but he takes it so much to heart. He feels he's letting the workers, the family, down." She stifled a sob, gained control once more and went on, her voice shooting out in a series of loud strangled volleys. "His grandfather and father ... built the business ... started with ten men ... five hundred now ... fathers, daughters, sons... Kelvin's worked there since ... university. He's never had another job and..."

"Mum, don't..." David began, but before he could finish he was interrupted by a harsh voice. "That's right. Ring the bell. Let everybody know. Tell everybody. Go on, announce it from the factory roof. Kelvin Morgan has bent the books, let all his workers down, put them all on the dole."

Kelvin had appeared in the doorway, ruddy, swaying slightly and spitting as he spoke. He looked so angry that Ravenna felt he would punch anybody who argued with him.

But Hilary spun round and challenged him. "That's not true," she declared.

Ravenna held her breath as Kelvin's hand slammed down

on the back of his wife's chair. "Tell that to the families who rely on us. Families who can't pay rent or mortgages and get turned out of their homes. What other work is there for them around here?"

"Everybody's life will change," Hilary said pointedly.

"Well, you won't have your fancy cars and sit in judgement on the bench, that's for certain," Kelvin stormed.

Mrs Morgan covered her face and burst into tears but her husband was unmoved. He glared at them all defiantly before walking unsteadily out of the room.

"Don't worry, Mum. He didn't mean it. He's been drinking," David said.

At this Hilary got up and ran from the room.

Molly, who had kept her head down, now looked across at David. "Trust you to make things worse," she said bitterly, and ran after her mum.

"I was just trying to be helpful," David muttered. He turned to Ravenna, shrugged his shoulders and spread his hands. "Just another quiet luncheon at the Morgan household."

"I'm sorry," Ravenna said. "I shouldn't have come."

"Don't worry. It wasn't your fault. Maybe we need a few big rows before we can begin to think straight. Dad's gone to pieces. I wouldn't have thought it would have altered him so much. He's always been so solid, reliable, but he's drinking all the time. He's not thinking about Mum or us, he just feels sorry for himself. All he talks about are the workers and how he's let them down. He forgets it's our lives too."

"Well, I suppose he feels responsible – doesn't know what

to do. It's the only thing he's known. He's probably frightened," Ravenna said.

David looked thoughtful. "I suppose you're right but he doesn't have to take it out on Mum."

He got up from the table and for a moment Ravenna thought he was going to walk out and leave her but he came round to her and put his hand on her shoulder. "I'll take you home. Molly will be up there with Mum for ages. Actually, she's doing a great job keeping her sane. More use than I am. Come on, I need to get out of here."

15.

"Ravenna ... is that you, Ravenna?" was Mum's inevitable call, as Ravenna opened the front door to her house.

Ravenna sighed and turned back to watch David's BMW purr away from the kerb and swish down the road, out of sight. For a moment she stood looking after it, wishing that David had taken her elsewhere, then she closed the door behind her, hung up her coat and went to face Sheila.

"Where the hell have you been? You know I've got to get the shopping done. How do you think I can manage pushing a trolley round Tesco's with Kirsty in tow, shouting for every mortal thing she sees?"

Mum, in flapping flowery shirt and white leggings, stood in the middle of the kitchen floor, dishcloth in hand.

"I've been scouring the bathroom – that sink was filthy. Nobody bothers if I don't. And whoever uses up all them toilet rolls, I'd like to know. I bought four the other day and..."

She waved the dishcloth menacingly as she spoke but Ravenna wasn't intimidated. In fact, she had to stifle a giggle – there was something oddly comforting about Sheila's irascibility. Cleaning always put Sheila in a bad mood and after the wretched day she'd had, Ravenna was glad to find something that hadn't changed.

Ravenna was, however, careful not to provoke her further. Humility, she decided was the best tactic. "I'm really sorry,

Mum. I had a lot of work to do in the library – I just forgot the time."

Sheila stared at her suspiciously, making Ravenna uncomfortable – she wasn't a natural liar.

"Oh, so what's with the T-shirt and where's the books?"

"I ... er ... I called at Molly's and left the books there. She's using them too."

Sheila smiled, a sort of secret knowing smile, then came over, put a hand on Ravenna's head and stroked her hair. Ravenna was taken aback. She was expecting an inquisition but instead she saw Sheila's smile turn into a grin.

"I saw his car, Vernie," she said triumphantly. "Well, you could do a lot worse."

Ravenna didn't know whether she should encourage this line of thought. It let her off the hook for the moment but, oh hell, her life was getting more and more complicated.

"Mum, it's not what you think. David just gave me a lift home," she protested.

Sheila was putting the cloth and cleaner back under the kitchen sink. When she straightened up, she was still smiling. "Make us a cup of tea, will you, while I get ready. Kirsty's asleep and Ian'll be back in a minute with the car."

Mum disappeared upstairs and Ravenna silently thanked David for saving her from an hour of retribution. Mum was obviously keen for her to hitch up with David, thought he was a good catch. Would she still think so after Monday?

Ravenna pictured David in the car, driving her home, one hand resting on the open window, a serious preoccupied look on his face, his forehead slightly furrowed. He really was very nice. Nice! What did she mean? Of course he was nice, he was

Molly's brother, she'd known him for ever. She'd built dens and tree houses with him, shared sweets and secrets, baked cakes, flown kites, arm-wrestled, fought and argued, tickled and giggled. Taught him to dance so he wouldn't be a wet log at school discos. He was like a brother.

So why was it that her insides did a funny little somersault when Sheila mentioned him? Did she fancy David? Impossible. They knew each other too well. They'd slept in the same tent; they'd even had baths together when they were little. She'd seen him nude for Christ's sake! Then she remembered that that hadn't happened for a long time and she blushed.

Reaching for the tea bags, she put two in the pot then wandered into the sitting-room to switch off the TV. If there was one thing she hated it was a TV playing to an empty room. What a waste of electricity and talent. Talent? She raised her eyebrows – the programme was darts. One hundred and eighty! She hated the triumphant way the commentator said this as if somebody had just scored the winning goal in the cup final or climbed Mount Everest on a packet of Weetabix.

The room smelt of recent cigarette smoke, the cushions on the sofa were flat and Mum's catalogue lay open on the coffee table. Cleaning? That would be the day! Kirsty must have been asleep all afternoon. The cigarette butts had been cleared away though. Who did she think she was fooling?

Ian arrived as Ravenna was pouring out tea. He'd had no lunch so she made him a sandwich. Then Mum reappeared. She didn't look any different except for more make-up and shoes instead of slippers.

"Kirsty's rattling the bars," she said. "Come on, Ian, down that sandwich or Tesco's'll be closed."

Ravenna shot up to her room, hoping to catch Kirsty before she started wailing. Kirsty hated waking to find herself alone.

"Hi, Kissi, Kissi. How's my beautiful bad girl?"

Big blue eyes looked accusingly over the cot bars. "Venna, Venna back. Venna back. Up, up."

Kirsty threw her arms around Ravenna's neck and clung on tightly, her warm face buried into her shoulder. Ravenna carried her into the bathroom to take off her nappy.

"Oooh, it's dry, Kirsty. What a good girl. You are getting grown up. Let's see if you can do a wee then I'll find you some clean pants."

Kirsty glowed with pride and toddled to the cupboard to pull out her potty, sat on it and did a long stream of steamy urine. "Wee, wee, wee, wee," she sang, getting up and stamping her feet in triumph.

Ravenna laughed and clapped. "What a clever girl."

She looked at Kirsty's plump little legs and the absolute joy shining on her face. For her life was so simple.

Plastic bags reigned supreme in the kitchen. Frozen food to put in the freezer, cans for the cupboards and toiletries to travel upstairs. The air was filled with the rustling of plastic whilst Ravenna, Ian and Brett scurried around like hoarding squirrels stowing everything away. Kirsty sat in their midst sucking on an ice lolly given to keep her quiet, and Sheila directed operations whilst smoking a cigarette.

"I'm only having one. Honestly, I need it after that supermarket. I thought going later it wouldn't be so crowded." Puff, inhale, puff. "I couldn't believe how much we spent. I don't know how other people live. Don't know how anybody manages on less than what we get – I mean we only buy the basics."

"I expect they don't smoke," Ravenna cut in.

"You cheeky monkey. If you'd have been back earlier we wouldn't have had to rush round and I wouldn't feel so frazzled," Sheila said, coughing on the last word.

"Listen to you. You should give it up, Mum."

"I have," Sheila declared.

Ravenna rolled her eyes at Ian as he pulled two twenty packs of cigarettes out from between biscuits and crisps.

Sheila snatched them from him. "They're only for emergencies," she said as she hurried out to stash them away.

"Can I have a packet of crisps now?" Brett asked.

"No, we're having tea in a minute," Ravenna answered.

"What's for tea?" Brett asked suspiciously.

Ravenna shouted the question through to Mum in the sitting-room.

"I don't know. There's a whole load of stuff there – have a look. Can't you cook something, Ravenna? It's that quiz show I like, then *Blind Date*'s on." Pause and distant coughing. "I'll have some chips and fish fingers."

Ravenna dipped in the freezer drawer to find a bag of frozen chips and switched on the oven. Spreading the icy sticks out on a blackened baking tray she thought of the bowls of delicious pasta and sauce on the Morgan's lovely oak table. Delicious food that had gone to waste. Then she remembered the smell of cooking in Beth's kitchen, the way Beth had been so pleased with the scones ... their golden roundness, Beth's smile of triumph... Don't ... don't ... it hurt to think about it.

"I want spaghetti. Mum bought a tin for me," Brett said, watching her.

"You'll have chips and fish fingers like everybody else," Ian said firmly. "And you can set the table."

"Aw, Dad, I want to watch telly."

"If Ravenna's cooking then you can set the table and watch Kirsty," Ian said as he opened a big white loaf of bread and started to butter some slices.

The telephone rang in the hall. Nobody answered it. It persisted, so Ravenna turned down the gas, stepped over Kirsty and grabbed the receiver.

"Ravenna? It's Selina. John and I are having a sort of party – well, er ... more like open house tomorrow afternoon ... barbecue in the garden if it's nice enough. There'll be a mixture of people, some dancers, friends, one or two you may have met at self-defence – we thought you might like to come."

Ravenna was surprised. After all, she didn't know Selina very well and John, Mr Barstow, was a teacher. She hesitated.

"Don't worry if you can't. I know it's short notice. We just thought because the weather had been so nice and it's ages since we've had a gathering. It's only an informal thing. People are dropping in from about two onwards."

"I'd like to but I'm not sure if I can and ... I don't know where you live."

Ravenna listened carefully to Selina's instructions, then put down the phone. She wasn't at all sure she wanted to go. There might be lots of other teachers there or she might not know anybody and be left standing by herself. She'd think about it.

The food was nearly ready when she went back into the kitchen. Luckily, Ian had flipped over the fish fingers, saving them from becoming charcoal.

Ravenna wasn't hungry after all the pasta she'd had at the Morgans' so she prepared some food for Kirsty whilst Ian dished up.

"Who was that on the phone?" Sheila asked as she collected her tray.

"Selina who runs the self-defence class, inviting me to her house tomorrow afternoon."

"You hardly know her," Sheila said suspiciously.

"I know, but there's a whole load of people going," Ravenna answered in between blowing on Kirsty's fish fingers.

Sheila splodged tomato sauce on to her plate. "Well, there's a car boot at Ecclestone tomorrow. Big one, roundabouts and everything. I thought we'd all go; we might not be back till late."

"I don't want to go to another car boot," Ravenna said.

"Thought you were quite taken with them last week." She looked hard at Ravenna. "Not that we ever saw what you bought. So precious you've stowed it away – out of sight. Anyway, you might not want to go but there's Kirsty to see to."

"I could take Kirsty to Selina's," Ravenna said recklessly, immediately regretting it when she pictured herself turning up at Selina's party with a pushchair.

"You will too," Sheila answered resolutely.

Ravenna looked to Ian for help but he was tuning the radio for the football results.

Much later, Ravenna lay on her bed reading over some

history notes. Should the US have stayed in Vietnam? Discuss. She had discussed and received a good grade for the essay but now Phnom Penh and the Khmer Rouge kept slipping away from her. She pictured Buddhist monks in saffron robes, temples with curly golden roofs, cool courtyards shaded by tall palms. Thought of the dancers she'd seen at school only last week, although it seemed a lifetime ago. She thought of Beth dancing that morning, whirling and flashing around the room, filling it with magic, her graceful limbs stretching and bending and then the two of them dancing together. It had seemed so right, so absolutely, perfectly right. She and Beth – two halves of a circle coming together. All the shadows disappearing from Beth's face, her spirits soaring. It had been so apparent, such a tangible thing, as if Beth had shed a layer of skin or shrugged off a dark cloak – untangled herself and broken free. But that freedom had been too much to bear. She had flown into a clear space, then lost her nerve, turned to face the past and it had shattered her.

Now Ravenna hated herself for having walked away from Beth, leaving Harry to collect the pieces and hold them together. She should have stayed. She should have comforted Beth. She wanted to go back now and find the answers. What was it that had shattered Beth's life? Or who was it – herself?

Her face flushed, stinging with shame, because she suspected why she'd left Beth crying in her studio. It wasn't because she'd felt helpless, not really. It was because she was disappointed. She'd thought she was sharing a dream that Beth would make come true and when it hadn't, she'd just walked out like a spoilt kid. She was no better than some of the shallow people she despised at school, no better than Faye Mellins or Dustin.

But Dustin was the last person she wanted to think about. She sat up, pushed her school books to one side, rose and paced irritably around the room. Her day had been difficult enough as it was. Perhaps seeing Dustin in the High Street that morning had been a bad omen. Whenever he was around, nothing good ever happened. It was as if Dustin's kiss had put a wicked spell on her. Since that moment, everything had gone wrong. Her school work was going down the drain, the meeting with Beth had turned out badly, Molly's dad had been arrested, the factory was closing, Molly was leaving school and probably the area as well.

What sort of atmosphere had David found when he returned to Badger's this afternoon? she wondered. She imagined him parking in the driveway and sitting in his car not wanting to go in. She wished she could be more help to them all, but what on earth could she do? She'd been naïve to think she could make any difference. It had been great to see David though and she pictured him, a lock of blond hair falling over his eyes, a frown creasing his broad forehead – and her heart turned over. If only *David* was pursuing her, not Dustin.

She heard Kirsty stir and checked the cot as she crossed to the window to close the curtains. Kirsty was lying face upwards, her eyes dark hollows, her lips puckered into a bow. Bending to tuck in the blankets which had tumbled down to her waist, Ravenna felt Kirsty's breath, soft as a moth's wings on her cheek. Little demon. She watched her for a moment, the small fist knuckle-tight, the blonde curls shining on the pillow. So different from the child in Beth's sketches – so different from herself.

Ravenna wondered about the child in the drawings and realized with a pang of jealousy that it might not be herself. Beth's heart was broken not because she'd given Ravenna up for adoption but because of another lost child – lost or damaged, dead or killed? The possibilities were all there. All dreadful. She had to go back and see Beth to find out – she had to know.

Turning to her dresser, Ravenna reached inside the bottom drawer and took out the shawl. Clutching it to her, she moved aside the history books, slipped under the duvet and lay down to sleep; the shawl a shimmering bundle held in her arms, her body curved around the soft silk.

All night she dreamed that she was dancing – she and Beth dancing in the silver light of a crescent moon, dancing in a damp, starstruck meadow, dancing as a shimmering sun rose to warm the hills. She and Beth whirling and waltzing and warming their souls – until Beth stopped and, stepping away, left her alone.

In the morning, Ravenna woke knowing that there were two certainties in the mess that had become her life: she wanted to see Beth again and she wanted to dance.

16.

All thoughts of dancing were banished from Ravenna's mind as she toiled up the hill towards John and Selina's house. For the moment she was concentrating on walking – pushing the heavy pushchair, extending her arms, thrusting forward, bracing herself against the slope and the brisk wind. She knew she'd arrive at the party hot and sweaty from the climb but at least Kirsty, after a boisterous morning, was now fast asleep.

Ravenna wondered what the house would be like. She'd never been in a teacher's home before and John and Selina were a bit unusual – for a start they weren't married and then Selina was black. Would that make a difference? She laughed scornfully at herself. What did she imagine – leopard-skin lingerie dripping from African masks? The sort of place the tabloids would call an exotic love-nest? She pictured John and Selina in a treetop – two giant birds perching on a kitchen table balanced precariously on a web of twigs, feeding each other spaghetti worms.

"Do have a little more wormiloni, dear."

Cringe and double cringe – she was spending too much time alone!

As she drew nearer to it, the stone terrace above her, with neat hedges and windows looking out over the valley, appeared extremely normal and she picked out Selina and John's house, the end one nearest the road.

When she reached the garden gate she paused to catch her breath and discovered that now she'd arrived she felt nervous about going in. There were lots of vans and cars parked around the house. There'd be a crowd of strangers inside and she wasn't sure any more that she should be there. She'd probably be out of place and Kirsty would be a nuisance.

After a morning spent at home by herself she'd decided to accept Selina's invitation; it was a chance to get out of the house and she couldn't get on with anything much when Kirsty was around. School work was impossible because Kirsty demanded playtime. She'd tried several times to ring Molly but each time it was a machine that answered. It was so frustrating – an answering machine with no answers.

Oh well, here goes, she thought as she opened the gate and struggled to steer the pushchair up the uneven garden path. No turning back now, not after that long walk.

Selina, dressed in a plain white shirt and jeans, opened the front door. "Hi! Great to see you. Come in."

Ravenna's doubts ebbed a little when Selina's broad smile beamed even brighter on seeing Kirsty.

"And who's this, then?" she asked.

"My sister, Kirsty. Mum and Dad are out . . . I have to look after her. I hope it's OK."

"Great. Don't worry, she'll be the main attraction. John loves kids. We'll set him on babysitting."

Ravenna hesitated. She could hear loud laughter coming from the back of the house and knew Kirsty would be in a bad mood if she woke before she was ready.

"Could I just put her in a quiet room somewhere? Just until she wakes up?" she asked.

"Course you can. Look, we'll put her in the study. She'll be fine in there."

Selina helped Ravenna lift the pushchair over the front step and into a narrow hallway. Then Selina took over, gently turning and manoeuvring the buggy through a doorway to the left of the stairs. Behind her, Ravenna waited, studying the colourful posters that lined the bright yellow walls: Winster Wakes, Edinburgh Festival, Hammersmith Odeon; dance, theatres, concerts, art exhibitions – she glimpsed the sort of interesting life she only dreamed of.

Inside the study it was cool and quiet. The stone walls were painted white and lined with full bookshelves, there were lots more posters; a collection of brilliantly coloured hats hung from a piece of driftwood and several guitars and assorted drums were propped in a corner.

Selina had wheeled Kirsty into the middle of the room. "She'll be fine in here. We'll keep an eye on her. Come and meet some people."

The noise hit Ravenna like a brick. So many people talking and laughing, all crowded into a small kitchen and adjoining living-room. The air was heavy with the smell of fried onions and garlic and the kitchen worktops were covered with dishes of food and bottles of drink.

People seemed to be heaped together in clumps so that at first it was hard to recognize individuals. Selina went to get drinks and for a moment Ravenna stood, hovering in the doorway, feeling like a lone gatecrasher. She recognized one or two women from the self-defence class and was half smiling at one of them when suddenly there was a hush. At first, Ravenna wondered if people had noticed her, an interloper, but then she remembered she'd been properly invited and through the silence she heard the faint soft strum of a guitar.

Ravenna followed the sound and saw John Barstow sitting amongst a group of young people. He was playing a guitar, his large fingers moving delicately, rapidly, making the air ripple with gentle sound. Then the sound grew and swelled. He'd been joined by another guitarist and Ravenna saw that opposite John Barstow, playing along with him, was David. Ravenna was so surprised to see him that she nearly spilt the drink which Selina was handing to her.

"Are you OK?" Selina asked.

"Yes, I'm fine. My hands got cold on the walk."

"Let's go and sit down. We'll find a bit of space on the sofa or the carpet."

Ravenna followed Selina weaving around and through two groups of people. There was no chance of a seat on the big red sofa which was already sagging under the weight of wedged bodies, so they sat on the floor with their backs resting against it.

Ravenna listened and watched the two musicians and felt the whole room listening with her. There was hardly a whisper. Music spilled from the guitars in intricate patterns, a rich mixture of bending blues and skimming cadences. Ravenna relaxed, absorbing the music, closing her eyes for a moment, lost in the pulsing rhythms. But she couldn't switch off for long. Part of her brain was trying to work out how David and John Barstow knew each other. David had always been away at school, then university. He and John Barstow would hardly move in the same circles – Rotary and golf club dinners. David had taken her a couple of times to the country club with the lovely swimming pool. It didn't seem like John Barstow's sort of a place. And how had David become such a good guitarist? She knew he played, had been in a band at school, but this was intricate stuff, difficult, very polished, professional. She certainly hadn't expected to see David here. He drove a BMW for goodness' sake! Had he parked it between the sardine-tin Citroëns and hippy vans outside?

"They're good, aren't they?" Selina whispered as they finished playing. "They did a gig at the Fox House a couple of weeks ago. Pity David's going back to uni soon. Natalie kept saying what a great guitarist he was."

Ravenna's eyes were drawn to a girl who'd just entered the room. She was stunning – long red hair falling in a thick veil to frame her pale face and creamy shoulders, hazel eyes fringed by long feathery lashes, lips that were full and softly smiling.

She moved sleekly and elegantly over to David and slid her long, long legs down to the carpet to sit, resting her back against David's knee. Somehow, Ravenna knew this was Natalie.

David bent over his guitar to whisper in the girl's ear. She turned to look at him, beaming up a dazzling smile, her teeth white and even, a sparkling half-moon. Ravenna saw David's fingers move from the strings to brush Natalie's hair, her cheek – the familiar caress of a lover. She felt a stab of jealousy; she was an outsider, shunned by the touching of their eyes.

She gazed at Natalie's hair. The light behind it had turned it into a flaming halo. Her shoulders looked marble-white. Between her small high breasts hung a large gold cross; on her wrist, a multitude of golden bangles jangled. She was wearing a red silky shift, long grey stockings, her legs rooted in heavy black boots. Ravenna was pretty sure she didn't live in

Maddock. She'd cause too much of a stir – too exotic for this place. But if she and David were a couple then why had Natalie never been to Badger's? Why had David never even mentioned her?

David bent to kiss the top of Natalie's head and as he looked up his eyes caught Ravenna's staring at them. Ravenna felt like a voyeur and flicked her eyes away but the next thing she knew David was beside her.

"Hi! Didn't know you were coming. I'd have given you a lift."

He was bending down to her, his face close to hers, a bright warmth in his smile, but Ravenna felt he was now part-stranger; no longer Molly's brother whom she'd grown up with, but a man who inhabited a world she knew nothing of. She blushed and stumbled over her words. "I only decided this morning and I . . . er . . . I walked here . . . with Kirsty."

David put his hand lightly on her shoulder. "I'll give you a lift back if you like. Kirsty can sit on your knee in the back. We'll put the pushchair in the boot. Where is she? Where've you hidden her?" he asked, looking around.

"Oh, she's asleep in the study. I . . . um . . . I'd better go and see if she's woken up."

But David was barring her way, a puzzled expression on his face. Ravenna guessed he was wondering who this person was, looking embarrassed and stumbling over her words.

She tried to speak more confidently, be more like herself, but the words seemed to keep getting stuck. "I . . . er, didn't expect to see you, er . . . here. It was . . . a surprise. Yes . . . um . . . a surprise. Didn't know you could play so well."

David laughed. "I wish. I don't get enough time to practise.

Too involved in Business Studies." His mouth curled with disgust. "Too much work, facts, figures, law, politics. Doesn't leave much time to play the guitar."

"Or for girlfriends?" Ravenna asked nervously.

David grinned. "Come and meet her," he said and, turning, called over to Natalie.

His face shone with pride as Natalie stretched, stood up, and, sleek as a cat, stalked over to them. She smiled a luminous smile as she slipped her arm through David's.

"Natalie, this is Ravenna."

Ravenna did her best to return the smile but all she could focus on was their arms and hands intertwined.

"Good to meet you. You're joining the dance group, aren't you? That's great," Natalie said.

Ravenna looked at her blankly. Natalie was looking pleased, welcoming, certain, but how could Natalie know anything about the dancing and her meeting with Beth?

Ravenna opened her mouth to speak but just a gurgling sound came out.

Natalie didn't seem to notice anything strange, however. She continued speaking: "Don't worry. Beth told me you hadn't had any training but she'll soon fix that. She's a brilliant teacher. It's great that she's dancing again. She's had such a tough time."

So many questions raided Ravenna's brain, fighting for utterance. The one that finally came out was, "How do you know about the dancing?"

"Beth was talking about you yesterday afternoon, saying how talented you were, what a natural dancer, what a great addition to our troupe you'll be."

Ravenna was astounded. She'd left Beth crying, seemingly heartbroken, and that's how she still thought of her. Beth's sobs had haunted her all night. But of course, Beth had been comforted by Harry, had blown her nose, stopped crying, gone back to the house, washed, eaten, talked to friends.

Natalie was Beth's friend. She could see that now. They all knew each other: Natalie, Selina, John Barstow, Harry, Beth. And David had been drawn into their circle too.

"Are you a dancer?" she asked Natalie.

"Absolutely. Beth was my first teacher – she's terrific. She came into our school one day, years ago, to run a workshop and she really fired me up. I'd never thought about dancing as a career. It was just something I did but Beth made me see it was possible. I grew too tall for classical stuff but I'm part of Arc dancers now. Have you seen us?"

Ravenna shook her head.

"It's tough, a lot of travelling, terrible floors sometimes, but I love it."

As she spoke, Natalie seemed to glow with energy. Ravenna could imagine her dancing; vibrantly, sensuously, her tall figure turning, swooping, bending. She would enjoy being part of a dance group with Natalie and Beth. And it might be possible – all she had to do was pluck up the courage to go back and see Beth.

Deep in thought, she was startled by someone saying her name. It was Selina.

"Kirsty's waking up. John's with her but if he's the first thing she sees when she wakes up she might think she's in Narnia."

"Or Beauty with the Beast," David laughed.

"That's nice, isn't it?" Natalie said, shaking David's arm.

"I'd better go," Ravenna said.

As Ravenna opened the door, she heard Kirsty chuckle. She was sitting on John Barstow's knee, pulling mischievously at his beard.

"Kirsty!" Ravenna chided, going over ready to lift her and take her from him.

"No!" Kirsty shouted, guessing Ravenna's intention.

"She's fine," John Barstow said. "Leave her with me. She's going to play the drums in a minute, aren't you, Kirsty?"

Kirsty's hands rhythmically slapped John Barstow's chest.

"That's it. Come on. Let's get the drums out," he said, rising to his feet and setting Kirsty on the floor.

Ravenna hovered uncertainly. "Be careful, Kirsty. They're proper drums not toys," she said as John Barstow leaned to pull a tall, finely polished drum into the middle of the carpet.

"She'll be all right. Off you go and enjoy yourself. Meet some people. I already know everybody. It's not often I get chance to play Daddy."

Ravenna smiled as John settled his burly bulk next to Kirsty and began to show her how to hit the tight skins to make different sounds. She held her breath when he gave Kirsty the drum stick but Kirsty held the stick still for a moment, a frown of concentration on her face, then she struck the drum lightly, delicately, as she'd been shown. John Barstow had judged it just right. He'd taken Kirsty seriously and she'd responded to him. Ravenna watched for a moment then turned back to the party.

More people had arrived in the short time she'd been gone. The kitchen was crowded and the noise level had risen again.

Selina was serving food from steaming casseroles. Plates and cutlery rattled and people were shouting to be heard. Ravenna stood for a moment, unsure where to go. She picked out Natalie's tall figure and beside her David's smaller, broad-shouldered shape. They were talking to a man with long wavy hair, light-brown with silvery streaks. He was cocking his head to one side listening, just as he always did. Ravenna realized with a shock that she knew this mannerism, as if she'd known him for years. It was Harry. He was talking to David and Natalie, laughing, gesturing with a glass in his hand.

Ravenna's insides began to divide and fizz. And as she stood watching, Harry turned to look straight at her as if he'd sensed she was there. He came over to her.

"Hello! Here she is, just the person we wanted to see."

The "we" made a volcano of Ravenna's insides.

He was twinkling, beaming, glad to see her.

"How are you?"

"I'm fine."

He threw his head back and looked at her with slightly raised eyebrows, then put a hand lightly on her shoulder. With only the slightest pressure, Harry turned her round so that she came face to face with Beth.

Ravenna's mouth went dry and her heart seemed to thump so hard she felt her ribcage vibrate. Beth's face was level with hers, creased with anxiety, her eyelids half closed, shielding her eyes.

"I wanted to apologize," she said. "I'm so sorry about yesterday. I shouldn't have let you go away like that."

Ravenna couldn't think straight. Beth was apologizing to

her but wasn't she the one who'd let Beth down? She'd walked out leaving Beth crying. Shouldn't she be saying sorry?

And yet Beth was looking at her, pleading with her to accept the apology.

"I ... er ... it's OK," she muttered.

"I want to talk to you. But not here," Beth said. "Will you come back to the cottage with us? Just for a short while. I want to explain things."

Ravenna could see what effort this was costing Beth. It was written in lines and shadows on her face but she hesitated.

"I've got Kirsty, my baby sister, with me."

"That's all right, bring her with you or leave her with John and Selina, they love kids."

"No," Ravenna said, more sharply than she intended. "She hardly knows them."

Beth looked upset and Ravenna spoke quickly to reassure her.

"I'll take her home first and come and see you this evening, if that's all right?"

Beth looked relieved and nodded her agreement. Ravenna, awash with emotion, turned away. She needed time to herself, time to calm down.

She found David with Natalie, deep in conversation with another couple. Ravenna hesitated then butted in.

"David, I need to get home right away. Will you take me?"

David turned, looked surprised for a moment but then said calmly, "I was just off anyway. Nat's got a train to catch and I'm needed at home."

Ravenna went to collect Kirsty who protested violently at being dragged so suddenly away from her drums and new friend but Ravenna was insistent. Bribing her with promises of return visits, a bath, a game and anything else she could think of, Ravenna said a hasty goodbye to John and Selina.

David carried the pushchair to his car, which was parked next to Beth and Harry's multicoloured wagon, and stowed it in the boot. Ravenna belted herself and Kirsty into the back seat and they drove down the hill and into town towards the station. Natalie chatted happily about plans for her and David to meet next week in Manchester, said she hoped she'd see Ravenna again, blew a kiss to Kirsty, and in a swirling tangle of boots, bags and goodbyes, was gone. David followed her and Ravenna averted her head from their kisses. She played Incy-Wincy spider and climbed up the spout more times than she could count before David finally returned to the driving seat and started the engine.

Natalie receded in a colourful blur. For a few moments Ravenna was silent. It was difficult having any conversation from back to front seat and she could see David's preoccupied expression in the mirror. He was concentrating on driving but also, she guessed, thinking about Natalie.

Snapshots of the party whirled in her head as the car sped along. There'd been lots of interesting-looking people there; she ought to have stayed and talked to some of them instead of rushing away. It had hardly been worth the long walk to get there. She was stupid sometimes. But how could she really relax and enjoy herself when she had Kirsty to look after? Even when John Barstow was playing with Kirsty she hadn't felt really free and then, of course, she couldn't have stayed after seeing Beth. When Beth spoke to her everything came flooding back: the hopes, the dreams. Her stomach was still churning nervously. Perhaps Beth wasn't her mother, but there must be some connection, there must. What did Beth want to tell her? She wanted to explain, she said. What was it?

The car lurched around the corner into the estate, interrupting Ravenna's thoughts and Kirsty's singing and drumming on the car seat. Ravenna looked again at David's face in the mirror and realized she hadn't asked him how things were at home. All last night she'd been worrying and wondering and now she hadn't even asked him.

She saw David blink rapidly and raise his eyebrows in answer to her question. "Not much different really. But at least Dad didn't go out last night. He shut himself up in the study and I think he slept in there. Things were pretty quiet this morning."

"Whenever I try to ring Moll, I just keep getting the answer machine," Ravenna said.

David winced. "Mum's still funny about talking to anybody and the press keep bothering us. I'll ask Moll to give you a ring. I expect she would have but she's been busy looking after Mum, trying to keep her spirits up. She keeps finding her things to do – they were cleaning out the kitchen cupboards when I left. It's a good idea, I suppose."

"I miss her," Ravenna said.

The car slowed and stopped outside Ravenna's house. David opened her door, then lifted the pushchair from the boot.

"I'll carry it up to the house for you," he offered.

"No thanks. I can manage."

David didn't argue. He wants to get home, see what's happening, Ravenna thought.

He turned to go but just as he was about to lower himself into the car, he hesitated and turned back to Ravenna.

"Did you like Natalie?" he asked, with an anxious tilt of his eyebrows.

"Yes, I thought she was lovely," Ravenna answered.

David smiled. "Thanks, Raven." Then he added cautiously, "Do you think Mum and Dad will?"

Ravenna smiled reassuringly. "Of course they will – she's a knockout."

"Hmm. . ." David said thoughtfully as he got into the car. "I hope so."

17.

It was a strangely silent house that Ravenna and Kirsty entered. Kirsty was chattering away as usual, but from the rest of the house there was no sound. No shouting, no radio blaring out and, amazingly, no drone from the TV set in the sitting-room.

Ravenna knew the family had arrived back because she'd seen the car outside, but inside, all was puzzlingly quiet. Where was everybody?

After checking the kitchen, Ravenna set the pushchair down in the hallway and followed Kirsty, who'd wandered off into the sitting-room.

The blank TV screen stared at Ravenna, its grey, glassy eye accusing her of neglect. Without its flashing pictures and bouncing sound it seemed like an alien squatting in the corner. Ravenna hardly recognized it – something was up. Her gaze swung round the room. They were there – all three of them sitting in silent contemplation: Ian, at the table, worshipping something wrapped in newspaper and Sheila and Brett sitting on the floor, facing each other across a chequered board scattered with ships and aeroplanes.

"What's wrong? TV broken?" Ravenna asked.

No one answered.

"Bomb," said Sheila, as Brett moved one of his counters.

"Isn't *The Clothes Show* on, Mum?" Ravenna asked.

"Spy," said Brett.

Ravenna looked at Ian who was now rubbing hard at a

tarnished lump of metal. Beside him, Kirsty was doing like-wise, copying his vigorous strokes, but sometimes missing the metal altogether and hitting the table.

"I'm home," Ravenna announced, stepping further into the room and spreading out her arms in mock greeting.

Her gesture had no effect. For once she felt something in common with the TV – they were both ignored. She shrugged and went over to the table, looking over Ian's shoulder to see what he was so busy polishing.

"What do you think, Ravenna? They're old miners' lamps, from the pit. Might even be from where my dad worked. There's real brass underneath. Look!"

Ian proudly showed her a bright golden speck, gleaming amidst the rust.

"I got five of them for a fiver. Cleaned up they'll sell for fifteen pounds a piece."

"Great," Ravenna said, as she took off her jacket and slumped on to the sofa.

"Bomb," Sheila announced triumphantly, sweeping aside Brett's counters. "That's it, I win."

"Aw, Mum," Brett moaned. Then he asked hopefully, "Can we have another game? That was cool."

Sheila got to her feet. "Not yet, love, Vernie's back."

"Amazed you noticed," Ravenna muttered.

Sheila rested a hand on Ravenna's shoulder. "Sorry, love, we were just entering the final battle – couldn't lose my concentration. Where've you been?"

"To Selina's – the party, you know, I told you..."

"Oh yes, I'd forgotten – had my mind on other things since then. Was Kirsty all right?"

"She was fine. She played the drums with Mr Barstow, didn't you, Kirsty?"

Kirsty laughed. "John, John," she shouted and drummed her feet on the floor.

"You'll get John," Sheila laughed. "He always seems such a nice man, though. I see him and his wife in the supermarket sometimes."

"They're not married – they just live together," Ravenna explained.

Sheila patted Ravenna's shoulder. "Who cares these days? She looks a lovely person – always smiling. We had a word about tofu one week – she's a vegetarian. Well, that might be her religion, I suppose. You sit down, I'll make a drink. You must be tired, walking back all that way."

Ravenna settled back and switched on *The Clothes Show*.

Brett moaned, "I hate this programme. You always say we watch too much television and you come in and put it straight on."

"Well, I happen to like this. Go out if you don't want to watch it."

Brett left to go up to his room and Ravenna was glad. She was tired, more tired than Mum suspected. She relaxed against the high sofa back, feeling drained of all her energy. So much had happened to her recently. She felt as if she'd been blown about in a gale, first one way then the other, then lifted off her feet and tumbled down a mountainside. Her head ached and her insides were all shaken up. She must rest before going to see Beth. But at the thought of that meeting she could feel the gale blowing through her mind again, lifting bundles of hopes and worries.

She watched skinny models gyrate along a cat walk. She saw brides and grooms, young farmers shearing sheep, frantic disco dancers and firemen modelling the latest in Latex. She admired Kirsty's lamp smeared with metal cleaner and assured her it was nearly shiny.

Sheila brought tea and Ravenna's favourite lemon cake. "I made it when we got back. It's still warm. Tell me if it's not lemony enough." Sheila set down a large, airy looking sponge cake, cut a large slice and handed it to Ravenna. "I thought you could do with cheering up, you've looked a bit peaky lately. Are you all right, love?"

Sheila sat down next to her, her warmth spreading over the couch like a plump duvet. And for once, Ravenna didn't move away from the odour of cigarette smoke mixed with a hint of sweat.

"Look at that hat, as if anybody'd wear that in the street," Sheila chuckled. She gave Ravenna a squeeze. "You could be one of those super-models, you know. You've got the looks and the figure. You ought to try for it."

"Mum! I want to do something more important with my life than that," Ravenna protested as she bit into a piece of warm lemon cake.

"I know you do, love, and you will. You're clever."

Ravenna frowned. She wasn't thinking about being a lawyer or professor, but about the joy she'd felt when dancing with Beth, the freedom she'd felt in her dream and the challenge that learning to dance would present.

Sheila put her fingers on Ravenna's forehead, stroking away the frown. "Don't look like that. You know you're clever and you've got personality, but a bit of money wouldn't go amiss, would it? When you're at college or for holidays."

Ravenna eyed one of the models. She was like her – tall, slim, long dark hair, big eyes. She would need money for dance school.

"I suppose not. Thanks, Mum. Might be an idea," she said and smiled. "It's lovely cake, very lemony."

After *The Clothes Show* finished, Brett returned and he and Sheila embarked on another board game battle. It seemed a good opportunity for Ravenna to slip away and she went up to her room to change.

As soon as she closed the door behind her, Ravenna felt a nervous excitement overtake her. With trembling fingers she struggled to unbutton her shirt and jeans, then flung open the wardrobe to find something to wear. Her nerves were jangling, telling Ravenna to grab anything that was clean, throw it on and zoom off to see Beth. But an obstinate streak of reason slowed her down, told her to relax and take her time.

She went into the bathroom and watched water gush into the basin; she scooped up trickling handfuls, spraying fountains on to her face and under her armpits. She'd only be a moment, she told herself; soon she'd be ready, rushing down the road to see Beth. But she was still there a full five minutes later, hesitating, delaying, slowly squeezing just the right amount of toothpaste on to the brush and meticulously brushing each and every crevice.

She looked in the mirror, examining her face. But it was Beth's eyes she saw and, shivering with apprehension, she seized a towel and began hurriedly drying her arms, hands and face.

There wasn't much hanging in her wardrobe at all – school uniform or jeans – but luckily she still had Molly's blouse, washed and ready to return, and the swirly skirt.

Nervous fingers fidgeted with shrinking buttonholes, the hairbrush was missing, shoes had to be located, earrings found. Finally, she was ready and ran over to the mirror for inspection. Not bad one thing was for certain, she didn't need any make-up, excitement added a feverish glow to her face. She raked her fingers through her hair, caught it in a loose pony-tail, then turned and ran down the stairs, shouting to Sheila, something vague about needing to borrow books, and fled down the street.

She'd done enough walking for one day so she waited for the bus into town. When it arrived it was almost empty so Ravenna sat by herself, staring out of the window. Every time she imagined what Beth might want to say to her, her stomach lurched and this, coupled with the bus driver's liking for skimming round corners, made her feel queasy – vomiting was a distinct possibility.

She tried to divert herself by focusing on Molly's problems. Poor Moll, it must be hell cooped up in the house trying to keep her mum cheerful whilst her dad drank himself silly. It didn't seem to be bothering David too much, though. He'd looked happy enough at the party, playing his guitar and being with Natalie. Strange that when he was so keen on her, he hadn't introduced her to his family yet. Molly didn't seem to know anything about her. Well, now was hardly the time to introduce a stranger to the Morgan household. But, Ravenna had to admit, David was probably playing it cool because Natalie was important to him. He loved her.

The bus finally arrived in the High Street and with relief, Ravenna gulped in cool air as she stepped down and made her way to the antique shop. Harry opened the door and took her into the kitchen.

"I'd offer you a cup of tea or something but Beth's up in the studio and I know she's anxious to see you. Have some tea when you come down, eh?"

Ravenna nodded in agreement. She must, however, have looked wary of returning to the long empty loft where yesterday her visit had ended so disastrously, because Harry gave her one of his warm, reassuring smiles and squeezed her arm. Then he beckoned for her to follow him across the yard and through the back door of the shop.

"Are you OK to go up on your own?" he asked.

"Yes," Ravenna said, more confidently than she felt.

"Go on then, she'll be waiting for you," Harry said, steering her towards the stairs but then leaving her.

The dark stairs stretched upwards lit only by thin shafts of light slanting down from above. Ravenna felt her way up, hands sliding over the cool plaster of the walls. At the top of the stairs, a spotlight blinded her eyes. She peered through the golden blur trying to see Beth. Was Beth waiting, watching for her?

The light seemed to scour her eyelids and she stood trembling; her nerves rubbed raw with excitement and trepidation, wanting Beth to come and take her hand and yet wanting to turn back and run away. No one touched her and the silence seemed vast. She heard no sound except for her own deep breathing. Then, with firm resolve, she ducked beneath the light and her vision cleared. Beth was sitting on the floor, slumped against the far wall.

An involuntary cry, a breathy gasp that had no words in it, came from Ravenna. For an instant she imagined something dreadful; Beth's huddled, lifeless figure made her choke with fear. But the figure moved, stretched, rose gracefully, glided forward into the light, reaching out a delicate, sinuous hand.

"Sorry, I didn't mean to startle you. I was just taking a moment to relax. I've been trying to get back in shape, having a real workout." Beth picked up a black sweater and pulled it over her tight stretchy practice clothes, then picked up a carton of juice and sucked on the straw. "Oh, that's better. I'm really out of condition." She gulped and swallowed then turned anxiously to Ravenna. "Thanks for coming. Let's sit down and talk. There are some things I want to tell you."

Ravenna's legs were trembling as she followed Beth to an old couch which had been singled out from the rest of the junk and dusted down. Beth sank on to it with a grateful sigh and patted the cushion for Ravenna to sit beside her.

Beth flexed her legs, stretching them out, pointing her toes; then pulled one ankle up to rest on her knee. As Ravenna watched and waited, her breathing seemed to blend with her heartbeat into one massive drumming sound, filling her ears.

The drumming only grew fainter when Beth began to speak.

"I'm really glad to see you. It's sorry I am, about yester-day."

She paused and Ravenna saw a shadow flit across her face, darkening it for a moment, etching out the scar and worry lines. "Sometimes I think it's getting a bit better, I feel happy for a while but then it all comes back again – do you see?"

Beth's Welsh accent was stronger than Ravenna had ever heard it. She was fighting to smile but her bottom lip was trembling and her eyelashes blinking rapidly. Ravenna looked away, trying to think of something comforting to say, but before she could speak Beth was reaching for her hand and laughing. Her laugh rang out high and clear across the empty room and for a moment Ravenna was afraid. Was Beth mad? Had some tragedy unhinged her mind? Beth was squeezing her hand, pumping it up and down, and Ravenna felt panic. But then suddenly Beth let her hand go and when Ravenna looked at her again, she saw her face was calm.

"I'm sorry. Promised myself I wouldn't drive you away again, I did. I'm just nervous. Hardly ever talk about it, it's too hard . . . but I want to explain, to tell you everything."

Ravenna's insides tightened. She almost wanted to tell Beth to stop. Suddenly she didn't want to know. She didn't want to be disappointed again or to have to share Beth's grief. She just wanted to be friends and for Beth to teach her to dance. She started to say, "It's all right, I don't need to know." But Beth stopped her, putting a finger to her lips.

"I have to tell you, Ravenna. I can't leave you guessing, wondering why you made me cry. It wasn't your fault. It was nothing you did." Beth gulped and pushed her hair back from her eyes. A shaft of light burnished the gold hoops in her ears and shimmered on unshed tears beneath her thick lashes, but her voice was steadier as she went on.

"When I saw you at the car-boot sale, I couldn't believe it. There I sat, painting T-shirts, and when I looked up, you were there. So beautiful. Your eyes deep-set and dark, like two little fishes, tails tilted upwards. Your hair black as ink, your skin smooth as polished copper."

Ravenna listened entranced, watching, waiting, hope pulsing through her body. She wanted Beth to put her arms around her but she seemed lost in her words so Ravenna sat still, breathing lightly, not wanting to break the spell.

Beth tilted her head slightly to one side as if listening, waiting for something, then she delicately licked her lips and began to speak again, hesitantly, sifting her words, her voice straining to form the sounds.

"So like her, you were. I'd always imagined her as she was, a little girl, then when I saw you, it was as if she'd come back to me – grown-up, strong, beautiful. I was filled with happiness and hope."

Ravenna didn't know how she could keep still enough to listen to the rest of the story. She wanted to throw herself into Beth's lap, yearned to move closer to Beth. She looked at Beth's face, the wide, deep-set, catlike eyes so like her own, her high cheek-bones and straight nose. Beth was speaking again and Ravenna listened raptly.

"When you asked about the shawl, I wanted to give it to you right away but I didn't, I don't know why. Perhaps I was worried that you'd think me weird and not accept it, so I said a low price, the first figure that came into my head, thinking you'd buy it. Then I waited, hoping you'd come back. But I told Harry and he started packing away – afraid I'd get hurt.

"When you came back to the van, I knew then I could give you the shawl. It didn't matter any more if you thought I was strange. All I wanted was for you to have something of mine.

And when I placed the shawl around your shoulders I felt really happy for the first time in years.

"When you'd gone, I knew I had to find you again. I told John Barstow about you and immediately he said, 'That's Ravenna.' I couldn't believe he knew you. He'd seen you that day when he was dancing.

"I wanted to see you again so much and was excited when you came to see me and we were dancing, but then suddenly I couldn't bear it." Beth blinked hard and swallowed. "I knew she would be a dancer, you see. Even when she could hardly walk she danced."

The drumming sound had returned to Ravenna's ears, the rhythm fast and furious. Who was this "she"? Herself or someone else?

Beth continued. "When you danced with me, here in this room, it was as if her spirit had returned. I kept telling myself after I'd seen you at the car boot, don't be silly, it's not Megan. But when we danced together, there was an understanding like we knew each other. As if there was some bond between us. It was just too much."

As Beth's voice weakened, Ravenna's hope was gone. She sat feeling it drain out of her like blood seeping from a wound. Her heart seemed to stop and start up again. For a moment she stared into a dark corner of the room, then she felt for Beth's hand and they sat linked by their beating fingertips. Slowly Ravenna turned to look at Beth, rested her eyes on hers for long moments, dared her eyes to ask the unspeakable question. What happened to Megan?

Beth's eyes were luminous, glittering with unshed tears. She looked at Ravenna silently then began again; her voice was gentle, unhurried, speaking now in a detached way as if telling somebody else's story, speaking rehearsed lines.

"We were in the car. I'd taken her to a dance class. I didn't want to leave her behind with a babysitter. She hadn't been well . . . nothing dreadful . . . just a bad cold. It was autumn, all the trees were shining gold when we drove there, but when we came out it was dark and foggy. I drove carefully, we went round a corner, not fast, but there was a lorry without any lights on across the road. Just suddenly. It was there right in front of me. I swerved and we went off the road and hit a tree. I don't remember it was a tree, but they told me. All I remember is the terrible tearing noise, a shattering, shuddering, splintering. It wouldn't go away. For months and months afterwards, I heard it."

Ravenna felt Beth's hand go cold in hers and when she looked at her face, it was like stone. The light had gone from her eyes and they were like empty caves. She stroked Beth's icy hand whilst the tears ran down her cheeks.

Beth made one last effort to speak. "When I woke up, I was in hospital and Megan was gone."

18.

Beth and Ravenna sat in silence whilst the windows darkened and the room grew cold around them. Ravenna felt she was sinking into a deep, dark hole, its edges jagged with pain and disappointment. Beth wasn't her mother; all her hopes and dreams were fantasies. Beth had lost Megan and she'd lost a mother. She and Beth weren't linked, they were two separate people.

Perhaps she'd been foolish for believing so readily that Beth was her mother. But she'd been convinced by something deeper than reason. She remembered Beth giving her the shawl, placing it around her shoulders as if it was the most precious gift on earth, her eyes glinting with pride. Ravenna hadn't been able to forget that look. It was as if Beth knew her, as if she owned a part of her. It was hard to believe there was no blood between them.

She glanced at Beth, seeing her tense white face creased with pain, her eyes staring into space, and Ravenna was stabbed with pity. She knew what it was like to lose someone you loved. Philip, her adoptive father, had died when she was six and the absence of her natural mother was like a deep, dark hole inside her.

That's why she'd wanted to get close to Beth, that's why she'd hugged the shawl at night. Suddenly Ravenna knew why the shawl had been such a precious gift.

"It was her shawl," said Ravenna thoughtfully. "Megan's shawl, wasn't it?"

"Yes," Beth answered, reaching up and wiping her face with the back of her hand, quickly, rubbing away the tears. "I gave it to her the day before she died."

She blinked and her voice strengthened, as if warmed by the memory.

"Megan found it in my things the day before the accident. 'Can I have this? Can I have this?' she sang."

A brilliant smile lit Beth's face as she remembered, a smile so radiant that it dazzled her pale cheeks for a moment, before fading as quickly as it came.

"I said it was hers to keep, for always; and she laughed. She sat on the floor smoothing the silk, singing a song, stroking the pretty birds. All that afternoon she danced, holding the edges of the shawl as she twirled round and round, laughing as she watched the light spin from the beads and gold threads. That night, when I put her to bed, she asked me to spread it over her and the next morning she trailed from the bathroom, the shawl draped round her shoulders, her feet tripping on the long fringes.

"Later, when we were going to the car she ran back for it, putting it over her anorak. I had to push aside the folds of silk when I did up her seat belt. The ambulance people said it was still wrapped around Megan when they found her. I didn't see her, I was too ill. But afterwards they gave me the shawl. There wasn't a mark on it."

The images that hurtled through her head stunned Ravenna into silence. She blinked away tears then asked in a voice hardly more than a whisper, "How could you bear to part with it?"

Beth smiled. "I never meant to sell it but when I saw you, I wanted to give it to you because . . . you were so like Megan and . . . something was changing in me, telling me it was time to let go."

They lapsed into silence, each busy with their own thoughts, then Ravenna asked, "The accident . . . that's how you got the scar?"

Beth nodded.

In the dim light her eyes were large and luminous. Ravenna thought she had never seen such sad eyes and she had to look away. She sat staring into the silence thinking, then she confessed, "Just before I met you, I'd been thinking about my real mum, wondering if she knows where I am . . . if she misses me."

Ravenna gulped. Tears were tearing at her voice and she struggled for control as she continued. "After I'd seen you at the car-boot sale, I couldn't forget you. I kept seeing your eyes, remembering the way you gave me the shawl, as if it was really important and I thought you'd come looking for me." Ravenna raised her eyes and looked into Beth's. "I thought you were my mother."

Beth's voice came back, barely audible, quivering and slight. "And I thought you were my Megan."

Ravenna felt Beth's fingers move to her hair, pause and tremble, light as a settling butterfly. She heard the breath beating in her throat like fragile wings and she waited, hardly daring to breathe herself, whilst Beth hovered on the edge of grief. Then Beth's hand moved around her shoulder and they embraced, holding each other, finding warmth and comfort.

Ravenna saw Beth's taut shoulders shudder then relax. She tilted her head back, sighed deeply and continued, "After the accident I was like a zombie, for months. Physically I got better but I didn't want to go on living without Megan. I saw her everywhere, heard her talking, watched her dancing. Saw her in her room at night curled up with her toy rabbit, she ran into my studio, she sat in the car. I could never get into the car without seeing her there in the back seat. Then one day I lost her. I couldn't see her any more, couldn't picture her face – I thought I'd go mad. I kept looking at photographs, forced myself to draw her. That was when I met Harry."

When Beth spoke again, her voice was controlled and clear. "Perhaps we were meant to find each other." She cupped Ravenna's face in her hand and looked at her, then stroked her cheek tenderly. "The accident was ten years ago – since then my life has been like a dark shadow. Nothing has really touched me. I've done things, painted, travelled, even danced, but my soul wasn't in anything. I was beginning to think I had no soul left."

Beth stopped speaking for a moment and Ravenna felt an echoing emptiness close around them. She wanted to say something but could think of nothing adequate. Finally, she raised her head and whispered, "I'm sorry." It sounded so pathetic that she felt ashamed, but Beth was getting to her feet, holding out her hand.

"Come on. I've been sad for too long. I don't want to make you sad too. I owe it to Harry, to Megan, to myself, to try and put some pieces back together. I want to make plans ... to dance again. Come and dance with me. Come on, I'll show you a new routine I've been working on with Selina and Natalie."

Shakily Ravenna got to her feet. Beth put on some music

and took her position in the middle of the floor. At first the music was sad, the sobbing strains of a violin filled the room echoing Beth's misery. Ravenna felt tears prick her eyes again but blinked them back as Beth began to dance.

It was a slow, sad dance, raw and painful, like the weeping of a broken heart. It was almost more than Ravenna could bear, but the beauty of it kept her transfixed. Beth's body keened and curled, sobbed and stretched, as if it were pouring out its grief. She danced like a tear-drop running down glass, like the last sigh of the dying, and Ravenna was filled with sadness. She thought of Megan, the girl in the sketches, the girl who had been so full of life but had died before she had time to grow up. And she thought of her own mother holding her for the last time before giving her away. She watched Beth through shining tears until the music died and Beth paused, stopped and sank gracefully to the floor.

There was a trembling silence for a few moments, then Beth looked up, gestured for Ravenna to join her. But Ravenna hesitated, still struggling to steady her emotions.

The music started up again but this time stronger, livelier, picking up pace and Beth's limbs shuddered into life, stretching, flexing, pushing back grief, lifting, rising in hope. Suddenly the room seemed lighter, airier. Ravenna's feet tapped, her fingers twitched, she wanted to join in but she didn't know the dance and she didn't want to interrupt.

Beth was leaping, flying through the air, her feet touching the ground, skimming light as a bird's wing, her hair streaming behind her. She was marvellous and Ravenna felt suddenly relaxed and exhilarated. All her problems seemed to float away as Beth moved towards her, put her hands around her waist and lifted her off her feet. They laughed as Beth set her down and Ravenna tried to follow Beth's steps, twisting her head to watch, checking her feet moving left and right. Beth suddenly changed direction and Ravenna nearly tripped over her foot. Beth stretched out a hand to stop her and together they rolled down on to the floor, giggling and breathless.

They untangled themselves and dusting down her skirt Ravenna got to her feet. She saw Beth was transformed, her eyes sparkling, cheeks glowing and she was filled with hope, seeing herself as Beth had once been, a beautiful young woman with her life before her.

"Let's go and see Harry," she said. "Get him to make us some tea."

Later, around the kitchen table, warmed by cups of tea and the friendliness of Beth and Harry, Ravenna poured out all her problems.

"It isn't that they're not kind to me," she said. "It's just that I feel I don't belong to them. They're not interested in anything I'm interested in, and I hate living on the council estate."

"Funny, I used to live in a great big mansion and I hated that," Harry said. "Used to make me different from the other kids. They called me a snob."

Beth smiled at him. "You could never be a snob," she said. She looked happier and more relaxed than Ravenna had ever seen her, sitting in a baggy black sweater, her hair tangled and damp with sweat.

Ravenna sipped her tea. "It's just that I don't know where I belong. I don't seem to fit in with the other kids on the estate. I've never gone around in a gang. All I want to do is dance. I love music, all sorts, not just rock and pop but the classical stuff Mr Jones used to play us in music lessons. One time he played 'The Sleeping Beauty' and everybody almost went to sleep, but I loved it and I wanted to dance, my feet kept moving under the table. I love dancing – when I'm dancing I feel so alive."

Ravenna looked searchingly at Beth then Harry, worried that she might be talking too much but they both looked sympathetic and interested. So she carried on. "Sometimes I feel like I'm weird. It used to be OK because I spent loads of time at Molly's – she's my best friend, her mum and dad are brilliant, really kind and understanding, but it's been difficult lately, I've had Kirsty to look after and they've had problems themselves."

"They own the factory that's closing down, don't they?" Harry asked.

"How did you know?" Ravenna asked, incredulously.

"John Barstow told me. There's not much John doesn't know about this town, though I think some things he'd rather not know. He told me to keep this under my hat but I must say I've been thinking about it a lot – what it'll mean for the town."

"I know," Ravenna said. "Half the people in Maddock work there. It's going to be terrible. First it was the pits and now this. There's nothing left."

"What about your parents? Is it going to affect them?"

"No, Ian's a printer," Ravenna said. "But then ... I suppose it will affect everybody eventually, won't it? If there's not much money around and lots of people are unemployed."

"Let's hope something can be done," Harry said.

"I don't think there's much hope," Ravenna said. "Well, not with Molly's family anyway. Molly's dad's gone to pieces. He just keeps drinking and her mum's hibernating. Besides, they don't own the company any more it belongs to shareholders. I've been trying to talk to Molly all day but it's useless. All I get is the answer phone."

Ravenna sipped her tea, feeling guilty for being so warm and cosy. She thought about Moll at Badger's. She ought to try and phone her again. Surely by now they'd switched off that wretched machine.

Beth seemed to read her thoughts. "Would you like to phone Molly from here?" she asked.

Ravenna went through to the little room at the back where the spiral staircase twisted upwards and the big work desk filled the room. She punched in Molly's number and waited. It was the same message: Mrs Morgan's icy voice, asking the caller to speak after the tone. Damn, she'd just have to go over tomorrow and force her way in again. She couldn't just let Moll face everything alone, she had to try and help her.

"Any luck?" Beth asked as Ravenna returned.

"No, just the answer machine. I hate it. I'd like to take a hammer and smash it," Ravenna said vehemently.

Harry laughed. "I know how you feel," he said. "I hate talking to them and I always have a sneaking suspicion the owner is there anyway, listening to the call, deciding if it's somebody worth talking to."

"You're just paranoid about any new invention," Beth

scolded him. "You'd still go about by horse and cart if you could."

"It'd be a darn sight safer," Harry replied.

Ravenna heard Beth sigh and close her eyes.

"Oh Beth, I'm sorry," Harry said.

Beth pressed her lips together and was stone-still for a moment, then she shook her head and looked up, smiling first at Ravenna and then at Harry.

"It's all right," she said. "It's OK. You shouldn't have to worry every time you mention cars or driving or fog or..." Her voice was tightening and becoming high-pitched and the smile changed to a tense grimace. Ravenna could see what an effort it was costing her to speak but she carried on.

"You shouldn't have to apologize all the time. And I should stop blaming myself for what happened. I can't ever put it right but I've put myself through enough hell – in fact both of us." She paused and swallowed hard. "I've decided ... no more running, Harry. Let's stay here. I want to build the studio and open it and do the summer concert. Lose myself in teaching, think about other people for a change and ... take care of you."

Beth reached across the table for Harry's hand and held it tightly. Ravenna looked away.

"We'd better get Ravenna home," Harry said, but he didn't stir and his voice lingered tenderly over the words as if he didn't want to let the moment go.

"I'll come too," Beth said, rising. "Just give me a minute to change."

Ravenna watched Harry's eyes follow Beth into the back

room then he leaned forward, clasped his hands on the table and gave a big sigh.

"You don't know how much you've helped," he said. "It's as though she's been given a new life. Even yesterday, in the studio when she cried and you left, afterwards she was making plans, thinking about teaching again, planning the summer concert. I was a bit worried at first. I thought, perhaps . . . you know . . . she was pinning too much on you, making you a sort of substitute for Megan, but it's not that. She knows you're not Megan but meeting you has made her happy and you've given her the will to dance again. I want to thank you."

Harry looked at her and smiled warmly. Ravenna felt embarrassed. "I haven't done anything," she protested.

"Yes, you have. She was going to refuse to do the concert, but after meeting you she began to change her mind. John Barstow told her he knew you and Beth decided there and then she was going to teach you to dance."

"Well, I'm glad we found each other," Ravenna said. "Beth's a wonderful dancer, brilliant. She must dance. The accident must have been dreadful, a nightmare."

Harry nodded his head, looking pained and thoughtful. "When I met her, she *was* like a zombie. She brought some of her paintings into a gallery I was working in. The paintings were very good technically but they had no life. Dead land-scapes, dead abstracts. The only things that were any good were some figure drawings. Sketches in pen and ink, precisely drawn, full of character and in each one of them was a little girl." Harry paused, his eyes moving away from Ravenna and looking into the distance. "I asked who it was and when I looked at Beth's face all I saw was pain. From that moment, I loved her."

"What happened to Megan's father?"

"They split up. It often happens. They couldn't bear it. Beth thought he blamed her."

At that moment Beth bounced into the room, full of life. "Come on then, we'd better get you back or we'll be in trouble for keeping you so long."

"It's OK, they hardly notice I'm there, except to put Kirsty to bed and read her a story."

"I'll believe that when I see it," Beth said.

"You're not coming in with me," Ravenna said, horrified at the thought of Beth and Harry going into the kitchen at home where the day's dirty dishes would be stacked and where Sheila would waiting, smoking her last surreptitious cigarette of the day.

"Of course we are. I want to meet them," said Beth cheerfully.

It was warm and comfortable in the van with them all squashed across the front bench seat. Harry put on some music and sang along with it, hitting the right note about one time in five.

"Don't tell him he can't sing," Beth whispered and Ravenna giggled.

"I know what she's saying," Harry said. "And I don't care," and he sang all the louder.

"Harry!" Beth protested.

Luckily there was no time for more because they swung into the estate. A gang of youths under a street light watched their passing and Ravenna hoped they wouldn't throw stones. She heard a thump on the back door of the van and quickly gave Harry directions so that they sped into her avenue.

Mum's answer to any invasion by strangers was to put on the kettle and get out the biscuits. Chocolate digestives usually, but taking a look at Beth and Harry coming through the door, she reached for ginger creams as well. Ravenna had to admit, they did look rather exotic standing in the red and white Formica kitchen. Beth was wearing one of her sweeping fringed skirts swirled with blurred colours and spangles and her hair was tied back with a bright sparkly scarf. Jangling hooped earrings completed her gypsy look and Harry was as usual sporting his long stripy scarf twisted around his leather coat like a gaudy boa constrictor.

"Nice to meet you," Sheila said. "Are you in the civil defence?"

Ravenna laughed. "Mum, it's self-defence but no, this is Beth, my dance teacher."

"Well, it's news to me. I didn't know you had one," Sheila protested.

"As from tonight I do," Ravenna said, smiling at Beth.

"How much is this going to cost, Ravenna?" Sheila asked, beginning to look anxious.

Beth caught her look and smiled at her. "Don't worry, it won't cost anything. Ravenna has talent and it will be a pleasure to teach her."

"What's this?" Ian asked, coming through from the sitting-room.

"These people are kindly offering to teach our Ravenna to dance for nothing," Sheila explained.

Ian laughed. "If it's for nothing, it's not worth it," he said.

Ravenna hoped Mum wouldn't get into one of her suspicious moods. She remembered only too well when she'd taken against the postman – just because he wore red socks.

"Is that a miner's lamp?" Harry asked Ian, indicating the now shiny brass cylinder that Ian was holding.

Trust Harry to save the day. Whilst Ian was showing him every bit of car-boot treasure trove stowed in the sitting-room, the tea was made and Sheila poured. Then, comforted by the warm tea and two types of biscuit, they all relaxed.

"I was only saying to Ravenna earlier that she ought to put herself forward a bit more. She could be a model. I hadn't thought about dancing though. What sort of dancing is it?"

Beth explained about the summer concert and the ballet training mixed with some jazz dancing and modern.

"I used to love dancing," Sheila sighed. "Can you remember, Ravenna? Philip and me, we used to go out every Thursday to the Assembly Rooms. No, I suppose you'd be too little to remember that. Phil's mum used to come round and babysit. Oh, he was a lovely dancer."

Ravenna had a vague recollection of a slimmer, much younger-looking, brown-haired Sheila in high heels and a swirl of chiffon. Why had she forgotten that until now?

"Well, you'd be welcome to come and try out my studio," Beth offered, "when it's ready."

Ravenna thought Sheila would laugh and refuse but she was surprised to hear her say she might just do that. "Do you do tap?" she asked. "I've always fancied having a go at that."

Harry returned from the lounge bearing a brightly shining miner's lamp. "They're in really good condition, these. I'm going to ask Tom if he'll sell them in his shop. They should fetch twenty pounds or more each."

Behind him, Ian was grinning.

Later, when Beth and Harry had left, Ravenna sat in her room, took out the shawl and spread it over her bed. Gently and thoughtfully she stroked the embroidered birds and fingered the long silk fringes. It gave her a slightly spooky feeling to think the shawl had been wrapped round Megan's body and she pulled her hand away, shivering. Perhaps the shawl was something that brought bad luck. But then she remembered how it had brought her and Beth together and how Beth had trusted her, sharing her memories of Megan. The shawl was something that bound them together, the three of them, and luck can change, she decided.

Reaching down she gathered the cool slippery silk to her cheek, and this time when she thought about Megan she didn't feel afraid but imagined a little girl with dark hair and green eyes twirling the shawl as she danced.

Lying back she closed her eyes. It had been a turbulent and stressful day but tonight she was warmed through with happiness and hope. Somehow she felt everything was going to turn out all right.

She hadn't found her mother but she had gained a friend and it was a friendship Ravenna hoped would last for ever. And Beth was going to teach her to dance, the thought of that thrilled her. She couldn't wait to get back to the studio and really begin to learn in a structured, disciplined way.

She hadn't dared to tell Beth yet that she wanted to make dancing her life. It had seemed too soon, too risky, but now, she realized, it wasn't a risk. Beth would understand.

Beth hadn't even laughed at Sheila's tap-dancing. Well, of course she hadn't, she was more sensitive than that. Ravenna had been amazed at how well all the adults got on together. She'd hated the thought of Beth and Harry coming into the house, but they'd enjoyed themselves. It had been past eleven by the time they'd left.

Ravenna slipped into bed and snuggled down beneath the duvet, feeling happy and peaceful. She hugged the shawl close and vowed not to care one jot about Dustin Harrows and his mates. She had her own friends now and her own purpose. She would ignore the petty gossip and scandals at school, she was going to study hard, pass her exams and then dance and dance. It would be brilliant to dance with Beth and Natalie and Selina – she just hoped she could keep up with them.

19.

Dustin stared down at Ravenna.

"Your friend won't dare show her face today."

"What do you mean?"

"As if you didn't know."

His mouth was a wide sneer, his eyes sharp as snakes. He stood over her, swaying slightly as he spoke, blocking her way.

"How did. . .?" Ravenna began.

Dustin shifted his weight on to his front leg and brought his face closer to Ravenna's. Any pretence he'd made at tenderness had been wiped from his consciousness. His face was cruel, twisted with spite.

"Thought it was a secret, did you?"

Ravenna wanted to spit in his eye. He was such a hypocrite. Trying to make out he was championing the cause of the factory workers when really he was only interested in getting his own back on Molly's family.

Well, she wasn't going to give him the satisfaction of an argument. She stepped back and glared at him. "I haven't got a clue what you're talking about, Dustin. Sorry," she said, and then, as nonchalantly as she could, she turned her back on him and retraced her steps along the corridor.

Finding Mrs Taylor to apologize about the missed tennis practice would have to wait. She needed sanctuary.

Hoping it wasn't Dustin's footsteps she could hear behind her, Ravenna turned the corner and sped towards the tutor room. She willed herself not to look back, fervently hoping he'd leave her alone.

The corridors were empty apart from the odd wandering latecomer and Ravenna rushed past the school office, past the library and towards her tutor room, but she couldn't shake off the heavy footsteps padding behind her. At the door of the tutor room she paused and gave thanks: Baker was at his desk. She darted quickly through the door and to her seat. It was only when she sat down that she noticed how quiet the room was. Heads were turned, curious faces were looking at her and then she realized that people weren't just looking at *her* – beside her sat Molly, in her usual place.

"Moll! What are you doing here?"

"I'm a pupil, remember?" Molly replied with characteristic sharpness, but the next moment her face darkened. "I'm beginning to wish I hadn't come, though. Everybody's looking at me, pointing, whispering."

"I didn't think people would know yet. I thought they weren't announcing it until this afternoon."

Molly's head sank so low that it nearly touched the table in front of her. "The news must have leaked out. There were two reporters outside the house this morning; I think everybody knows."

"Well, don't listen to any nasty comments. Just shrug your shoulders and say it's nothing to do with you. Tell them to mind their own business. Don't get drawn into any arguments."

Ravenna said this as firmly and cheerfully as she could whilst at the same time wondering if it was Dustin's shadow that was haunting the classroom window. She pulled her chair in front of Molly's, hoping to shield her, but it was in vain. The next moment Mr Baker boomed out, "What do you want, Harrows?"

Molly looked panic-stricken and clutched Ravenna's arm. "He knows I'm in here," she whispered.

Ravenna turned and saw Dustin hovering in the doorway like a monstrous stick insect. She looked at him with loathing.

"Just came to see if Molly Morgan was here. I've got a message for her."

"Come here, lad," Mr Baker rasped.

Dustin loped across the room, hands in pockets.

The class was silent.

"I don't know what you're all listening for – get on with some work," the form tutor snapped.

Some people made a show of turning pages in their books and one or two mumbled to each other but the teacher and Dustin were still centre-stage.

"I don't know what you want or who's sent you, but I don't want you bothering Molly or anybody else in my class. Not today or any other day. Do you understand?"

Dustin, leering over Mr Baker's balding head, was full of contrite, "Yes, sir, no, sirs". But as he lurched out of the classroom his grinning face turned towards Ravenna and Molly, and he threw a quick question loaded with sarcasm, "Sold the Merc yet?"

"Great stupid dolt!" Ravenna threw back.

She watched as the teacher rose and Dustin, sensing danger, dashed for the door and disappeared. Then she turned to Molly, who was miserably biting her lips to stop the tears spilling.

Ravenna felt a surge of anger towards Dustin and wished she could tell everybody why he was stirring up trouble. But all she could do was sit and listen to Molly's anguished voice.

"Trust Dustin, he'll set everyone against me. I was stupid to come. I thought I should face it but Mum warned me not to. I suppose she was right. But I'd half convinced her and myself that we shouldn't hide away like criminals – it's not our fault the factory's closing."

"Course it's not your fault. You were right to come. There's no reason for you to hide. Don't worry about Dustin. I'll think of a way to sort him out."

Ravenna had no idea how she would sort him out but she knew she'd have to do something. For one thing the class had gone completely quiet again and her last words were heard loudly and clearly by everybody. Oh well, she'd take advantage of their attention and set them straight on a few things.

"I don't know why everybody's blaming you. Your family sold the business years ago – they're not responsible. It's just stupid people living in the past who think they are. If they want to blame anybody they should blame the government," Ravenna said loudly and clearly. "And I can't think why anyone listens to that despicable toe-rag, Dustin Harrows, he just wants to stir up trouble."

Then she lowered her voice for Molly's ears only. "We'll stand up to them. If you get through today it won't be so bad, we've got friends, they won't all agree with Dustin. We can count on Rachael and. . ."

Ravenna's words did nothing to dissolve the knots of worry on Molly's face. Impatiently she cut in. "Faye and her mates have already been having a go. She must have spotted Mum dropping me off, and by the time I got here she'd rounded everybody up to start whispering when I went past. Where were you? I was looking everywhere for you."

"Sorry, I was looking for Mrs Taylor. I forgot tennis practice on Saturday."

"No! She'll kill you."

"I know. I thought I'd confess and be slaughtered quietly before she did it in public, but Dustin stopped me in the corridor, so I headed back here sharpish."

At that moment the door opened and Mrs Taylor came in. Ravenna sighed, the air hissing from her like a deflating mattress. She watched the teachers smile at one another, the way teachers always did, like conspirators, then she heard the words she knew would come: "Can I have a word with Ravenna Collins?"

Ravenna got up immediately and went to the desk. Mrs Taylor beckoned and Ravenna followed her outside.

Mrs Taylor was young and pretty and popular. She was easygoing and fun but, when riled, she was formidable. She waited a moment then fixed Ravenna with a piercing stare. "I don't have to tell you how disappointed I am, Ravenna, not to say ... surprised. The first practice of the season. We waited. Where's Ravenna? Is she ill? No, she'd surely have sent a message. She's reliable, conscientious. She wouldn't have her partner waiting around on the court for nothing. Not Ravenna. She's not like that."

Mrs Taylor's glittering eyes turned to splinters of ice and Ravenna shuddered. Although the teacher had paused for breath she could think of nothing to say in her defence and Mrs Taylor started up again.

"I thought this match was important to you too. I was thinking of making you team captain this year, but how can I when you don't even come to the first Saturday practice? And you were late the other day; you've let your partner and everybody else down. What's your excuse?"

It all sounded familiar to Ravenna. She'd heard it before, rattled out like machine-gun fire on dark corridors – irate teachers spitting out the same old clichés – they were disappointed, had hoped for better, pupils were letting themselves down, letting the school down. But this time it was different – it was aimed at her. She was so mortified that the excuse she'd prepared went out of her head.

"I'm sorry, Mrs Taylor."

"Well, what was it, Ravenna?"

"I wasn't ill."

Why had she said that? That was going to be her excuse. What excuse could she give now?

"Well, Ravenna, I'm waiting."

Ravenna swallowed hard, then said weakly, "I . . . I forgot." Mrs Taylor looked shocked.

"Is that all you've got to say?"

"Yes, Miss. I'm sorry. I just forgot. That's the truth."

Mrs Taylor looked hard at her for a moment, scanning her face, then she exploded.

"I thought you were one of the few people in this school I could count on. Somebody I could trust. What's the matter with you? Julia had no partner to play with on Saturday – she's new to the team and needs all the practice she can get and you forgot. You'd better come at lunchtime without fail and make up for it – get an early lunch pass."

Mrs Taylor strode off down the corridor, leaving Ravenna worried and miserable. She liked Mrs Taylor and hated her disapproval. What was worse, she would have to go to practice just when Molly was counting on her to stay close and help fend off Dustin and his clutch of menacing mates.

Today, she decided, was a disaster – and yet last night she'd been full of hope. True, her emotions had been turned inside out and upside down, going from wanting to sob her eyes out because Beth wasn't her mother and because Megan had died, to wanting to jump for joy when Beth had promised to teach her to dance. But she'd ended the day relishing her friendship with Beth and Harry and she'd begun to see that even Sheila and Ian had their good points. The thought of Beth and Harry visiting her home had made her cringe with embarrassment and yet all the adults had got on really well together. That had made her happy and she'd gone to bed looking forward to the future and imagining that somehow everything would sort itself out. Now, back at school, that happiness seemed like a dream – things were going from bad to worse.

The bell above her head went off, dazzling her ears, but she couldn't escape it; she had to stand aside and wait to collect her belongings from the classroom whilst the rest of her form trooped out, bludgeoning their way with heavy bags and folders. When they'd filed past, Ravenna went back to her table where Molly was waiting for her.

"Gosh, I could hear what Taylor was saying. She really went for you."

"It doesn't matter."

"It does. I'm sorry. It's all my fault. If I hadn't asked you to come to the house on Saturday, you'd have remembered the tennis."

"Look, you've got enough to worry about. It was my fault. I went to see Beth. That's why I forgot."

Molly's eyes widened, her problems forgotten for a moment, quashed by intense curiosity. "Why didn't you tell me you'd seen Beth? What happened?"

Ravenna smiled, picked up her things and began to explain as they walked out of the classroom. "Well, she isn't my mother but she's really nice, and she's a brilliant dancer and she's going to teach me to dance and there's. . ."

Ravenna broke off suddenly when she saw Mrs Taylor had returned and was talking to Mr Baker, outside in the corridor. Grabbing Molly's arm, Ravenna hurried her past the teachers, but unfortunately not fast enough to avoid hearing Mrs Taylor's remarks.

"I can't understand it. Ravenna of all people. She's never forgotten before. It's that Dustin Harrows. I knew he'd have a bad effect on her."

Ravenna was furious. Hadn't people got it through their thick heads that she loathed Dustin Harrows?

This time it was Molly who grabbed Ravenna's arm and pulled her down the corridor.

"Don't say anything. It's not worth it," Molly warned. "Come on, don't worry. Dustin's yesterday's news. Tell me about Beth. I want to know everything."

On the way to the drama studio, Ravenna told Molly the whole story about Beth and the dancing and the accident, and was just getting round to mentioning David and Natalie when they arrived at the door to the drama studio. The room was unusually quiet when they walked in, as if everyone had suddenly stopped talking, but by the time they'd found themselves a seat, loud whispering had begun. Miss Devlin was late and Dustin had time to gather Faye and Dean and more of his buddies around him. They clustered together, whispering and giggling like a gaggle of geese. Dustin made a loud but inaudible comment and his flock exploded, flapping and hissing with appreciation. Dustin preened himself, then led them over towards Molly and Ravenna, grinning mawk-ishly and nudging Dean as he spoke.

"What shall we work on today? A little play entitled 'Closure'?"

Dean giggled at his friend's joke.

But Faye looked daggers and moaned, "It's not fair. I can't go skiing now."

Dustin took no notice of her but carried on, speaking in an affected, stagey voice. "Or shall it be 'Repossession'? A high drama about poor unemployed factory workers being evicted because they can't keep up their mortgage payments. Inter-cut, of course, with scenes set in the factory owner's house. 'Oh dear, we can't have steak tonight, it'll have to be chops and I don't think we'll be able to afford Barbados this year – we might have to settle for Benidorm instead. Never mind, we've still got the swimming pool.'"

Ravenna wanted to hit him but knew she'd have to settle for words. She tensed her jaw, drew herself up and was about to give a stinging reply but Molly stole her thunder. Molly's words were fired like arrows before Ravenna could speak.

"You don't understand anything about us. I've never been

to Barbados in my life and if you must know I'm a vegetarian and we don't have a swimming pool, just a tennis court – make something of that if you like. And we'll probably be moving out of our lovely old house soon because my dad's lost his job too."

Molly, with eyes blazing and fists clenched, leant threateningly forwards and Faye and another girl stepped warily away from her.

But Dustin wasn't so easily quelled. He wanted drama, a fight. "No swimming pool. Oh dear, don't tell me you've sold the Merc and the BMW and, oh dear, not the Range Rover as well? Poor little rich girl."

"I'm not rich. We're well off, yes, but not rich. We probably will have to sell the cars. Will you be satisfied when you see us driving around in a beat-up old van? You never know, we might end up living in the flats next to you, Dustin Harrows."

One or two people laughed in an embarrassed way at Molly's reply and Ravenna actually heard simmerings of sympathy as people began to drift away. Dustin wasn't ready to let go yet, however.

"Why was your dad at the police station? Bet they're trying to find where he's stashed the money," he said in a loud voice.

Molly glared at him for a moment, then blinked and crumpled. Dustin had hit her where it really hurt.

"There isn't any money," she said, her voice breaking. "We haven't got any. Dad's at home now worrying himself sick about the place having to close."

"Poor man," Dustin muttered.

Ravenna had had enough. "Leave her alone! You're not interested in the factory, none of your family work there – it's just an excuse for you to bully somebody. It's what you do best, isn't it?''

Dustin looked like a simmering kettle about to whistle, but before he did Rachael stepped forward. "What do you know about workers anyway, nobody'll give your dad a job, that's why he's sleeping rough.''

Ravenna saw a glimmer of panic in Dustin's eyes and a faint flush come to his cheeks before his head dropped, and with a Neanderthal grunt he sloped off into a corner without replying.

As he walked away, Ravenna heard several people expressing sympathy for Molly. "She can't help it." "She's always been all right with me." "She's not stuck-up." "It's not her fault.''

This time Dustin had judged it wrongly and he stood like a solitary lamppost in the back corner. Even Faye left him and joined the rest of her group so that when Miss Devlin appeared most people were working.

Course work was far from the minds of Ravenna, Molly and Rachael at this moment, however. Molly was wiping her eyes and sniffing. "Dustin Harrows is sick," she was saying. "I wouldn't be surprised if it was him who's been making the obscene phone calls and upsetting Mum. As if she hasn't got enough to cope with!''

Ravenna said she wouldn't be surprised either, but her mind was on what Rachael had said to Dustin.

"I thought Dustin's dad was in prison?" she asked.

Rachael was only too eager to give the news. "He came out a few weeks ago. Dustin's mum won't have anything to do with him. He was hanging about the school gates last week, looked a right tramp. He's sleeping in the park – Dustin's dead embarrassed about it."

Ravenna and Molly exchanged glances.

"It must be awful for him," Molly whispered.

Ravenna shook her arm. "Moll, don't you dare go all soft. Dustin and his dad deserve everything they get."

"Yeah," Rachael agreed. "Even if his dad has been in the nick, it doesn't give Dustin the excuse to bully people."

"It must be horrible knowing your dad is homeless, though," Molly said.

Ravenna sighed. She didn't want to feel sympathy for Dustin. He was cruel and twisted and she wasn't going to soften towards him. "Come on," she said, "his dad's a criminal." Then getting out her folder, she said, "Oh, sod Dustin! Let's get on with some work."

The drama lesson got underway and Dustin kept out of their way. Miss Devlin called them together to take some notes and discuss comedy so that they were busy for the rest of the lesson and it wasn't until break that Ravenna had more time to talk to Molly and ask how things were at home.

"Not much better. Mum and Dad are hardly speaking but at least Dad's stopped going out to drink. He just gets drunk at home now."

Ravenna was stung with sympathy for Molly. Her happy, secure life was being rocked at its foundations. She badly wanted to protect Molly but she couldn't even be with her at lunchtime – she'd got tennis practice.

Moll looked desperate when Ravenna told her. "I can't face lunch by myself," she moaned.

"You can come home with me," Rachael offered.

But Molly was wary of leaving the shelter of the school buildings.

"I think I'd rather stay in school. Dustin and his mates will be hanging around outside."

Ravenna had an idea. "I know who'll help us. I'll ask John Barstow to go down to lunch with you. And I'll ask him to have a word with Dustin."

"I can't keep getting somebody else to fight my battles for me. I've got to brave this out on my own," Molly argued.

"You've also got to know when to ask for help," Ravenna replied. "And John Barstow's my friend, as well as a teacher. Come on."

As John Barstow listened carefully to what Ravenna had to say, his face creased into a worried frown. "I think I need to have a strong word with Dustin Harrows," he said. "There's something wrong with that lad."

20.

"I want you to be captain, Ravenna. Don't let me down, will you?"

Ravenna looked up as Mrs Taylor strode past, then watched her retreating back with resentment. She hadn't even waited for an answer.

I might have refused, might not want to be captain. Too much responsibility for someone in the habit of letting people down. I don't want the job, Mrs Taylor, if you can't trust me. I've faithfully attended every practice and match for three years and the first time I miss, you make a big deal out of it. Well, I'd just like you to know that I've had a lot on my mind recently. My best friend might be moving to the other end of the country, Dustin Harrows and his cronies are constantly harassing me, I've been searching for my real mother, and I can't concentrate on my school work just when it's most crucial. It's not only teachers who have problems, you know – kids suffer too.

Ravenna glared at Mrs Taylor's long legs now striding across the playground towards the changing rooms.

"I'm not going to lick your gym shoes because you've made me captain," Ravenna muttered. "I've earned the right to be captain. And what's more, I haven't forgiven you for the insensitive remark you made to Baker this morning."

Ravenna stooped to pick up two tennis balls from the gutter and slammed the netted gate behind her as she left the court. In the distance she could see Mrs Taylor's blonde head bobbing as she counted in the tennis balls. Two more here, Mrs Taylor – balls to you!

At the changing room door Mrs Taylor put a hand on Ravenna's arm to detain her.

"Is everything all right, Ravenna? You haven't been your usual self lately. You played well today, put in some cracking shots, but forgetting practice last week, that wasn't like you. And you've been walking around school lately looking as if you've got the cares of the world on your shoulders."

Ravenna saw Mrs Taylor's lovely blue eyes examining her. She was so pretty, so self-assured. She imagined Mrs Taylor's life: orderly, straightforward, everything cut and dried, no doubts, no indecisions. What could she know?

"I'm fine," Ravenna said. "Just a lot of work to finish and exams coming up."

Mrs Taylor flashed another pearly white smile, her teeth shining with perfection.

"Oh, you've got nothing to worry about. You'll do brilliantly."

"Thanks for the confidence," Ravenna said, more sarcastically than she intended, and as she walked away she immediately regretted it. If she was honest, Mrs Taylor was all right and she supposed she ought to feel pleased about being made tennis captain. But she couldn't conjure up any excitement. Now that practice was over, all she wanted to do was find Molly as quickly as possible and make sure she was safe from the horrible Harrows.

Going into the changing room was like stepping into a tropical rain forest. Ravenna made her way through steaming bodies, underwear fluttering white as lilies and drops of heavy-scented deodorant dripping on to the damp floor. A fine mist of pungent hair spray hung above the girls' heads and strange, shrill cries rang from the showers.

Ravenna elbowed her way through tennis and netball players, most of whom had already darted under the showers and were hurriedly dressing so that they could go for lunch.

Her clothes were not where she had left them. It was enough to make you spit. It always happened. Those who arrived first would clear a space for themselves, confining anybody else's clothes to three inches of wood at the end of the bench, and then somehow the clothes would end up scattered on the floor.

"I left my stuff here. Have you seen it?" Ravenna demanded. The girl who was in her space shrugged. Ravenna darted under an arm-pit smelling of orchids and prodded amongst bags, shirts and shoes. Eventually she retrieved her skirt from a far peg; her shirt, damp and trampled, from the floor; and one shoe, which had been kicked under the bench.

By the time she'd showered most of the girls had left. Ravenna caught up the crumpled shirt, smoothing it over her breasts, tucking it tightly into her skirt, then she searched and managed to locate her missing shoe. The door banged for the last time as the remaining girls straggled out, and suddenly the steamy room was quiet.

It was an eerie place without the usual sounds of chatter and laughter. Pieces of clothing hung from hooks, limp and shapeless, the concrete floor was cold as a prison cell and the dripping water echoed loudly, hissing through the silence.

Ravenna pulled a brush through her tangled hair, stowed everything away in her sports bag, then leaned over to tie her shoes. The outside door creaked. She looked up but saw no one. Probably younger boys playing dares. Just let her catch them at it! She'd tell them how funny it was to push a boy into the girls' changing rooms.

Scraping her hair back she screwed it into a pony-tail then rifled the pockets of her blazer for chewing-gum to stem the pangs of hunger. Finding nothing she pulled on the blazer and looped her tie around her neck. It was time to go.

The door bumped again, followed by a scraping sound. Ravenna picked up her bag and turned. For a moment she didn't believe what she saw. Her breath turned to ice as she recognized the tall, slim figure of Dustin standing in the doorway.

The heavy door flapped shut behind him and he stood with his back to it, his face in shadow but his eyes glinting through the dim light.

Ravenna backed away. "What do you want?" she asked, trying to make her voice sound as bold as she could, though inside she was quaking. Dustin didn't reply but just stood there, glaring at her.

Her mouth went dry. She realized she was trapped. Mrs Taylor had locked the other door which led into the gym.

"You're not allowed in here," she rasped.

Dustin merely grinned.

Ravenna thrust her bag in front of her body, preparing to push past him, but Dustin was too quick. He caught her by the shoulders then slipped his arm around her neck, holding her in the vice of his elbow. His face was against hers, his lips on hers, his tongue pushing to the back of her throat.

Ravenna felt sick, the sourness of his breath, the thickness of his tongue filling her throat made her gag. She struggled for breath as he pressed his face down, his mouth engulfing hers, his stubble scratching at her skin. His arm was pressing on her throat and she knew if she panicked and squirmed, she would lose consciousness. It was like trying to breathe through cotton wool but she hung on and then she heard Selina's voice gently commanding her, *Knee him, Ravenna, poke at his eyes.* But she couldn't do it. She was like solid rock, unable to move, unable to think.

Now Dustin's hand was slipping inside her blazer, moving over her sweater, feeling for her breast; pressing, kneading. His body was pushing hard against her so that she would have fallen if he hadn't been gripping her tightly. His hand was on her leg now, sliding upwards. She could feel all her strength oozing away but, just as everything began to turn black, Dustin relaxed for a moment. His mouth loosened, his eyes flicked open, the amber light gleaming like fire.

"You've been avoiding me," he said huskily, his breath hot on her face.

It was a chance Ravenna couldn't miss. She felt the weight of her sports bag still dangling from her hand and with one quick, fluid movement she wriggled sideways and swung the bag upwards with all her might, thumping him in the groin. Dustin crumpled and gasped, staggering from her. The bag fell with a thump on to the floor and Ravenna was outside and running.

An agonized gasp followed her but she didn't stop until she reached the science labs. Hurtling through the doors she almost catapulted into Molly.

"What's happened?" Molly demanded.

"Dustin," Ravenna breathed.

"What's he done now?"

Ravenna grabbed Molly's arm and pulled her to the side of the corridor. She didn't want anyone else to hear. Between deep choking breaths she said, "He came into the changing rooms. It was awful ... horrible ... he ... he..."

"He what?"

Molly's eyes were round as plates.

Ravenna looked away. Suddenly she couldn't find the words; her anger was turning to shame and she felt her cheeks burning. She struggled to get her breath. "He tried to kiss me and ... feel me."

"He what?"

Molly was aghast. She stared at Ravenna for a moment and then, as Ravenna didn't answer, she asked again, "What? Where?"

Ravenna sighed. Now the bursting anger was subsiding, she didn't want to explain, not even to Molly. She was too tired. She just wanted to shut it out. Forget it. She shuddered as she remembered Dustin's eyes glinting, glowing – with what? Desire? Evil? A strange cold shivering set into her bones and she knew she was afraid of him. Afraid of what he might do next time.

She heard Molly say her name, felt a hand on her arm, shaking her slightly.

Looking up she saw Molly's eyes; anxious, caring. "Tell me, Raven, what happened?"

"He grabbed me and I thought he was going to rape me," Ravenna whispered.

Molly's reaction was instantaneous. "We've got to report this."

She was already tugging Ravenna towards main school but Ravenna hung back, close to tears. Her feet ground to a halt and she planted them firmly so that Molly couldn't move her. "No," she said loudly.

Molly swung back to face her. "But Ravenna, you've got to. You can't let Dustin get away with it."

Ravenna knew she was right. But she couldn't talk about it now. She'd go to pieces.

"I need time," she said. "Nobody will believe me. Everybody'll say I asked for it. Just think what Mrs Taylor said this morning."

"It's not true, Ravenna. What Dustin's done now is different. You've got to tell. If you won't, I will."

Ravenna saw Molly tilt her chin upwards and recognized that look of determination. Molly would tell, and Ravenna knew she was right. But she couldn't face it yet. She needed time to think. There'd be questions, lots of them, and she knew how clever Dustin was. She wasn't in any fit state at the moment to stand up to him. He'd say she led him on, asked him to meet her.

Breathing deeply she tried to calm herself, tried to show Molly she was in control. "Look, just leave it for now. I'll tell somebody later. I'll go and see John and Selina tonight and tell them. But not now. I don't want to do it now."

Molly hesitated a moment then raised her eyebrows and sighed. "All right," she agreed. "But promise me?" she demanded, putting a finger delicately on Ravenna's nose and looking into her eyes. "Promise me you'll see Mr Barstow and Selina tonight?"

Ravenna nodded. "I promise."

Dustin wasn't in any of Ravenna's afternoon classes – but he made his presence felt. He was in her head, in her mind. She could still taste his breath, feel his hands. Her body felt dirty. She wanted to go home and have a bath. She hoped she'd hurt him when she hit him with the bag. She hoped he was still sprawled on the changing room floor.

But he wasn't. At afternoon break when she and Molly went to retrieve her bag from the changing rooms, he was leaning against the wall leering at them, the collar of his school blazer turned up, his shoulders hunched, his hands shoved down hard into his pockets. He'd chosen his post thoughtfully, knowing that Ravenna would have to pass within a few metres on her way to the gym. Ravenna averted her head but knew his eyes were following her and she felt his power.

Molly held Ravenna's arm. "Glare at him. Show him you're not frightened," she urged.

But Ravenna couldn't. Only when they reached the gym did she dare to glance again in his direction but he'd disappeared.

"Don't worry. I'll go inside and get your bag for you. Anyway, he's gone," Molly reassured her.

"At least he had the decency to keep out of my way," Ravenna said, sighing with relief.

"Decency?" Molly argued. "Didn't you see him? He was watching us all the time. He's scared you'll tell."

"I hardly looked at him," Ravenna confessed. "I couldn't."

"You've got to show him you're not afraid. Show him you're as strong as he is."

Ravenna tensed as Molly went inside the changing room and shivered as the door slammed on the echoing emptiness. But as Molly returned with her bag Ravenna glimpsed the large expanse of dull concrete floor and remembered Dustin spread-eagled there. She put her hand to her mouth and giggled nervously.

"What's funny?" Molly asked curiously.

Ravenna was laughing now, her shoulders shaking. She fought to control herself but the laughter kept bubbling out of her as if she was crazy; her eyes streaming, her nose running. Eventually she was aware of Molly shaking her and Molly's eyes staring at her.

"Stop it, stop it!" Molly was saying.

Ravenna stopped laughing and hugged Molly. She was shaking but felt calmer now.

"Hell's teeth, Ravenna! I thought you'd flipped," Molly said anxiously.

Ravenna let go of her friend. "I'm OK now – just reaction, I expect. It shook me up more than I realized." She grinned. "I bet it wasn't great for him either. No wonder he was propped up against the wall. I bet he can hardly walk. I really whacked him. Like this. . ." she said, seizing her sports bag from Molly and giving a quick demonstration.

"Watch it," Molly said, stepping aside.

"He just might not try anything else in a hurry," Ravenna said thoughtfully.

"Yes, but you've got to make sure," Molly answered firmly. "I'm coming with you to tell John and Selina."

"OK," Ravenna agreed, and this time she had some of her old confidence back as they strode from the changing rooms and across the playground. After all, she reflected, it wasn't the first time she'd come off best in a battle with Dustin.

For the rest of the afternoon Ravenna was in better spirits, although in lessons her concentration kept slipping. She wondered what would happen after she told John and Selina about Dustin's attack. If the story got out, somebody would be bound to say she'd asked for it, arranged to meet him there. But Molly was right, she couldn't let him get away with this. If she did, he might try it again.

At the end of school, Molly telephoned home to say she was staying with Ravenna. She was on the phone for ages convincing her mum that she was fine and school had been OK.

"Hurry up," Ravenna nudged her. "Everybody's going."

"What's the rush?" Molly asked as she replaced the receiver.

"I want to catch him now," Ravenna said urgently.

"Who? Dustin?" Molly asked, her eyes all agog.

"No, John Barstow. I want to tell him now. Get it over with."

Ravenna hurried Molly towards the staff car park. Now she'd made a decision she couldn't wait. But when they arrived, cars were already leaving and John Barstow's van was nowhere to be seen.

"Damn. He must have gone home early," Ravenna moaned. She kicked at the gravel of the path, feeling irritable. After being all keyed up, rehearsing what to say to John Barstow, now she wasn't going to get her chance.

"Oh well, there's always tomorrow," she shrugged, turning to walk down the drive.

Molly caught up with her. "Oh no, you don't. Come on, we'll walk down to Rachael's, see if we can leave some of our stuff there and phone Mr Barstow or Selina. Maybe we could meet them in town."

Ravenna reluctantly agreed and they set off towards Rachael's house, emerging minutes later from the path that ran between school and the new housing estate.

A boy from school was already delivering evening papers, an orange bag slung around his shoulder. But apart from him, all was quiet and there was nobody else to be seen.

"Wouldn't like to live here. Too quiet. No litter, no broken bottles, no car engines revving – don't know how people exist," Ravenna said.

"Everybody's inside having tea, I expect," Molly answered.

It seemed to come from nowhere, belching out of the calm evening sky and enveloping them: a thrusting, roaring wall of sound crashing against their ear-drums.

There was no time to run. Molly clung to Ravenna's arm as the motor bike thrummed towards them, the light glancing off it in steely splinters, the rider heading straight for them, keeping to the middle of the road, bearing down on them at a furious speed.

Ravenna saw the black gloved hand tightly gripping the throttle, saw the letters on the helmet – DMH. She stood transfixed, watching the letters grow larger, the wheel coming towards her until it seemed she was right underneath it.

He knows I'm going to tell and he's coming to get me, flashed through Ravenna's mind.

At the last moment, something snapped into place inside her. She leapt to one side and at the same time pushed Molly with all the strength she could muster, trying to fling her on to the pavement out of the path of the lethal whirring wheel.

Ravenna was aware of the ground trembling beneath her, aware of her legs, soft as gravy, aware of her stomach heaving with fear and then all was still. Acrid fumes stabbed at her nostrils and the roar subsided into a low whine as the bike disappeared up the road.

Molly was lying crookedly in the gutter, not moving. For a moment Ravenna thought she was dead. She stood there shaking, trying to call Molly's name but not managing a sound. After a few moments, she somehow manage to make her liquid legs walk over to her friend and bend down to her, without falling over.

"Oh Moll, I'm so sorry," she whispered. "It's my fault. Oh God, I thought he was going to kill us."

Molly lifted her head and looked at her with dazed eyes, staring unseeing. Her face was washed white. Ravenna thrust a quivering arm underneath Molly's armpit and, mustering all her strength, pulled her to the kerb. Molly lolled against her as they sat shivering in silence.

Then Ravenna began to curse under her breath. "The bloody stupid idiot, the stupid sodding idiot. . ." She went on for several minutes, using up every damning word she could think of until her trembling was quelled and replaced by a hard, rigid anger. Then she became aware of Molly's grave silence and dead weight upon her.

"Oh God, Moll. You look terrible."

She stared at Molly's ashen face as a voice rang out. "Are you all right?"

Craning her neck round to see over Molly's head, Ravenna saw Rachael's mum running towards them.

"Oh my God, what was he trying to do? Are you hurt?"

She bent down and put her arms around both the girls, rubbing their shoulders and smoothing their hair. "Come on, let's see if we can get you inside."

At the sound of a new voice, Molly suddenly seemed to come to life, wincing and groaning as she moved. "My ankle... It feels like it's on fire."

Between them, Rachael's mum and Ravenna managed to raise Molly on to her one good leg and support her as they walked the few metres to Rachael's house.

"That boy's a maniac," Rachael's mum muttered.

"Did you see him?" Ravenna asked, as they turned into the driveway.

"I was looking for the paper-lad... I saw the motor bike and you two. He drove straight at you. I couldn't believe it."

"Well, I know who he is," Ravenna said, her voice hard as steel. "And he's really done it now. He won't get away with this. This time I can prove it."

Rachael answered her mother's shout, coming to the door with a half-eaten hamburger in her hand.

"What happened?" she asked.

"People could be murdered in our street and you wouldn't know," Rachael's mum said, as she and Ravenna staggered past with Molly hanging limply between them.

"Sorry, I was watching T V," Rachael replied, taking a bite

out of her burger. "What's Molly done?" she asked, following them into the sitting-room, then munching and standing in front of the settee.

"Get out of the way, Rachael," her mother ordered. "Make yourself useful and phone Molly's parents. She's had a nasty accident."

Rachael's mum settled Molly on to a sofa, then shouted after Rachael, "Don't alarm them, though. Tell them it's her ankle," and to herself she muttered, "Thank God it's nothing worse."

Then she set about trying to untie Molly's laces and ease off her shoe.

Ravenna saw Molly close her eyes tightly and bite her lip but she made no sound. When the shoe and sock were off she saw the ankle was swelling rapidly, bulging with fluid and already tinged blue. She stood by the sofa, her eyes fixed on the swollen joint. She realized she was trembling and couldn't seem to keep her hands still; she was rubbing them together, clasping and unclasping them and her stomach was churning like a food mixer. It had happened so suddenly. The motor bike coming from nowhere. Dustin must have been following them but why hadn't they seen or heard him? Had he meant to hurt them or just give a warning? Either way it was a crazy thing to do – he must be deranged. Why ... how ... had she got herself into this mess? And now Molly was hurt.

She felt useless, standing like a gibbering wreck. Rachael's mum had taken charge but she should be the one who was helping Molly. It was all her fault. She wished Beth were here. She wanted to have a good cry and tell her everything. She thought about last night when they'd been dancing and making plans for the future, but this only made tears well up in her eyes.

Rachael came in from the kitchen, bringing tea.

"I've phoned your mum, Molly. She's on her way."

The minutes passed slowly. Rachael went to get some frozen peas from the refrigerator for her mum to hold against the damaged ankle. Ravenna sipped at her tea but couldn't keep still.

Molly was sitting with her foot propped up on a stool, her ankle swollen now to twice the size of her other one, her face set in rigid lines of pain. Ravenna was stabbed with pity and remorse and went over, perching on the arm of the sofa next to her.

"I could kill him, I could just kill him," she moaned, clenching her fists and thumping her knee. "If I'd have split on him straight away, this wouldn't have happened. It's my stupid fault. I'm so sorry, Moll."

"It wasn't your fault. It was Dustin's," Molly said through clenched teeth.

Rachael's mother rose from her knees. "I shall report him. I know who he is. We've had enough of him riding round here before any of this happened. Now he's got even more to answer for," she said.

In the street outside a car pulled up. Rachael ran to the window.

"Your mum's here," she announced to Molly.

A look of relief mixed with anxiety passed over Molly's face. She tried to shunt herself more upright but flinched with pain. Ravenna patted her shoulder. "It'll be all right," she said. "I'll tell her what happened."

Hilary came anxiously into the room, checking Molly over with her eyes as she hurried to her side. "Are you all right, darling?"

Molly nodded her head. "I'm fine," she said.

Hilary dropped to her knees and hugged her. Ravenna turned away, rubbing her hands over her arms, up and down, up and down. She felt nervous and edgy, worrying for Molly, hating herself and dreading the questions that would surely follow.

Vaguely she was aware of Molly telling her mum what had happened and then Rachael leaving the room and returning with their bags. Then there was a loud knock on the door and this time Rachael returned with Kelvin.

He dashed into the room red-eyed and angry, and Ravenna's first thought was that he was drunk. Oh no, this was all they needed. He stood in the middle of the room for a moment, clenching his fists and looking as though he would burst with rage. The room suddenly seemed very quiet. Ravenna heard him breathing loudly as if he'd run there and then he went over and sank to his knees in front of Molly.

Everyone seemed to be holding their breath. For a moment he just knelt there, his head bowed, his whole body sagging. Ravenna felt desperate. This was embarrassing ... excruciating. Moll had nearly been killed and Kelvin was drunk. But then he raised his head, looked calmly into Molly's eyes and asked, "How are you, love?"

Ravenna shuddered with relief and tears spilled down her face.

She saw Molly smile at Kelvin. "Apart from my ankle, I'm fine," she assured him.

The wild-eyed anger had faded and Kelvin looked gently at his daughter. "Thank God," he murmured.

Thank God he's sober, Ravenna thought as she wiped the tears away with the back of her hand.

The next moment, Kelvin was standing next to her, putting his arm around her and squeezing her shoulder. "You're both all right, that's the main thing," he was saying. Then he turned to Rachael's mum and thanked her and assured them that the doctor would be with them any minute. It was the solid, dependable Kelvin of old, dispensing warmth and comfort to everyone, and Ravenna felt cheered.

Molly was looking from one parent to the other and smiling. "I'm glad you both came," she said.

"Of course we both came," Kelvin said. "And don't you worry, everything's going to be all right."

And somehow Ravenna knew he meant more than the ankle.

21.

"He's really done it this time."

Ravenna lay on her bed with these words echoing around her brain. Dustin had done it. He'd proved that he was more than just a yob; he was malicious, capable of exacting terrible revenge.

And Ravenna felt ashamed. Dustin had taken her for a fool. He'd said a few tender words, smiled softly and she'd fallen for it. Had she thought she could change him, bring out the best in him, turn his intelligence to something positive, uncover hidden depths of humanity? Or was it more likely that she hadn't been thinking at all? That at the school disco she'd seen a boy who held the stage with a sensuous voice and a body that oozed sex?

Ravenna wriggled impatiently, kicking her bedclothes. It was torture even to think about it. It was her fault that she and Molly had almost been flattened by Dustin's bike and Molly had come off worst. She couldn't even genuinely wish it was her ankle that was broken because then there'd be no dancing. And that just proved what a rotten person she was. She was still thinking about herself even when Molly was in hospital.

Molly's mum had rung from the hospital about half an hour ago. Molly's ankle was broken. They were going to operate to set the bone and if all went well, Molly might be home tomorrow.

Ravenna sighed, rolled over and sat up, pushing her school books aside. There was some work she needed to do but she couldn't get on with it. Her head ached and she couldn't concentrate. The picture of Molly lying in the gutter kept coming into her mind. Poor Moll, she was probably having her operation at this very minute.

The thought of this sent her nervously pacing around her room. She picked up a mirror, sat making faces at herself, then pulled out the drawer that contained the shawl. She reached for its shiny folds, fingering the beads, stroking the silk, but even this didn't seem to comfort her. She wanted to see Beth, talk to her – but she couldn't even phone her, she'd gone to an exhibition with Harry.

If only there was someone to distract her. Usually the house was a hive of noise and activity but tonight Kirsty was fast asleep, Brett was playing on his computer, Ian was cleaning miners' lamps and other treasure trove and Sheila was out at bingo. The walls of her bedroom echoed with silence – if she didn't get out of her room, she'd go mad. Pushing the shawl back in the drawer, she closed it firmly and headed across the landing.

In the bathroom Ravenna rummaged in the cupboard and found some aspirin, took two then wandered downstairs. In the kitchen she made for the fridge. She hadn't eaten all day and was hungry, but there was nothing to tempt her: a half-eaten yoghurt, a loaf of white bread, a jar of salmon paste and a few squishy tomatoes – hardly a feast. She thought of the wide refrigerator shelves at Molly's house packed with olives, sun-dried tomatoes, soft cheeses and packets of crisp ready-mixed salad. Of course, all this could change soon. The Morgans might have to sell Badger's. Hell, she thought she had problems, Molly must be feeling really miserable.

The outside door rattled and Sheila entered, dripping wet and shaking an umbrella.

"It's raining like stink out there. Rotten weather."

She unbuttoned her mac, hung it on the back of a chair and ran her fingers through her damp hair, trying to fluff it up.

"Are you making a cup of tea?" she asked, hopefully.

Ravenna scowled. "No, I wasn't."

Sheila looked at her, examining her face with sharp eyes.

"What's the matter, Vernie? You look terrible."

"Thanks a bundle," Ravenna answered, sinking into a chair. Sheila sat down opposite, her eyes intent on Ravenna's face.

"Come on, I wasn't born yesterday. You come back late from school looking as white as the Queen's knickers, you go straight up to your room without any tea, and now you look as if you're on a sinking ship without a lifeboat."

Ravenna sighed. Trust Sheila to make it all sound like some extravagant soap opera.

"I've just got a bit of a headache," Ravenna sighed.

Sheila put her hand on Ravenna's forehead and smoothed her hair, then squinted closely at her face. "Come on, tell your Auntie Sheila all about it and she'll blow all those nasties away."

Sheila's lips puckered and she blew a stream of air on to Ravenna's forehead.

"Remember how we used to chase those bad dreams away?" she asked.

Ravenna did remember and found it strangely comforting. She didn't even mind when Sheila just sat looking at her expectantly, with a silly sort of sympathetic smile on her face.

She wants to help, Ravenna thought. Well, I might as well tell the whole story. She'll find out sooner or later anyway. What was there to do between bingo games except gossip?

Ravenna cleared her throat and swallowed. Her mouth felt as if it was full of fizz-bombs and her voice sounded harsh and jerky. "I was walking home from school ... with Molly, crossing the road ... and this lad on a motor bike came at us ... drove straight at us. I didn't think he was going to stop so ... I pushed Molly out of his way and ... she fell and she's broken her ankle. She's in hospital."

When she'd finished speaking, Ravenna felt as if the fizz-bombs had exploded. Her mouth was dry and stiff as if coated in powder. She gulped and looked anxiously at Sheila.

Sheila blinked a few times then her mouth puckered as if it had sucked on sour lemon. "What! All this happened and you didn't even tell me when you came in?" Her voice was shrill, reflecting her disappointment.

Ravenna felt guilty. "I'm sorry. I just needed to think, get it straight in my head."

"Were you hurt?"

Ravenna shook her head.

"And this boy, who was he?"

"Oh, nobody you know."

Sheila folded her arms on the table. "I might, try me."

"Dustin, Dustin Harrows."

"I do know him. He lives in the flats. I know his mother. She comes to bingo. Ever such a nice woman, though her husband's no use. She talks a lot about Dustin. He's very good to her by all accounts."

Ravenna felt as if she was trying to swallow a brick. Oh,

trust Dustin to be the loving son. "Wouldn't you just know?" she muttered.

"So what's between you and this boy, then?" Sheila asked, eyeing Ravenna suspiciously.

"Nothing."

"Well, he wasn't coming after you for nothing."

"He's just stupid, that's all. Thinks he's so cool because he's got a motor bike."

Sheila sucked in her bottom lip, making a clucking noise. "I think I get the picture. This lad likes you, you give him the cold shoulder, he chases after you on his motor cycle and unfortunately it's Molly who – cops it."

Ravenna stared at Sheila. She'd certainly grasped the situation.

"Yes, I suppose that's about it."

"And now you feel miserable because you think it's all your fault that Molly's got a broken ankle."

"Yes."

"Well, let me tell you this. It isn't. That boy didn't need an excuse. He's a delinquent. Anybody who drives a motor bike dangerously deserves to be put behind bars."

Ravenna looked at Sheila's podgy round face, her blue eyes clear and unwavering, her plump chin wobbling with conviction, and she smiled.

"Thanks," she said. "Thanks, Mum."

Sheila patted Ravenna's arm and then rose from the table. "I'll make you a cup of tea and some toast. You must be starving, having no tea. You just sit there. I'll get you something and then I want you to tell me all about this lad and what happened. He's going to have me to reckon with tomorrow."

As Sheila got up and plugged in the kettle, Ravenna leaned over the table and propped her head in her hands, relief washing through her like the incoming tide. Sheila had absolved her of guilt. Molly's accident wasn't her fault, Sheila had said so, and Sheila always said exactly what she thought, you could rely on that – she was straight and if Sheila took her side then maybe others would see it her way too.

And it was Sheila's advice that sent Ravenna back to school the next day.

"Stay at home and you'll worry. Face it and it won't be easy, but you'll show you've got nothing to hide. And, I guarantee you, you'll feel better at the end of the day." Squaring her shoulders, she pulled herself up to her full height which, although, well below Ravenna's chin, made her look threatening. "I'll be down there to see what's what as soon as I've dropped Brett off at school and Kirsty at nursery."

In spite of her worries, Ravenna smiled. Sheila was right; she had to face the questions and tell her side of the story. She just hoped Dustin wouldn't be at school.

It didn't take long for the rumours to spread. In maths, Molly had a broken leg, in science, she was crippled. Luckily, few people seemed aware of Ravenna's part in the drama and Rachael fielded questions. The girls did listen attentively, however, when Malc said Dustin was at the police station.

Mid-morning Ravenna was pulled out of lessons to be interviewed by the Head and the police. Sheila was there too, slightly overwhelmed and silent, but nevertheless a solid, comforting presence. Ravenna told the story as simply and directly as she could – the school disco, Dustin following her,

Dustin inciting people to gang up on Molly, Dustin in the changing rooms, and then the accident outside Rachael's house. She didn't minimize her part in events, but telling the whole story helped her get things in perspective.

It was difficult for Ravenna to talk about some things that had happened, particularly about Dustin molesting her in the changing rooms. She could hear Sheila listening intently as she described Dustin kissing her and trying to feel her up. At that moment Ravenna actually wished Sheila wasn't in the room, although she had to admit she didn't fuss. In fact, to give her her due, Sheila didn't butt in or make any comment – she just sat there quietly, oozing sympathy.

When the interview was over Ravenna felt drained. The policewoman suggested she take the rest of the day off but Ravenna knew she needed all the lesson time she could possibly get at the moment. She had a lot of catching up to do.

It wasn't easy to concentrate on lessons during the rest of the day, however. Ravenna kept seeing the hurt look on Sheila's face. She'd tried to cover it up but Ravenna knew she'd upset her by not confiding in her. Then there was the look of horror on the Head's face when he knew what had happened in the changing rooms. He seemed to take it personally that such a thing could go on in his school. Ravenna saw he had a hard job controlling his anger.

Most of the afternoon she tried to put everything out of her mind and study – but she didn't always succeed.

After school, Ravenna walked to Badger's, hoping that Molly would be there. Poor Moll, she must have had a rough time in the hospital. She'd hate spending the night away from home.

Mrs Morgan smiled brightly when she opened the door and saw Ravenna. Well, that was a good start: the Morgans weren't holding her responsible for the accident, it seemed. On the contrary, Hilary welcomed Ravenna warmly and immediately took her through to see Molly, who was lying on the sitting-room sofa.

Molly was reading, a nest of plump cushions supporting her shoulders, the thickly plastered leg lying like a huge lump of rock on the dark blue velvet sofa. Ravenna glared at it, as if it had kicked her. She couldn't ignore it, or the guilt its presence engendered.

Once again, she was stung with regrets about Dustin and the accident. Sheila had assured her she wasn't to blame, but when faced with the rock-solid evidence of the broken leg, Ravenna felt guilt creeping back like a bad cold.

She mustn't be miserable for Molly's sake, though. Steeling herself to look cheerful she smiled and, motioning to the piles of fruit, magazines and chocolate, she said brightly, "Well, you look as if you're having a relaxing time."

Molly smiled back at her. "I've been well looked after. Mum's been dancing attendance on me since I arrived back."

Hilary, hovering in the background, laughed. "I'm just pleased you're all right." She turned anxiously to Ravenna. "She looks fine, doesn't she? A bit pale perhaps but. . ."

Molly cut in before Ravenna could reply. "Mum, what can you expect? It was only last night that they operated. I was lucky to be able to come home today."

Hilary nodded. "I know, darling."

There was a pause in which Ravenna noticed dark shadows

under Molly's eyes. She shuffled uneasily, watching Hilary pick up an empty glass and wipe the coffee table.

"Well, I'm sure you two have a lot to talk about and I'd better get on with dinner," Hilary said, hesitating for a moment, as if uncertain, then she turned to Ravenna, "You'll get her anything she needs, won't you?"

Molly laughed. "Mum, don't fuss," she said, but Ravenna nodded, pleased to think she might be of some use.

The tension eased when Hilary left and Ravenna settled down in an easy chair close to Molly.

"Was it awful?" she asked.

Molly grimaced and shrugged, signalling that she didn't much want to talk about it. "Not too bad," she said dismissively. She tossed back her hair and held out a magazine she'd been reading. "I've never read so many magazines in my life. Look! Cosmo, Seventeen, Sweet Dreams, Wet Dreams – Mum bought the lot. They're all crap. Just ask me, go on, what are the 'in' colours for summer, the right lipstick to wear, what goes on the beach this year, one-piece, two-piece or butt-naked? What is the best chat-up line in the jacuzzi?"

Ravenna laughed wickedly, spiked her fingers and screwed up her face. "Hubble, bubble, toil and trouble," she chanted.

"That's not what they recommend," Molly protested.

"Go on then, tell me what great line they suggest," Ravenna demanded.

Molly's face puckered. "Can't remember," she giggled.

"Well, let's hope you're not stuck in a jacuzzi with the man of your dreams this summer then. You'll have to be content with, 'Do you come here often?'"

"That sounds like a wet dream," Molly giggled.

"You rude person," Ravenna said. "Just you wait – I've got something to bring you down to earth." She picked up a school bag and swung it forwards. "I hate to remind you but before we're soaking in jacuzzis on tropical islands this summer there's the little matter of exams to settle. Geography!" Ravenna announced, opening her bag.

Molly's top lip curled in disbelief. "They haven't! Not already? I don't believe it!"

"Yep. What did you expect ... sympathy?" Ravenna said, unloading Molly's folder, file and textbook. "My dear, you've only broken an ankle. Course, word got round that Dustin had knocked you down and paralysed you for life. I almost didn't feel like correcting that one – let him stew."

"Was he there?" Molly asked anxiously.

"No, thank God. He was at the police station for most of the day, I think."

"Did you see Dad? He went down to see the Head this morning."

"No, but I spent ages with the Head and the police. I don't know what they'll do. I mean, it wasn't actually Dustin who knocked you down – I pushed you."

"Yes, but only because he was heading straight for us. How do you know he'd have swerved in time? I thought he was going to kill me." A look of sharp anger scored Molly's face and she winced in pain.

"Does it still hurt?" Ravenna asked.

"No, not really – only when I get mad about Dustin. It aches but I've had some strong painkillers. Most of the time it's OK. It's just when I remember. I hate thinking about it."

"I know, I had bad dreams all night. I dreamt Dustin had killed you but somehow it was all my fault. I woke up crying."

Molly looked up and held Ravenna's eyes for a moment. "Raven," she said firmly, "it wasn't your fault."

Then she dropped her gaze and asked, "Did you tell the Head about what happened earlier?"

"You mean Dustin coming into the changing rooms?"

"Yes."

Ravenna pursed her lips and rocked silently back and forth for a moment. "Yes, I told him."

"And..."

"And ... he said Dustin was out of order."

"Was that all?" Molly asked, her voice crackling with out-rage.

"No," Ravenna said, smiling at Molly's flash of temper. "He said he'd got to listen to Dustin's side of the story."

"That's just typical of teachers," Molly sighed.

Ravenna moved forward and sat on the edge of her chair. "Well, he's got his job to do. I think his sympathies were with us but he couldn't say so without speaking to Dustin, could he?"

"I suppose not," Molly reluctantly agreed.

For a few moments there was silence as they sat thinking. Then Molly said softly, "Do you think Dustin's worried? I mean, perhaps he couldn't sleep either."

"Oh, Moll. Don't think about him. Think about yourself. Why waste your thoughts on him? He's not the one with a broken leg."

"Ankle," Molly corrected.

"OK, ankle, sorry. Look, Dustin's a real shit, a nut-case. I

don't care if he's expelled from school and fails all his exams –
he deserves it."

"I suppose you're right but I can't help feeling sorry for him
somehow. His mum lost her job and his dad's living rough."

Ravenna shook her head. "Moll, did they X-ray your head
last night?"

Molly giggled. "All right, I know I'm nuts but I can't help
feeling sorry for the underdog. I think I might be a politician
when I grow up."

"I hate to tell you, Moll, but you'll never get elected on
those sort of policies," Ravenna said.

Molly moved aside a pile of magazines and leaned towards
the overflowing fruit bowl. "Would you like a mango? Look,
I've got three. Mum bought me the whole fruit shop."

Ravenna took a big red and yellow fruit, held it to her nose
and sniffed. "I can smell the luscious juice through the skin.
This mango has been ripened by tropical sunlight and picked
by a hunky young man with rippling muscles, beautiful white
teeth and skin the colour of ripe plums."

"Dream on," Molly laughed.

"I'll go and get a knife," Ravenna said, as she twirled and
chasséd out of the room, keeping time with a reggae tune that
was lilting inside her head. Suddenly she felt much better,
lifted by laughter and music and thoughts of sunshine. If she
were in Beth's studio now she'd leap and touch the skylights.

Dancing into the kitchen, Ravenna found Hilary making
dinner.

"You're looking pleased with yourself," Hilary said.

"I know. I'm so glad Moll's getting better. I felt terrible last
night after you'd all gone off to hospital."

"I'm sorry, Ravenna. We didn't give you a thought, did we? We were so concerned about Molly. It must have been awful for you too."

Hilary came over, put an arm round Ravenna and gave her a hug. Ravenna felt the boniness of Hilary's body and reflected how thin she'd become. This factory business was dreadful. But the next moment Hilary was smiling and, despite the gauntness of her face, Ravenna saw happiness in her eyes. After the trouble with Dustin, and Molly's broken ankle, Hilary actually looked happier than Ravenna had seen her for some time.

"Don't blame yourself," Hilary said. "We know you wouldn't do anything to hurt Molly – it could easily have been you that ended up in hospital."

"Yes, but it wasn't," Ravenna replied tightly.

Hilary slipped her arm around Ravenna's shoulder. "If anybody is to blame it's me. I was responsible for Dustin bearing a grudge. If I hadn't..."

"Molly told me," Ravenna cut in. "You were only doing your duty. It wasn't your fault Dustin's dad was a burglar."

"I don't suppose either of us is to blame. The best thing we can do is to help Molly keep her spirits up." Hilary gave Ravenna a hug and smiled. "And don't forget you were very brave. You may have saved her life. Molly's aware of that and she's grateful. In fact, she doesn't seem bitter about any of it. She was quite worried last night that Kelvin would be too hard on Dustin."

"I know. I've told her she's nuts. How is he?"

"Dustin or Kelvin?" Hilary teased.

"Kelvin, of course," Ravenna replied.

"Amazingly better. Molly's accident really knocked him for six. You should have seen him. He was beside himself when we got back from the hospital – threatening Dustin, blaming himself. We talked for hours but just ended up going round in circles. I went to bed some time after midnight."

Hilary let go of Ravenna and nervously smoothed her hair.

"This morning, when I woke up, he wasn't in bed. I was so worried – thought he'd gone off again – but I hardly had time to think about it before he waltzed into the bedroom with a breakfast tray looking ... transformed, smiling, wide awake and ... well ... back to normal. He said he'd done a lot of thinking, sat up all night, and he talked much more sensibly about what had happened to Molly. Then he started to talk about the factory, said he had plans, though he wouldn't tell me what, until..."

At that moment the phone interrupted her and Hilary turned to answer it. Ravenna lingered, remembering the unwelcome intrusion of news reporters and threatening phone calls. But Hilary spoke warmly, cheerfully, her sleek bobbed hair swinging around her fine cheek bones.

"No, she's fine, darling. Don't worry. She came home this afternoon."

Reassured, Ravenna slipped out of the kitchen. But before she was out of earshot, she heard Hilary say, "No, of course, it's no trouble. We'd love to meet her," and Ravenna's heart went thumping into overdrive. She knew who Hilary was talking to.

The thick yellow juice of the ripe mango ran down Ravenna's fingers as she peeled and sliced the sweet-smelling fruit.

"Don't you hate how big the stone is? It's a cheat," Molly said as she speared a slice.

"I scrape it with my teeth," Ravenna replied, demonstrating so that juice ran down her chin.

"I've tried that but all the bits get stuck, like string."

"All the better to bite on," Ravenna laughed, gnashing her yellow stained teeth.

"Ha ha! And here comes the big bad wolf," a deep voice boomed and Ravenna turned to see Kelvin standing in the doorway holding an armful of flowers. He looked smart, clean shaven, his eyes twinkling with good humour as he came forward and with a flourish uncrossed his arms and held out two separate bouquets.

"One for the patient and one for her saviour," he said.

Ravenna blushed, feeling uncomfortable. She took the flowers but couldn't accept the praise. "I was probably responsible for breaking Moll's ankle, flinging her on to the pavement like that," she said. "Dustin missed me, didn't he? And I was the one he was trying to get."

It all came out in a rush, sounding fierce and angry. As she spoke her hands clenched and a cold shiver shot down her arms. She saw again the wheel spinning towards her, the determined grip of Dustin's hand on the throttle, the roaring noise. She shuddered and sucked in a gulp of air.

Kelvin put his arm around her shoulders and said gently, "Look, we don't know what Dustin intended. He says he didn't mean to hurt anybody, but it was a stupid action. You can't mess around with motor bikes like that. They're lethal weapons. How did he know he could swerve? He could have killed you, himself or Molly."

Ravenna knew there was sense in what Kelvin was saying. He looked full of concern, his face etched with deep, unfamiliar lines.

"We all do stupid things at times," he went on. "I've done some myself lately. I could have killed somebody the other night when the police pulled me in. There's never any excuse for drinking and driving." He pursed his lips and swallowed hard, shaking his head slightly as he spoke. "I can't believe how stupid I've been, but thank God, I've got time to put things right."

There was an awkward silence. Molly and Ravenna looked at one another across the fruit and flowers, then quickly looked away. Kelvin stood stroking his face, gazing thoughtfully into the distance.

It was Ravenna who broke the silence, getting to her feet. "I should be going," she said. "I ... er ... I just came to bring Molly some school work."

Kelvin was startled out of his thoughts and reacted swiftly, putting an arm around Ravenna's shoulders. "Nonsense. I won't hear of it. You must stay to dinner. David's coming, bringing a friend, and Hilary's planning on your being here too, I'm sure. I'll go and see."

Ravenna watched him stride firmly and purposefully into the kitchen.

"It's going to be all right, Moll, isn't it?" she whispered.

"Yes," Molly agreed. "Somehow it'll all work out."

Ravenna hoped so. Everybody at Badger's seemed much happier and that made her happy, but it would be tough seeing David and Natalie here together.

She looked across at Molly, who was neatly piling her school books at the side of the sofa.

"Moll?" Ravenna began.

"Yes?"

"Oh, nothing," Ravenna said.

"It must have been something."

"Well . . . have you noticed something odd about your leg?"

"Which one?"

"The broken one, of course."

"What do you mean?" Molly asked a little anxiously.

"Well," said Ravenna picking up a pen. "Nobody's drawn on your pot yet. It's bare. Hasn't anybody told you, that's the fun part of having a broken bone?"

"I didn't realize there was a fun part," Molly replied, looking ruefully at the lumpy plaster. Then she sighed. "I wonder who David's bringing to dinner? I don't think I'm up to making sparkling conversation tonight."

Ravenna didn't reply. She was rooting in her school bag, her face averted. "Don't worry, no one will expect you to be the life and soul," she said. "Everybody understands you're tired." She went over and sat beside Molly, pen poised. "Oh no, I can't think of anything to write. I mean it's a big responsibility to be the first one. You have to write something witty or meaningful."

"Daz woz 'ere, or something like that, you mean."

Ravenna didn't answer, she was busy writing; SORRY was appearing in big block capitals.

Molly watched, waiting for Ravenna to finish. Then she caught up the pen. "Not accepted," she said firmly. "Because will you get it into your stupid head that it wasn't your fault.

Now," she said, giving Ravenna back the pen, "write something I want to read."

Ravenna thought for a moment; then, smiling, she wrote as stylishly as she could on the shiny new plaster, "DON'T FORGET TO DANCE".

Molly laughed. "Some hope!" she said.

22.

Molly and Ravenna were watching TV when the door burst open and in walked David and Natalie. Ravenna saw Molly's eyes widen with surprise.

"Hi, David, who's this?" Molly demanded.

David reached out and drew Natalie close as he replied, his voice full of warmth and affection, "This is Natalie."

Dressed in a loose linen orange jacket over a long skirt of blood-red, tangerine and gold stripes, Natalie glowed like tropical sun against David's navy sweater and black jeans. She was just as deliciously attractive and colourful as Ravenna remembered.

For a moment, Molly was dumbstruck; Ravenna could tell she was trying to work out how her brother had become connected with his beautiful stranger.

Natalie held out a slim hand, her wrist jangling with gold hoops. She shook hands with Molly and smiled warmly at her.

David was beaming too. "We met when Natalie came to dance at the festival last term," he explained.

Molly's eyes were on stalks. "Great to meet you, Natalie," she stammered.

Natalie held out a small package which she placed in Molly's hand. "We bought you this. Thought it might cheer you up."

Molly struggled to open the neatly taped parcel. "Oh great, a CD," she said, as she gave up trying to undo the tape and ripped open the paper.

"The Indestructible Sound of Soweto," David read for her. "Natalie chose it. It's great dance music."

"Sounds wonderful," Molly said. "It'll have me rollicking around the room in no time."

Natalie laughed. "Sorry. Thoughtful, wasn't it?"

"I'm sure I'll love it," Molly replied.

They were all laughing when Hilary and Kelvin came into the room. Ravenna registered the looks of surprise on their faces when they saw their pale, shy son with a tall and beautiful woman. But they soon recovered. Hilary greeted Natalie warmly, then Kelvin kissed her on both cheeks.

It wasn't long before Ravenna could see the Morgans had taken Natalie to their hearts and she was beginning to feel like a cold outsider. Kelvin was playing the affable host just as he used to, making sure everybody was comfortably seated, offering drinks. Ravenna was amused to note that when he spoke to David, there was a tinge of admiration in his voice.

"Well, David, what would you like to drink? I must say, you're a dark horse. How long have you two known each other?"

David was sitting on the small sofa, nestling close to Natalie, holding her hand. Ravenna saw him wince at his father's question and he answered shortly, "Since last term. Natalie came to dance – it was part of the performing arts festival – I was playing."

"Didn't know you were still in a band," Kelvin said.

"Oh, I just stood in for someone – played bass," David said quickly.

"Well, no harm in keeping your hand in, I suppose,"

Kelvin replied. He turned to Natalie. "So, you're a dancer?" he asked.

"Yes, I trained with Beth Owen who lives here now, in Maddock, and then I went to the Royal."

Ravenna saw David squeeze Natalie's hand and they glanced at each other, sharing a swift secret smile.

Natalie leant against David and began to talk about their first meeting. She relaxed as she spoke about the dance festival, laughing about David turning up at a workshop one morning, thinking he'd be able to watch and hating actually having to join in.

"I couldn't think how else I would get to see her again," David explained.

"You should have seen him, he was brilliant," Natalie laughed.

"So brilliant, they asked me to stand out for the final dance," David reminded her.

"Yes, but that was only because they needed another drummer."

"So you say," David said, shaking Natalie's arm.

Ravenna watched the two of them. They looked so happy together. David, who was normally quiet and self-effacing, was bubbling over with pride now that the ordeal of Natalie meeting his parents was over. And Natalie just sat there glowing, looking lovely. What was it that made her so beautiful? Ravenna wondered. It was partly, Ravenna decided, the way she held herself, as if she expected to be noticed, and then there was a sparkle about her, as if she was lit up from the inside. Like Beth. Beth looked beautiful when she was happy.

Perhaps no one was truly beautiful until they were happy inside.

Ravenna was shaken out of her thoughts by hearing her name.

"I met Ravenna at John and Selina's party," Natalie was saying.

Ravenna started as the spotlight fell on her. She'd been so absorbed in watching everybody, that she'd thought herself forgotten.

"Ravenna's a dancer too," Natalie said.

"Oh, I'd hardly qualify as that," Ravenna replied.

"But you will." Natalie smiled.

At that moment, they were interrupted by the telephone ringing and Kelvin went to answer it, whilst Hilary checked on dinner.

As soon as the parents were out of the way, David demanded to know the exact details of the accident and what had happened to Dustin. David was more angry than Ravenna had ever seen him as he listened to their tale of Dustin's pursuit and harassment. The usually gentle, taciturn David looked ready to tear Dustin apart.

"He needs sorting out," David said.

Kelvin returned, looking worried and thoughtful. "The police are charging Dustin with dangerous driving. And," he lowered his voice, "he's admitted making anonymous phone calls."

Molly sat bolt upright. "What ... those obnoxious phone calls that Mum had? Those! That was Dustin! Damn him, I suspected it all along."

Kelvin nodded.

David let go of Natalie's hand and thumped the sofa. "He needs locking up," he said angrily.

Ravenna was so angry that she could hardly contain herself. "He should be made to feel as bad as he's made all of us feel. I could kill him."

"Well, you may not have a chance to murder him," Kelvin said heavily. "Apparently his mother is so distraught she may get there first. She's so angry with him Dustin doesn't want to go home. He's still at the police station."

"It serves him right," Ravenna said. "He deserves everything he gets. As if Hilary didn't have enough to worry about without him making it worse."

"Well, he was pretty nasty to you and Molly too, Ravenna. Actually, the Inspector said he's really sorry. Wants to apologize to us all."

"That's just a con," Ravenna said firmly. "He probably thinks he'll get off lightly if he apologizes."

"I don't know. Perhaps we should give him a chance, if he wants to," Kelvin said. "He didn't appear such a bad lad in some ways. He seemed genuinely worried about Molly, and I think he cares about your opinion, Ravenna. He's had a tough life, saw his mum knocked about, his father jailed – perhaps with a different background, different upbringing he might have put his mind to good use ... he's a bright lad, you know."

Ravenna snorted. "You'll be giving him a job next."

"Well, we'll see what Hilary thinks. After all, she's the one with the experience of court and criminals," Kelvin replied.

He didn't continue the conversation, however, when Hilary came in to say that dinner was ready, and nobody mentioned

Dustin. They'd all had enough of feeling miserable, Ravenna supposed.

It was a much happier occasion than the last time Ravenna had stayed to dinner. Then, she remembered, Kelvin had appeared in a drunken rage, and Hilary had left the table in floods of tears. Now they sat down, calmly and sociably, pleased to be together. Kelvin was charming and sober and talk flowed easily. Natalie told them about her dancing with "Arc" and her plans to teach workshops in schools. David talked about his guitar playing and his plans to form a new band.

Ravenna was surprised that Kelvin mounted no opposition to this. "Think about your studies – put them first," Kelvin might have said at one time; although easygoing about some things, he'd always been strict about David's education. Perhaps the factory crisis had reminded him there was more to life than making money, or perhaps he'd realized, seeing David with Natalie, that David should now be trusted to make his own decisions.

Ravenna ate heartily. She loved Hilary's cooking – pancakes filled with spinach and feta cheese, asparagus with a tangy sauce, grilled garlic mushrooms with lemon – she relished everything, never failing to compare it with Sheila's slapdash approach to cooking which usually involved a knob of lard and a frying pan. But this time, remembering the lovely lemon cake Sheila had baked on Sunday, she felt guilty. It wasn't Sheila's fault she'd never had the time or money to experiment with expensive ingredients. Five eggs to Sheila meant a meal, not a fancy dessert.

As they were finishing off their meal with chocolate soufflé and coffee, Ravenna heard the telephone ring and Beth's voice on the answer machine.

"It's Beth. Can I answer it?" Ravenna asked.

As Hilary nodded, Ravenna raced to the phone before the message finished.

Beth's voice was anxious. "Oh, Ravenna. Poor dab. I only just got your message. How's Molly? Are you sure you're not hurt? Can I come and see you?"

"Molly's fine and I'm completely unscathed," Ravenna reassured her. "But I'd love to see you. If David will bring me over later and if I can manage it after all the food I've eaten, could we do some dancing?"

Ravenna patted her face with a towel, then wiped her forehead and neck. She was spangled with sweat, her leotard sticking to her back; her thighs and crotch, wet and itchy.

"Wow, that was tough!" she exclaimed, pulling down on her leotard, easing it free of her body's creases for a moment.

"Yes, I'm out of practice too," Beth breathed, as she pulled a sweatshirt over her head.

Ravenna threw down the towel, grabbed a bottle of water and slumped into a chair.

"I really enjoyed it, though. And I nearly got that last part." She sniffed. "Yuk! I smell really sweaty."

Beth laughed. "Part of a dancer's baggage. Fresh sweat's all right – it's when it dries it stinks."

Ravenna wrinkled her nose, gulped some water and stretched her legs out in front of her.

"The barre work was difficult. I kept wanting to break away

but it paid off later. It really loosened me up. I was much more supple when we started dancing."

"Well, that's the theory. It's important for a dancer to keep the muscles warm and exercised because you're asking a lot of them. And it's important to keep warm afterwards," Beth said, motioning to Ravenna's cardigan, which was lying on the floor.

Ravenna picked up the heavy multicoloured cardigan, slipped her arms into the sleeves and pulled it around her. It was something Sheila had knitted for her – chunky bright colours. She thought she'd never wear it and had brought it to the studio because it didn't matter if it got sweaty and dirty. Now she snuggled into it, glad of its warmth as the hot flush of exercise seeped away.

"Am I improving?" she asked Beth.

Beth put her hand lightly on Ravenna's shoulder. "Of course you are. You were terrific, but don't expect miracles. You can't be a dancer in one lesson – you've got a lot to catch up on. You can't learn technique overnight, no matter how committed you are."

"I know. I wish I'd started when I was five."

Beth sipped some water and wiped her mouth with the back of her hand. "Don't worry. You're learning quickly. And it's never too late. I used to run a beginners' tap class for senior citizens. They were excellent, learnt really fast."

"That's the one for Sheila," Ravenna laughed.

"You be careful," Beth warned. "You never know. Sheila might be able to show you a thing or two."

Ravenna didn't reply. She had become suddenly still and very thoughtful.

"What is it?" Beth asked her.

"I want to ask you something, but I don't know if I can," Ravenna said, fiddling with a long strand of hair, twisting it round her fingers. "It's just that, I don't just want to do this as a hobby. I want to be good. I mean, really good. I feel I've wasted so much time. I can't explain it very well but when I'm dancing ... well, I feel as if I'm really me. I know it sounds corny but I feel like I've come home ... as if I've discovered what I really want to do with my life."

Ravenna gulped and continued, her voice shaking slightly, "Only I don't know if I'm good enough."

She looked at Beth anxiously, hope shining in her eyes.

Beth gently took the strand of hair that Ravenna was winding and unwinding, smoothed it round her cheek and smiled. "I understand. I'm a dancer too, remember? I never feel whole if I'm not dancing. I turned my back on it after Megan died. It was the wrong thing to do – but I couldn't see it at the time – really I needed it more than ever. But when you dance, if you *really* dance, you put your heart and soul into it and I suppose I didn't have any heart or soul to give. I was too damaged."

She took Ravenna's hand and gently stroked the knuckles with her thumb. "I can't honestly tell you if you're good enough to really count. You've got masses of talent, you move wonderfully, you have strength and grace, you're eager to learn. Whether you will be great, only time will tell. But if you're serious, you'll give your life to it. It's a big sacrifice."

"I know," Ravenna sighed.

Beth squeezed Ravenna's hand then let go and rose to her

feet. "Well, I don't know about you, but right now I need a rest and a drink."

In the kitchen, Beth set out mugs and put the kettle on to boil whilst Ravenna found milk and spoons. Harry was working in the room at the back so the two dancers sat together at the big cluttered table and drank hot tea, their hands cupped around the steaming mugs.

Ravenna felt happy and relaxed. She loved this kitchen with its bright disorder.

"Did you ever want to do anything else but dance?" Ravenna asked.

"Not really. I like to paint but I'm not that good. And I'll only ever be like hundreds of other amateur painters. But when I danced, right from when I was a child, I was me. Nobody danced like me."

"That's how I feel," Ravenna said. "That's exactly it. It's me dancing, heart and soul and spirit. All of me. Lots of things I do are just brainwork. At school I use my head – even when I play tennis I'm thinking, thinking all the time – but when I dance, my brain can switch off. I mean it's there, working away, but I'm not aware of it. It's so natural, it's as if my feet, my hands, my body – they think for themselves and then it's as though I'm not thinking, just feeling. It's so exhilarating."

Beth laughed. "I know what you mean and I can't fault you for enthusiasm. You may well make it to the top but there are no certainties. I want you to understand the drawbacks. You've got years of hard slog ahead of you. It's tough, excruciating at times. Sometimes I would hear the alarm clock and wonder how I was going to drag myself out of bed, let alone dance. Pain was something we all lived with. You learnt to dance with it, through it."

"But there must have been good times too?" Ravenna asked.

"Yes. The times when I was asleep," Beth laughed.

"No, but you wouldn't have. . .?"

Beth finished the sentence. ". . .given up. No, I don't suppose we would. If you want to dance more than anything, then that's what you do, and despite the pain, you love it."

Ravenna cupped her chin in her hands and smiled. "You're not putting me off."

"Then you can count on my help," Beth said. "I'll be with you all the way." She rose and poured more tea. "Selina is taking me to the community centre at the Meadows tomorrow night. I want to pull together as many cultures as I can in the summer concert, and Selina said there are some brilliant dancers that perform there. Would you like to come?"

"It sounds exciting. I'd love to go," Ravenna said. "But I'll have to check with Sheila."

Beth nodded then said, "Tell you what, I'll ask Sheila. I'll phone her. If it's OK we'll pick you up about six-thirty."

"Will Natalie be coming too?"

"No, she's away."

"Not tonight she isn't. She's staying at David and Molly's."

Beth frowned. "Oh, how did that go?"

Ravenna caught the anxiety in her voice. "What do you mean?" she asked.

"Well, Natalie thought David had been putting off introducing her to his parents. She thought he was afraid they wouldn't like her."

"Why?"

"Well, they're very conservative, from what I hear. Very church on Sundays, roast beef and good works."

"No, they're not a bit like that really," Ravenna said. Then thought for a moment. "Well, I suppose they are but ... in a nice way. I think they were a bit surprised. She isn't the sort of person you imagine being with David. She's elegant, beautiful, extrovert, and David's always been fairly quiet, a bit of a loner in some ways. But they did like Natalie. I could tell."

"I should think so too," Beth said. "She's wonderful."

Ravenna sighed. "Yes, she is," she agreed.

"And David seems a pretty nice sort of guy too," Beth said, quizzically.

"Yes, he is," Ravenna agreed again.

Beth looked at her closely.

"You'll find someone for you one day," she said. "But if you're going to dance, you may have to wait a while."

Ravenna smiled. "How can you can read my thoughts?" she asked.

"Because we're soul sisters," Beth said. "I knew it as soon as I saw you. You don't have to be blood-related to feel a connection, you know."

23.

When Ravenna came home from school the next day, Sheila was playing loud music and dancing around the kitchen, a slice of toast in one hand, a knife in the other.

"Did I tell you about the time I met Ray Davies?" she asked.

"Yes, about a million times," Ravenna answered, as she plugged in the kettle.

"Well, he's still writing great songs. Listen to this."

Sheila danced on, breasts bouncing, elbows out, fingers clicking, her feet surprisingly light and nifty in fur-lined slippers.

"*A nice bit of old, with the right attitude,*" she sang.

"Well, the words are appropriate," Ravenna muttered.

But Sheila didn't hear. She was accompanying the raspy voice on the tape whilst she dripped syrup into Kirsty's rice pudding. "*Don't forget to dance, Oh, no, no, don't forget to smile.*"

So that's where she'd heard it. Ravenna smiled as she remembered the words she'd written on Molly's plaster and found herself singing along, "*Don't forget to dance, Oh, no, no, forget it for a while.*"

"Pink, pink," Kirsty shouted, banging her spoon.

"She likes jam in it," Ravenna explained. But Sheila was lost in the music.

"Oh, just listen to this. How can anybody keep their feet still when this is playing? Not like all that electronic stuff they

have now. That's not proper music – turns you into a robot."
Sheila's flowered leggings jiggled over to the cassette player
and she turned the music up even louder.

"Jeez, it's like a madhouse," Ravenna complained. But she
was smiling, happy that for once she didn't have to make
Kirsty's tea and pleased to see Sheila in such a good mood.

"*You do the thing you do the best . . . that separates you from the
rest,*" Sheila sang as she opened a tin of spaghetti hoops.

Ravenna picked up Kirsty's spoon, found some jam and
stirred it into the rice pudding.

"It's pink now, Kirsty, eat it up."

Kirsty smiled contentedly and spooned the pink mixture
into her mouth. Ravenna picked a box of crackers out of the
cupboard, found a tub of cottage cheese and sat down at the
table. Sheila turned the music down and came and sat beside
her, balancing toast, butter and a mug of tea.

"How was Molly yesterday?"

"Oh, quite cheerful, getting around on crutches. Things at
the house have improved too. Kelvin's got plans for the factory, though they're a bit hush-hush at present."

"That's good. And how about the dancing? How's that
going?" Sheila asked. "Are you going to stick at it?"

Ravenna crunched a mouthful of biscuit and cheese and
swallowed.

"Yeah, absolutely. Beth's brilliant – a great teacher. I love
it. Actually, I wanted to talk to you . . . about the dancing, I
mean."

Sheila's face was bright, eager for confidences. "Well, go
ahead."

Ravenna hesitated. She didn't know quite how to put it.

She felt like a diver on the edge of a high board, butterflies fluttering in her stomach – she paused, then plunged.

"I want to learn to dance properly. I mean, make it a career. Try and get a place at a school or college. Do an audition; see if they'll take me."

She looked at Sheila, waiting for an explosion, but Sheila sat quite still, eyes half closed, sipping tea. Had she listened? Had she taken it in?

The music was oozing softly now. *Don't forget to dance.* Was Sheila remembering the time she'd danced with Ray Davies, contemplating missed opportunities or . . . Ravenna's future?

The eyes flickered, closed for a moment then flipped open. They were a startling blue as they glared at Ravenna. "You mean give up on university?"

Ravenna, taken by surprise, replied a little more hesitantly than she wanted to. "Well, yes, I suppose so."

The blue eyes blinked. "Oh, Ravenna. I don't know. When you've got brains it's a shame not to use them. I imagined you as a solicitor or doctor. You'll regret it if you throw everything away."

Right, Ravenna thought, if this is going to be a fight I have to win the first round. So, with all the nerve she could muster, she leaned forward and stared intently at Sheila. "I don't want to be a solicitor or a doctor – I want to dance. I want to do it more than anything else in the world."

"But dancers don't earn much, Ravenna. You might have a family to support one day. Look at me. What could I do when Phil died except get married again?"

"Good dancers get well paid. One day I want to choreograph, maybe work in the theatre or films. I'll make a success of it, you wait and see."

Sheila sighed and set down her cup. "Well, it seems as if you've got it all worked out. But I'm not happy and I don't know what Ian will say."

Ravenna's heart was thumping. "I've just got to do it, Mum."

Sheila shut her eyes and in the silence Ravenna held her breath. She could almost hear the tug o' war going on inside Sheila's head – a sound education versus something arty-farty. And as if to illustrate this, Sheila frowned, shook her head and blinked. Ravenna's heart sank. She was sure Sheila was going to oppose her, but then she saw she was smiling.

"Well, I suppose we should all have a go at doing what we want once in our lives. If you can't do it now you never will," Sheila said.

Ravenna leapt off her chair and hugged her. "So you mean it's all right?"

Sheila smiled, her eyes sparkling, sharing the dream. "I didn't say that, but if it's what you want I can't see us stopping you. Now, aren't you going out?"

Ravenna gave Sheila another hug, kissed Kirsty and ran upstairs to get ready. She felt a new sense of freedom and joy. She was going out with friends, off to enjoy herself and not expected to babysit.

After a quick bath, she returned to her room and pulled on the swirly skirt, smoothed a blouse into the waistband and brushed her hair. She was just leaving her room when she ran back for something which she placed carefully in a duffle bag and carried with her.

When Ravenna walked into the sitting-room at Badger's, Molly was surrounded by school books and files.

"See how industrious I've been. Can you see my halo?"

"I'm suitably impressed," Ravenna replied. Then she saw that Molly wasn't the only member of the Morgan family who was working. At the opposite end of the room Kelvin was at a desk, poring over thick sheaves of paper and files.

He looked up. "Hallo, Ravenna. Make Molly rest, she's working too hard."

"So are you," Molly rapped back at him, but her face was glowing. Ravenna looked from Molly to Kelvin and back again. Something had happened. Something important. They were grinning at one another, looking as if they'd just won the lottery.

"So what's going on?" Ravenna asked.

"You tell her," Kelvin said, rising to his feet. "I need a break – I'll make some coffee."

"Dad's done a deal. It's strictly secret at the moment, but it should all go through. He's taking over some of the factory orders. He thinks he'll be able to employ about twenty workers to start with and more later on."

"Oh, that's brilliant. He looks tons better, too," Ravenna said, as she settled down on the sofa next to Molly.

Molly propped her pot leg up on a small stool. "Ever since he planned this new deal he's been like a different person. And Mum's been really solid. We'll have to sell Badger's but she doesn't seem to mind."

Ravenna shot her a quick glance. "Do you?"

Molly blinked. "I can't say I don't but, well, it is a great mansion of a place. David's rarely here and I suppose I'll be going away in a couple of years. Mum and Dad will rattle around in it by themselves . . . you have to look forward, don't you?"

Ravenna agreed, but felt the need to swallow a great deal and she and Molly avoided each other's eyes for a few seconds.

"Look, I've finished my drama project at last. Stuck in all the photos, even done the bibliography." Molly, determined to be cheerful, handed over a handsome black folder.

Ravenna flipped through it. "It's excellent. Should get an 'A'."

"I hope so. It's taken me ages and I've done that French translation, look."

"Are you coming back to school, then?"

"Course, I am. As soon as possible. I'll manage to limp round somehow. Dustin won't be there and I can put up with Faye and her mates. Besides, when news gets out about Dad's new enterprise they might not give me such a hard time. And it's not for much longer. We'll be at college in September."

Ravenna's face fell.

"What's the matter?" Molly asked.

"I've changed my mind about college. I mean, I'm not certain and I may not get a place but. . ."

"What?"

"You know I've been dancing with Beth. Well, I've decided. That's what I want to do, more than anything – I want to dance – for a career, I mean. It'll be hard work but I want to do it. Beth's going to help me try for scholarships or a college place on a performing arts course."

Shock exploded across Molly's face. "What? You mean not do A-levels?"

"I might still do some but most of the time I'll be dancing. I'm not quite sure how it works yet, there are different courses, but if I can, I want to concentrate more on dance than anything else. It's what I want to do, Moll. I've got to go for it."

Molly looked anxious. "But, Raven, you're clever. You could do really well – Stanton was talking about Oxford. The Head will have a fit."

"I know. I'm prepared for everyone to be against me but I want to dance. Beth says I've got talent and —"

Molly looked grave and cut in sharply. "Is this because of Beth? It's not just her idea, is it?"

"No, it isn't. It's mine," Ravenna said firmly.

Molly was convinced. She smiled. "OK. I'll back you up. I always knew you'd do something extraordinary. I should have known you'd be a dancer, ever since the time you danced on Miss Devlin's car."

Ravenna threw her arm around Molly's shoulder and gave her a hug. "Thanks, Moll."

Kelvin came in with a tray of coffee.

"What's the celebration?" he asked, as he set down the tray. "You both look pleased with yourselves."

"Ravenna's going to be a dancer," Molly explained.

"That's wonderful," Kelvin smiled. "I wish you every success."

Ravenna raised her eyebrows in surprise.

"Aren't you going to tell her how hard it is, how difficult to get a grant, how impractical?" Molly asked.

"I'm sure she already knows all that," Kelvin replied. "It hasn't put you off, has it?"

Ravenna shook her head. "I'm prepared to fight for it," she said.

"Well, life's never easy. Go for it," Kelvin encouraged.

"I am," Ravenna said.

A shout came from the hall. "Beth's arrived!" Natalie announced.

Ravenna reached for her bag and said hasty goodbyes before running out to the waiting van.

Beth reversed down the drive and into the road, handling the big van smoothly and easily, chatting to Ravenna sitting beside her and Selina and Natalie in the back. It felt exhilarating to be going off together – like a school outing – as if they'd been liberated; though in their case, Ravenna couldn't have said what from.

"I'm looking forward to this," Beth enthused. "I hope the Bengali dancers will perform in the summer concert. They're really exciting to watch and I want to make it a night to remember."

Natalie laughed and nodded in agreement. "Exactly. What we need is a great celebration."

"Many people – one dream. Dance is great for that – something we can share," Selina joined in.

When they arrived outside the community hall, it looked a long way from dreams and celebrations. It was a dirty brick building with heavily meshed windows and litter blowing against iron railings. Beth parked in the side street where two dogs idly sniffed each other and a boy skateboarded past, surfing from asphalt to tarmac.

"He's good," Beth said, pointing at the boy's disappearing figure. "Balance, poise, he'd make a good dancer."

"Come on, you can't recruit everybody," Selina laughed, taking hold of Beth's arm.

The four of them entered a dank-smelling entrance hall, Selina leading the way. She nodded to an old grey-bearded man dressed in white tunic and trousers.

"Just wait here, I'll see if I can find Ayesha."

Ravenna stood next to Beth whilst a group of women in strong, bright colours floated past. She gazed at them, fascinated by their elegance and poise, and then with a shock of recognition she realized she had seen some of them before. They were the same dancers who had entertained her at school two weeks ago.

The door into the hall opened and a clutter of sounds spilled out. Fragments of an unknown language, wailing trills of unfamiliar music, shouts of children. Selina appeared with a woman who was a vision of liquid gold. Her eyes were lustrous amber, her ears dripped golden drops, her wrists jangled bright hoops and her body was encased in shiny satiny yellow.

"Welcome. I'm Ayesha," she said, smiling broadly and showing large sparkling white teeth. "It's good to see you. Come on in and join our festivities."

She led the way into the hall, which resembled a bustling Eastern bazaar full of sound and colour. Standing together at the far end of the hall were the dancers, stretching their arms and legs and talking excitedly.

Ravenna lost track of names. She nodded and smiled, noticing their lustrous black hair, high cheek-bones and slender, painted hands. The women were pleased to see the newcomers and said they were looking forward to taking part in Beth's summer dance festival.

"Tonight we will dance for you and we hope you will join us."

Ravenna trembled with anticipation, remembering the last time she'd danced with them. Nobody here is going to laugh or make stupid comments though, she thought. And with a thrill of pleasure she reminded herself . . . Dustin Harrows is vanquished.

Ayesha clapped her hands and the people began to organize themselves. Bearded men in traditional costume seated at the front, behind them women with veiled heads and children scattered on knees and floor.

Ravenna stood between Beth and Natalie, and as the music began and the dancers glided forward, she knew her friends were watching every movement of the delicate scooping hands and gliding feet and sharing her enjoyment.

The dancers swayed their shimmering satiny bodies, weaving a magic spell that entranced Ravenna just as it had before, and her fingers and toes tingled to join in. She glanced at Beth and knew she was thinking exactly the same thing – she could almost see her body aching.

"Aren't they wonderful?" Beth whispered. "So graceful."

Ravenna slipped her arm into Beth's and nodded.

As the drumbeat faded and the dancers froze in a shining tableau, Ayesha stepped forward and took Beth's hand, pulling her in amongst the dancers. Then the girl who'd beckoned to Ravenna before in the school hall came to take her hand and gather her into their midst, along with Selina and Natalie.

As the music started up again, Ayesha clapped her hands and smiled broadly. "Just follow us," she shouted.

Ravenna copied the dancers, arching her feet, turning out her toes, stepping lightly. She tried to mimic the exact hand gestures, the tilt of the head, the dip of the shoulders, but it required skill and concentration and as the music became quicker, precise movements became impossible.

As the music grew wilder, Ravenna gave up hope of synchronization. She lost herself in a haze of swirling light, stamping her feet and throwing out her arms. Her body took over, pulsing and bending to the beat of the drums. The air rippled as the dancers shook their heads, shoulders and hips. The room rang with the jangling of golden bangles and anklets. Ravenna danced on until she became aware of empty space around her and suddenly she realized that she was dancing alone. She felt uneasy, sensing the other dancers watching her. Had she made an exhibition of herself and offended them? She hesitated, reined in her flying hair and legs and paused, her heart thumping, her eyes casting about her like a frightened deer.

She needn't have worried – the women were smiling and clapping her, and she saw she hadn't been dancing entirely alone. Natalie was performing her own ballet, interpreting the music in a wild catlike dance. Ravenna moved to the edge of the circle and watched as Beth and Ayesha joined Natalie.

Beth's orange skirt flowed like sunshine, Natalie's long legs moved like rippling trees and Ayesha twirled spinning threads of gold.

Ravenna hesitated, wanting to join them but standing nervously on the edge of the circle, her heart fluttering. Then she darted to the side, opened her duffle bag, pulled something out of it and returned. She moved forward slowly towards the dancers and with as much grace and agility as she could muster, joined them, swaying and sliding, her arms outstretched, holding the beaded shawl. She saw it flash in the light then let its soft silkiness slither down her arms. Her eyes caught Beth's and they smiled at each other, moving closer and dancing together, twisting the shawl around their shoulders and entwining their arms. The other dancers dropped away as Ravenna and Beth danced, stepping sideways, their hands resting lightly on each other's shoulders.

Beth's arms were sure and strong, providing support as Ravenna stretched and leapt around her. Ravenna felt as if she were flying until Beth caught her and they stood still, facing each other, curving their backs, each lifting one leg high behind them, their toes brushing their hair.

As the music died they folded and collapsed against each other, their limbs dangling lifelessly as if suddenly unhinged. Ravenna blinked. Around her people were clapping and chattering. Sweat dripped into her eyes but she didn't care, she was still soaring and tingling with excitement. She and Beth had danced together like practised partners, each reading the other's mind to perform swift, sure movements, and she saw by the crowd's reaction that it had worked. She and Beth smiled as the crowd applauded and the Indian dancers surrounded them with congratulatory pats and hugs.

Food was served and Ravenna's mouth sizzled with spicy vegetables, sauces and sweet-tasting semolina balls. Mint tea clinking with ice cubes was passed around. Sitting beside Beth, Ravenna sipped her cooling drink. She was glowing with happiness. She had danced with Beth, following her secret instructions. Without words, with only looks and touch, they had danced in unison.

She watched Beth and thought how happy and relaxed she looked – her eyes bright and clear, unclouded by sadness.

"You look really happy," Ravenna told her.

"I am," Beth sighed. "Happier than I have been for years. It's as if I've come out of a long tunnel."

"I'm glad," Ravenna smiled.

Beth squeezed her hand and looked serious for a moment. "You've helped me," she said. "You were the one that gave me the push I needed to start dancing again."

Ravenna, embarrassed by the praise, looked down at her folded hands.

"You were dancing," she said. "You'd never given up."

Beth shook her head. "It didn't have any meaning until you came along."

"I thought you were my mother," Ravenna whispered.

Beth smiled softly. "I know. You told me."

"Do you think I'll ever find her?"

"I don't know."

Ravenna was quiet for a moment and then said thoughtfully, "Two weeks ago it was more important than anything for me to find my real mum. I wanted to know who I was and where I came from, or I thought I'd never feel whole."

"And now?" Beth asked.

"Now I realize I've got to know myself. Find out who I am before I go looking for anyone else. You can't really rely on other people to make you happy. And things aren't that bad. I hate the estate, but so what? Soon I'll move out. And Sheila and Ian, they're OK. Sheila went on about university but I think she quite liked the idea of me being a dancer."

"I think she's nice," Beth said. "Did she tell you I'm going to teach her tap-dancing?"

Ravenna laughed. "She said she was going to ask you, but I didn't know if she was kidding."

"No, she wasn't. A lesson every Tuesday, we've fixed it up."

They were silent for a moment and Ravenna smiled as she imagined Sheila bouncing around in black leotard and red tap shoes. It made her hot just thinking about it. She pulled out the neck of her blouse and blew gently down her front.

"Phew, I'm boiling. That dancing was wild." She wiped her forehead, pushing back her hair and looking about her. "I like it here. Everybody's really friendly. And that's another thing – if you don't know who you are, you can belong anywhere. You're free. I could be anybody," she laughed.

"You will definitely be somebody," Beth said.

Ravenna looked pleased. "Yes," she said, "I want to be a great dancer and make you all proud."

Beth put her hand on Ravenna's cheek and rubbed it gently.

"Don't do it for us, do it for yourself," Beth said.

Ravenna grasped Beth's hand. "Oh, don't worry," she said. "I will."